The Linguist

Sebastian Beaumont was born in Scotland in 1960. He gained a degree in Visual Art and Creative Writing before moving to Brighton, where he now lives with his partner Simon. He is the author of four previous novels: *On the Edge* ("An elegantly written, finely paced first novel" Tom Wakefield), *Heroes Are Hard to Find*, *Two* ("Formidable both in its technique and its story-telling" *Gay Times*) and *The Cruelty of Silence* ("A tough black comedy, I read it at a single sitting" Patrick Gale).

THE LINGUIST
Sebastian Beaumont

The Linguist by Sebastian Beaumont

First published 2000 by Millivres Ltd, part of the
Millivres Prowler Group, Gay Men's Press, PO Box 3220,
Brighton BN2 5AU, East Sussex, England

World Copyright © 2000 Sebastian Beaumont

Sebastian Beaumont has asserted his right to be identified
as the author of this work in accordance with the
Copyright, Designs and Patents Act 1988

A CIP catalogue record for this book is available
from the British Library

ISBN 1 902852 18 4

Distributed in Europe by Central Books, 99 Wallis Rd,
London E9 5M telephone: 020 8986 4854 fax: 020 8533 5821

Distributed in North America by Consortium Book Sales and
Distribution, Inc. 145 West Gate Drive, Saint Paul, MN
55114-1065, USA   telephone: 651 221 9035 / 800 283 3572

Distributed in Australia by Bulldog Books,
PO Box 300, Beaconsfield, NSW 2014

Printed and bound in the EU by WS Bookwell, Juva, Finland
Acknowledgements: I would like to thank Leonie Gayton,
Darren Howe, Simon Lovat, and Martin Swan for their help with
my manuscript. Also, Toni Manzanera for the translation and
Robert Cochrane for the poetry.

for Simon

ONE

1999:

The persistent ring of the bedside phone didn't wake Howard immediately. It was his companion who roused him with a nudge of her knee and a murmur of annoyance. In a brief, definitive instant it occurred to him that inviting her home the previous night had been self-delusion of the worst kind - a wilful disregard of previous experience, prompted by the demands of his libido. He sighed, briefly, as he reached for the phone and noticed that the puckered sheets had left an imprint on his forearm, where he had slept heavily on it. The irregular pink lines looked like a diagram of some kind, or an Abstract Expressionist sketch. His fingers tingled with pins and needles.

"Mmm?" he murmured into the receiver.

"Howard?"

"Uh-huh."

"It's David here. David Tanner."

Howard glanced at his watch and tried to remember who David Tanner was. It was just after 8.00 a.m., on Saturday.

"I'm sorry..."

"You remember," he said, "from Leamington. Matthew Rickard's friend."

Matthew Rickard? Howard hadn't seen Matthew for two years; not since the embarrassing dinner-party conversation that, in spite of Matthew's legendary Christian charity, had caused them to become estranged. Sitting up abruptly Howard half opened one curtain with a flick of his hand, letting in an enervated trickle of light from the quiet Hampstead street outside.

"Right," he said, "I've got you now."

"It's Matthew," David continued. "He's ill. Well, to be precise, he's dying."

"Oh," Howard said, trying to activate his sleep-sodden mind and feeling a mournful beat of sadness. "Dying imminently you mean?"

"Pretty well. He wants to see you."

"Me?"

"Yup."

"Why?"

There was a hesitation before David spoke.

"He regrets losing touch with you," he said. "Can you come up to Leamington today? This morning?"

Howard glanced at The Woman, who was watching him with interest.

"I... I'm not sure."

"Come on, Howard. I'm not asking you for your sake, or my sake. This is for Matthew's sake. He's obsessed with the need to talk to you again and I don't think he'll be able to sleep properly until he does."

Howard nodded to himself.

"Okay," he said, "I'll be there. I can be with you by... ten-thirty?"

"Fine," David said, and then proceeded to give relevant directions.

Howard replaced the receiver and turned to his companion who was, by this time, also sitting up. It was a morning that, but for the phone call, might have been lost in a dark plangent haze of eroticism, during which he'd probably be filled with an obscure yearning to be doing something other than going through the motions of ecstasy. He noticed, as he forced himself to smile, that The Woman had a tiny tattoo of a scarab beetle on her hip, enclosed in an ornate circle the approximate size of a ravelled condom.

"I know, I know, you've got to go," she said. "I heard. You've got to rush to the bedside of a dying friend."

"That kind of thing," Howard admitted. "Though, sadly, I can no longer, truthfully, claim him as a friend."

He got out of bed and rummaged for some clean underwear. Last night's clothes were wildly strewn across the carefully sanded floorboards, socks tangled with stockings, trousers crumpled on top of a green silk blouse; evidence of the frenzy with which they had embarked on their passion.

"What's wrong with him?" The Woman asked.

"I don't know," Howard told her, realising only now that he hadn't thought to enquire.

"Who was he, then? Why did you sound so surprised that he wanted to see you?"

"Amongst other unforgivable things," Howard said slowly, carefully buttoning his shirt cuff, "I killed his wife."

The woman laughed, momentarily, before she realised Howard was serious.

"You mean," she said guardedly, "I've been sleeping with a murderer?"

"I didn't murder her, no," Howard said. "I killed her, which is different."

***

The M40 was less busy than Howard had expected and he found himself in the strangely relaxed state that sometimes follows the rush and then the forced inactivity of unexpected journeys. After a hasty breakfast, he'd let The Woman out of his flat with a brief apology for running off - an apology accepted with seeming unconcern and lack of interest regarding a repeat performance - and he now found himself sitting behind the wheel of his Audi Cabriolet with no other thought than his looming meeting with Matthew.

Matthew who had, until Corinne's death, been one of Howard's closest friends.

Corinne! Why did her name rise into his consciousness so seldom, when her absence was one of the all-encompassing facts of his life; one of the great inhibitors when it came to meeting new people? Would he have managed more than the pretence of abandonment with The Woman of the previous night if he hadn't seen the ghost of Corinne in her eyes? Would it have helped if he had been able to ignore the similarity of her breasts? Or maybe it was something more subtle, to do with gender itself, that was enough to cause some deep rumbling of pain...

Howard tapped the wheel as he drove. The car hummed in a luxuriously muted fashion, as though tempting him to put his foot down. At eighty-five, the only appreciable noise came from the closed hood which allowed a subdued intrusion of the clamouring wind outside. He grimaced slightly as he thought of the car - the object that he referred to as *my possession*. It had been an unexpected acquisition, bought for his thirty-second birthday the previous month by Sally, an admirer with whom he'd spent an alcohol-sodden month in Madrid. It still shocked him slightly that she should have chosen to make this gesture, despite the fact that she'd often referred to her practically limitless fortune. On previous encounters with her, she'd bought him clothes, scent, jewelled cuff-links, a gold watch... but a sports car!

Just sitting in the figure-hugging driver's seat gave him a contradictory sense of success and failure; success because it was an expensive car, given in a moment of cheerful generosity when his job had been to make Sally happy; failure because, in some obscure way, Sally, by making this gift, had somehow purchased exactly the detached, self-sufficient part of himself that he'd promised would never be for sale.

The emotional dynamic he'd felt with Sally had been weird. He'd never been attracted to her, but he'd been able to lose himself so completely in their love-making that it frightened him when he thought of it. There had been no connection between them other than his position as paid companion, and yet, the passion that he'd faked with her had been so close to being genuine that, for whole days at a time, he found he couldn't tell the difference. But he hadn't loved her - hadn't even liked her. What was that, the curious sad passion that overwhelmed him in situations like these? It was as though he was using sexual friction to try and wear away an indelible stain of loss. Maybe that was what these occasional patronesses found so endearing about him; the fact that his intense sexual striving could be read as love, when in fact it was merely vulnerability (perhaps the most beguiling emotion of all for those who are lonely?).

He didn't often accept work as a gigolo. He was a part-timer, an opportunist prostitute. After a welter of work in the first six months of being offered employment of this kind, he'd settled down to accepting commissions maybe three or four times a year, and never as a one-night-stand. Usually it was for a long weekend, or a week; only once had he worked for longer than a fortnight. This extra income allowed him to take whole periods of time off for himself, especially in the summer. Initially, he'd used this time to travel, to get away into another milieu where independence was paramount, and fellow travellers were rarely boring.

The rest of his time was spent on his 'real' profession of translating. He specialised in Spanish to English by choice, but was also fluent in French, German and Italian, hence his bread and butter work of handling brochures, for razors, electric toothbrushes, and endless useless gadgets for cluttering the home. He also worked as an interpreter, which took him abroad to political conferences and inter-departmental meetings of global companies, and which, over the years, had given rise to certain commissions for work peripheral to interpreting that could euphemistically be described as falling within the field of 'companionship'.

Howard liked the word prostitute. It had a glamourless realism to it that appealed to the cynic in him. It was also a word that he had initially been unable to accept, as though it had been inappropriate in some way; as though prostitutes were, necessarily, different from people like himself. But now that he felt comfortable, if not always happy, with this area of his livelihood, he used the label, in certain circumstances, as part of an obsessive aspiration for complete personal honesty (an aspiration born of having been less than honest in the past).

In a rather complicated way he felt that by using this label of himself he had finally achieved a personal integrity in which he felt both physically and morally relaxed.

He lived without extravagance in the flat he'd bought near Hampstead Heath. In his first frenetic six months of prostitution he'd earned enough money to put a 50% deposit on the run-down two bedroomed apartment. Over the next year he had spent at least two days a week doing it up; learning the skills of carpentry, bricklaying, and some elementary rewiring. He'd laid a parquet floor in the hall, replaced the skirting boards, stripped the doors... the only work he'd had done for him by a professional was the replastering, which he'd tried but found himself unable to do. By the time David phoned him to say that Matthew was ill, Howard had bought the flat outright, thus liberating himself from the feeling that he was constantly in the act of making a purchase, a feeling that made him ill at ease because, for him, acquisitions of any kind represented both a financial and an emotional tie.

He never went shopping, except for food, unless he *had* to, and always refused any daytime meetings that might incorporate purchasing anything other than coffee or a meal. This lifestyle enabled him to manage a fifty-fifty split between work and leisure time. Six months a year was quite enough for anyone to work, he reckoned, if they could manage it.

He was intensely aware that his frugality was in stark contrast to the thoughtless extravagance of his clients. It was largely their wastefulness that made him feel a kind of repugnance towards unnecessary purchases. He'd come to dislike domestic *objects*, too, because of the tie that they represented, and he lived with only the barest essentials. That was why he suffered a mild discomfort about the car that he was driving now. (His gold cufflinks and expensive suits were kept separate from his 'real' life, shut away in drawers, or the wardrobe, and were only used when he was 'working'.) The only objects that he allowed to accumulate in the flat were books, which he couldn't imagine living without. Still, he acknowledged, as he pulled out to overtake a long-distance coach, a car was one of the few possessions, if you could afford to run it, that liberated as well as fettered. If he felt like it, he could rent his flat out for sixth months, or longer, jump into the car - and drive.

He was grateful to Sally, not only for buying him the car, but also for helping him to overcome his nervousness around the whole business of driving. This was the first time he'd owned a car since the accident, and being able to drive at all was one of those truly surprising developments that he would never have foreseen, even three months ago.

There was a sense, in that purr of movement, that the road ahead of him led anywhere and everywhere. If he wanted, he could ignore the Leamington turn off, keep driving, and be in Manchester for lunch, Glasgow for tea, or he could turn tail for Dover and be on the Continent in time for an aperitif - a prospect that suddenly filled him with yearning.

He knew that this sudden urge to go off somewhere new was caused by nervousness about his imminent meeting with Matthew. It was a time-honoured strategy for evasion that Howard had used, either consciously or subconsciously, all his life, sometimes to great effect, and sometimes with disastrous consequences (he had, for example, run away for a month in his final year at university, thus ruining his chances - so his tutor had angrily maintained - of gaining a First).

The hospital that David had given Howard directions for was four or five miles from Leamington, on the outskirts of Warwick. The area was superficially the same as ever, though Warwick itself was even more traffic-bound than Howard remembered. He drove in by the old outer walls of the castle and was held up in a traffic jam for ten minutes. The place was so loud and congested that he couldn't imagine peacocks from the castle grounds strutting along the side streets now, as they had when he was young, except perhaps during those quiet moments in the evening when even the busiest of provincial towns seem to slumber. Still, the familiar beamed and mullion-windowed buildings that he passed helped to settle in Howard's mind the context of what he was doing. This was the past. Leamington and Warwick were where he used to live, his old life - the life which had contained Matthew, and Corinne.

The radiotherapy wing of the hospital was an ultra-modern building - a cross between an over-inflated bungalow and an early nineties super-market, with its long Spanish-style tiled roof. Howard parked outside and walked into the waiting area, which smelled new and slightly antiseptic. Institutional-style chairs had been arranged in informal clusters round magazine-strewn coffee tables, and the place felt as though an effort had been made to make the unit a more inviting place than its predecessor.

David was already there, with his sleepy eyes and laconic expression, and he strode from the tea counter towards Howard as soon as he entered the building, extending his hand whilst he was still some distance away, so that he looked unintentionally comic. He was wearing small round glasses that suited him but accentuated the fullness of his face.

"Hullo," he said. "Thanks for coming."

Howard smiled and tried to look friendly, but was aware that *trying* to look anything always made him appear insincere.

"No problem," he said. "Where's Matthew?"

"He's having a word with the consultant. I must get back to him. I'll come and get you when he's free."

"Wait," Howard said, reaching forward and grasping David's elbow as he turned to leave, "what's wrong with him?"

"Oh," David stalled, blinked a long blink of disorientation and exhaustion. "Didn't I tell you?"

"No."

"It's a cancer of the lymphatic system. One of those kinds that seems to fizz through your whole body at once. You'll have to ask Matthew for further details. I just can't... I can't take it all in right now."

David hesitated and Howard wondered briefly if he should embrace him, but decided it would be inappropriate. David had always been dis-tant and would surely take a show of physical intimacy now as a kind of hypocrisy.

"Well," David murmured. "I'll be back shortly."

As he walked off, Howard thought how sad it was that circum-stances had prevented them from ever becoming friends.

He crossed to the gents, in which one of the lights had blown so that he was standing in gloom. Beside a grizzled-looking man, he splashed water onto his face before glancing at himself in the mirror. His short hair was spiky and looked dark in the dimness, though it was in fact pale brown in daylight. His eyebrows were straight and low on his forehead, overshadowing his eyes and making them look, in his opinion, mean. People had told him that he looked like a young Clint Eastwood; a man who also, in Howard's opinion, had mean eyes. Still, his straight nose and wide, expressive mouth gave him a cheery self-confident demeanour, and his wiry frame had a certain elegant poise that suggested an athlete at rest - a long distance runner, perhaps, whose physique was on the borderline between lean and scrawny. He noticed that his eyes were particularly clear that morning. Whenever he suppressed emotion or succumbed to unhappiness, his eyes became icy and glowed with an inner luminescence that, in spite of the paleness of their blue, suggested, paradoxically, heat of a fervent and slightly insane kind.

Back in the waiting area, whose smoke free atmosphere nevertheless seemed heavy with an odourless fug, Howard wondered how helpful Matthew's faith was now, how comforted he felt by his closeness to the God he believed to be waiting for him. Matthew's faith had always been a backdrop to everything he did, and Howard thought, then, that perhaps if religion did offer any reward in this life, it was in providing comfort at moments like these.

Howard was sufficiently absorbed in his thoughts to jump with surprise when David tapped him on the shoulder.

"Matthew's ready to see you now," he said. "It means a lot to him that you've come."

As they walked along the clinically impersonal corridor to Matthew's private room Howard felt both shy and nervous. He pondered, briefly, the fact that it was two years since they had last seen each other. So little of his life seemed to have had much relevance in that time, the time since Corinne's death.

David stopped at a door, knocked quickly, and then ushered

Howard into the private room. It was pale and sparsely furnished, with two institutional chairs, a bedside table with a television on it, and a large vase of flowers on the windowsill. David followed Howard in, then crossed to sit on the edge of the bed and take Matthew's hand.

Howard was shocked by Matthew's wraith-like face. He looked so thin and aged. He tried to remember how old he was. Was it thirty-four or thirty-five?

"Hi," Howard said quietly from just inside the door.

Matthew smiled and beckoned him towards the bed, then grasped his hand and shook it repeatedly and said, "Well...well," over and over, tears welling in his grey eyes, his smile as professional and non-committal as ever.

"David," he said, turning to his partner, "could you... could you leave us alone for a while?"

It was clear to Howard that this request annoyed David, even though he smiled and nodded. When he left, he closed the door a touch harder than was necessary. Matthew raised his eyes and shrugged.

"Don't take it personally," he said. "He's been frighteningly possessive since I've been ill. Please, sit down."

Howard did so, in one of the chairs, whose sludge-green cushion sagged on overstretched springs, making him feel trapped instead of comfortable, enveloped in soft, unnatural fabric as though he was being prepared for an awkward interrogation.

"Don't say anything about my illness," Matthew said. "It isn't necessary. I haven't asked you here to embarrass you. Actually, I seem to have resigned myself to what's happening, so you needn't feel sorry for me."

"Your faith must be a big help," said Howard.

Matthew smiled; would probably have laughed if he wasn't clearly too exhausted to do so.

"Ah, yes," he said, "that's one of the reasons I've asked you to come. You see, I've lost my faith. It's extraordinary."

"Oh?" It occurred to Howard that he should say something like, 'that must be terrible for you'. But religious faith of any kind was such unknown territory to him that he couldn't begin to imagine what *loss* of faith might feel like.

"Let's just say I realised I was wrong," Matthew said. "It's quite an interesting story, but I'll tell you another time - you'll be able to come back and see me again?"

"Yes, of course."

"Good."

Matthew closed his eyes. After a couple of minutes, Howard wondered if he'd fallen asleep and leaned forward to have a closer look at him. The veins on the back of Matthew's hands stood proud of the skin like blueish cords laid there. The skin itself had a dry sheen to it which reminded him of how his grandfather's had been when he was in his eighties. His full head of extremely thick hair looked oddly dark against the pallor of his forehead, and his rather shapeless nose had been accentuated by the wastage of his cheeks. There was something dignified about the set of his jaw and chin that had, if anything, been emphasised by his illness, making him look like a biblical martyr.

He opened his eyes.

"Yes," he said, speaking in a halting, breathy voice. "Losing my faith. I always saw things as being either good or bad. And I judged them accordingly. Towards the end, I came to think of my relationship with Corinne as bad."

"You did so much for her," Howard said quietly.

"Except force her to be strong enough to live without me," Matthew wheezed. "I should have been more aware of *why* she chose to stay with me. Why she clung to me. For both her sake and mine I should have ended our marriage so that we could move on. But that's not what I wanted to say to you. I wanted to say that, after the accident, I was too disturbed and confused, myself, to acknowledge that you were also hurt. A part of me irrationally felt that you were responsible for her death."

"I *was* responsible for her death, Matthew."

"No, you see, that's the point. You weren't. I wish I had made that clear to you at the time. Later, when I was with David and I was settled for the first time in my life, then I realised that I was so distant and uncommunicative with you after the accident because you'd fallen in love with Corinne, when, in fact, I'd always hoped you'd fall in love with me."

Howard looked down at the floor, embarrassed by this declaration of something that he'd always understood, but which had previously remained unspoken.

"If only it hadn't been Corinne that you fell for," Matthew sighed. "If only your love for each other hadn't been so close to me... *that's* what I found hard. When we went to the Frankfurt conference, do you remember, at the time you were so happy? I deliberately made sure Corinne couldn't come with us."

"I can understand that," Howard murmured. "Corinne was your wife, after all."

"Okay, if you want to look at it like that, fine," said Matthew. "That's how I pretended I was seeing it, too. But really, all I was doing was trying to hurt you for being happy when I was so *un*happy. That's why I made David phone you today, because I wanted to apologise unreservedly to you for the way I cut you off after the accident. *You* were the one who'd lost the most, because you were the one who was in love with her. I was just her husband."

Matthew paused, waiting for Howard's response. Howard reacted by evading the central issue.

"But what has this got to do with losing your faith?" he asked.

Matthew smiled a slight, private smile.

"That's simple enough," he replied. "Since I stopped believing in God, I no longer have any outside criterion by which to make my judgements. I don't have to worry about what He might think at all. I don't have to wonder if what I've done is good or bad, or right or wrong. I don't have to worry about the whole business of dying and then somehow *explaining* myself to someone who will pass judgement. I tell you, Howard, that's quite a relief considering the balls-up I've managed to make of things."

He leaned forward slightly in order to cough, propping himself up with a scrawny arm as he cleared his throat with a pathetic, feeble hacking sound. After a short time he fell back against his pillows. Howard stood to help him in some way, but Matthew motioned to him to return to his seat and lay for a while, eyes closed, trying to regain his breath.

"And, of course," he continued, shakily, after a while, "since I lost my faith, my attitude to the past has changed. I have total freedom over it. I can forgive *myself* for all my mistakes without wondering whether God would forgive me too. It's been hard - to forgive myself - but I think I've genuinely managed it. Nevertheless, there was this last piece of unfinished business. To talk to you. To tell you it wasn't your fault. To tell you that it's time to stop blaming yourself; to forgive yourself, if you haven't already done so - which you clearly haven't."

"But how could I?" Howard asked.

"You were just the driver, Howard, and Corinne wasn't an innocent passenger."

"What does that mean?"

"*I know what happened,*" he whispered with a conspiratorial smile.

The door opened and David came in, looking concerned and residually annoyed. He was accompanied by a nurse.

"Right, Matthew," she said. "Time for your injections."

"What do you mean, *you know what happened?*" Howard asked.

"I'm afraid I'm going to have to ask you to leave," the nurse told Howard, who ignored her.

"It's true that you were there and I wasn't," Matthew said. "I know that, but I also know things about Corinne that you don't - about what she was going through at the time. Incidentally, you should talk to her sister about all this sometime. You'd find what she has to say very interesting."

The nurse stood beside Howard's chair, expectantly, exuding a contradictory air of tolerance and irritation.

"Look," Matthew whispered, "I need to talk this through with you. There's a lot I never told you about Corinne that I feel you should know. I'll talk to you some more tomorrow. Can you come in at around the same time?"

Howard nodded and got up slowly as the nurse put her tray of medical accoutrements on the bed.

"And thanks for coming," Matthew wheezed, baring his skinny forearm for the nurse. "See you tomorrow."

***

Howard sat motionless in his car for a moment. The internal silence that he had experienced on the journey from London was still with him, but it now seemed like an affliction. It was an empty, incurious, self-perpetuating silence; a deadening emotional blanket through which only muffled feelings percolated. Now was the moment to be clear and insightful - now was the time to work out exactly what he felt about his conversation with Matthew. Was Matthew right about the need for self-forgiveness? The question pressed around him but didn't give rise to answers, just a vague and melancholy reverberation.

Instead of facing these thoughts, he gave himself up to the ritual of carefully putting on his seat belt. It was something that had become a moment of poignancy for him - that movement of gently pulling out the dark, silky belt and pushing home the fastener with a reassuring snap into its trustworthy socket. No one who has ever come as close to losing their life in a car crash as Howard had can ever view seat belts as mere *belts*. Sometimes, when braking for traffic lights, or steering round a sharp corner, a vision of how it might have been would flash before him and he would find himself clutched by a debilitating panic, a dread that sometimes affected him so strongly that he needed to pull over and stop the car until the ghastliness had passed. In those moments of post-panic quiet, he would sometimes get flashes of what he imagined might have happened to Corinne - who hadn't been wearing a seat belt either - of how she might have looked after her neck was broken. Had she bled at all? He didn't know. But in his imagination there was always blood, and a strange sickly smell of loss. Of course, he thought about this at other times, too, particularly during those limbo moments at night, between wakefulness and sleep, when the same grisly possibilities would sometimes replay themselves for him in endless permutations.

Howard sat and took ten deep, slow breaths - something he did whenever this suggestion of dread drifted over him. He sat with his hands loosely on the steering wheel and closed his eyes, managing for moments at a time to let his mind go blank. Then, he started the engine and set off. He opened the window, wondering for the first time since getting the car, if it was warm enough to take the hood down. He decided that, although it probably was, the journey was too short for it to be worthwhile.

As he drove along Warwick New Road, it felt like more than two years since he'd been to Leamington - he hadn't returned since the disturbing dinner party when Matthew had been so moody with him. That one evening had cast a distancing shadow over everything about his life in Leamington, and it wasn't just because he'd witnessed Matthew's intense discomfort, it was also because that display of emotion and loss had clarified Howard's own sense of loss. And after that, Leamington had felt too bereft of Corinne's presence to be anything other than painful. Sometimes he wondered if, by moving down to live in London so soon after the accident, he had been running away from what had happened to him. But, in the end, it was a pointless question because it was so unanswerable.

That image of Matthew's blank face was the image that had coloured Howard's memory of him since then. Now, it was the new, sunken features that predominated over all other memories. But somewhere amongst those hushed and curiously inaccessible moments from the past, was the Matthew who had laughed, joked, chatted, and even - it was stupid to deny this, now that it had been stated - loved him.

Putting these thoughts aside, Howard focused on the need to find something to eat. He was prone to overwhelming feelings of nausea and dizziness if he went too long without food.

He managed to park beside the Spa Centre on the north side of Jephson Gardens and walked to The Parade, via Euston Place, whose tall sycamore and beech trees gave pleasant shade in the sunshine. He walked up past the Town Hall and the slightly askew statue of Queen Victoria (displaced an all-important inch by a German bomb). The café he'd hoped to find, on Regent Street, was now a meritless boutique, so he retraced his steps to the still foliage of Jephson Gardens, opposite which stood the fluted columns of the Pump Rooms. Here, where from Victorian times people had come to bathe in the invigorating spa waters, there was still a somewhat institutional, but functional, restaurant and tea room, where he bought himself a salad with chips.

He sat beneath a high cupola, facing a stained glass window that depicted the signs of the zodiac. Two women smiled and chatted to each other at the table next to him, and a pallid waitress stood behind the seventies-style fake-wood counter waiting for food to come through from the kitchen. There was something reassuringly shabby about the place, and conscientiously unfashionable. Comfortingly, it was exactly the same as when he'd last come here, just before Corinne's death.

Our lives were so entwined, then, he thought. It was extraordinary to recall the casual way in which Matthew had habitually called round for a drink, to discuss his work or a future project; or to recall the urgency with which Corinne would sometimes dash round during her lunch break from the florist shop that she ran, for a blinding half-hour of passion.

When he allowed them to surface like this, there was no sequence to Howard's memories. They seemed to be filed in his mind in order of scale rather than chronology - so that, bizarrely, his first memory of Corinne was that of her death.

I need to unravel all this, he thought as he ordered coffee. *I need to put it all in order.*

TWO

1995-1996:

In the year before he met Matthew, Howard had a particularly lazy summer. He lived in a small, rented flat on Bindswood Avenue, a wide street lined with linden trees that in hot weather spattered a light, sugary glue onto everything beneath them. He was unemployed at the time and half bored, half entranced by his empty life. There was a firm in Birmingham, Sheldon Translation, that gave him a small amount of cash-in-hand work, on brochures and such-like, with which he supplemented his Income Support and which allowed him to run a small, battered, rust-ridden Citröen. He also managed to visit Spain occasionally, for short, intense bursts, so that he could dabble in its culture, a culture that he felt was still burgeoning in an extraordinarily self-indulgent (and not altogether positive) post-Franco fizz that had been going on for years and showed no sign of letting up. Sometimes with friends, and sometimes alone, he would search for the drop-out culture; on Formentera, perhaps, or Valencia, or the crumbling Tetuan area of Madrid. Here he could indulge in the kind of fervent conversations that would sharpen up his Spanish (at twenty-nine, seven years after graduation, he was acutely aware of how easy it was for the extensive bulk of his second language to diminish, like an iceberg caught in a warm current). He also had an opportunity in these ephemeral, polyglot mêlées, to practice his other languages. It suited his sense of solitariness to attempt to seduce a different woman each night, in a different language. He might wander the bars and cafés in search of someone German, or Italian, or French. The result of this was that, in the first few years of his life as a professional translator, he found it difficult to concentrate on the mundane realities of plugs, wires and sockets when his previous experience of those languages had been of using words for seduction (and it occurred to him, then, that a language tends to be at its most languorously beautiful when describing the exotic or erotic).

Back in England, and still specialising in Spanish, he made do with authors such as Javier Marías, or Juan Goytisolo, whose *La Cuarantena* or *Las virtudes del pájaro solitario*, kept him on his linguistic toes. There was no one he knew in Leamington who spoke Spanish to a level that was useful to him and so he put the majority of his cash-in-hand money aside for trips to Spain.

During that summer his boss in Birmingham, Mr Fischer, arranged his first job as an interpreter. He was asked to accompany a Spaniard who was trying to open up a market for his cheap, and exceedingly tacky, olive-wood *objets d'art*. Howard worked for the man - a rather tedious materialist - for a week and earned enough money to take a flight to Alicante for a fortnight, where he hired a car and spent his time experiencing the wavering heat and dusty, undeveloped backwaters of Murcia.

His second job as an interpreter took him to Madrid with a wealthy American industrialist; his third, to Hamburg, Munich, Paris and Milan. His fourth was the first on which he was 'encouraged' to offer his services as a 'companion' - to a rich German widow who was an acquaintance of one of the delegates at the conference where he was translating. This business of companionship was an area in which, it turned out, Mr Fischer had a secondary interest, being a part-owner - with his brother - of an escort agency with offices in London, Manchester and Birmingham...

Although at the end of that life-altering week Howard had laughed to himself at the ease with which he'd earned a spectacular sum of money (by his standards), he was also deeply shocked by what he had done. For someone who regarded himself as an unthinkingly liberal person for whom 'anything goes', he discovered that he was carrying a wealth of prejudicial baggage around with him. Whilst on holiday, for example, it was completely acceptable for him to seduce a stranger and then part from her in the morning without a transaction of *love* having taken place. But when he was paid to perform exactly the same service for someone to whom he was not attracted, it became, not exactly sordid, but false. He realised, and was not entirely comfortable with the fact, that he was being paid not as a lover so much as an actor - to *appear* to be attracted.

He found it interesting, in a disconnected way, that it was so easy for him to perform under these circumstances. After dining with the German widow on his first evening with her, and finding her charming but sexually unmoving, he'd wondered, as they reached the bedroom, if he was going to be able to achieve a sufficient erection to perform intercourse. In the event, a strange transformation had taken place and he'd ended up being deeply affected by the intensity of the sexual side of their liaison. There was a definite erotic charge in being an object of lust for a client.

Language could be used as an effective analogy for this: it was as if he was tailoring every nuance of the language of his body to fulfil specific needs that were being requested in the subtle vocabulary of desire - an idiom that had to be translated like any other. In a bizarre and confusing way, Howard was both a spectator and a participant, and, curiously, just as in his work as a linguist, he discovered (with a certain wry humour) that he achieved a genuine sense of satisfaction at a job well done.

His work as a prostitute did not make him arrogant, because there was no-one to whom he felt inclined to boast. In fact, in many ways, it was a humbling experience, and taught him a great deal about the inequality of sex; for example, the fact that in a sexual assignation, no matter how consenting it is, it is rare for both parties to have the same agenda. (That was why, later, it was such a shock for him to meet Corinne - a woman who was in tune with him in a way that he had, cynically, come to believe was impossible.)

Howard, over the course of those first six months, prided himself in being able to offer his services without discrimination. He was assigned to a dozen or more women, all but one of whom gave him good reports and rewarded him well. He reckoned this was because of his easy-going nature and lack of narcissistic posturing - he was to come across many men, in that milieu, for whom sex was an ego thing. Howard, however, was incapable of deintellectualising to the extent necessary for him to be able to make sexual prowess into something that might embody *superiority* of any kind.

He was also detached, but in a cordial, concerned way that allowed him to be lavish with his attention when it was necessary and self-contained when it was not.

Another reason for his success, he came to realise, was the fact that, after that first few months, he accepted work of this kind relatively infrequently. He was aware that a conveyor-belt mentality would not only be bad for his clients, but probably disastrous for himself. There was something deeply sad about the way in which so many people - both amongst his clients, and amongst the majority of those they purchased - regarded sex as a consumable commodity on about the same level of profundity as a bar of chocolate.

The realisation that this was not the case for himself came early on when he accepted an assignment with a male. He assumed that the gender of his client would be of no significance, given that he reckoned his emotional involvement was zero. This proved not to be the case. On this occasion Howard accepted an extremely lucrative commission requiring him to take on the dual role of interpreter and bed-partner for Ian Gray, a cable television entrepreneur. The interpreting went extremely well. The sex was a disaster. It wasn't that Howard was disgusted, or rationally disinclined; it was that he was unable to physically respond, or find enough erotic charge in what he was asked to do to summon an erection. Of course, there are plenty of ways to perform sex that don't require an erection, but Howard's flaccidity certainly cast a shadow over the proceedings. Still, apart from the sheer embarrassment of that hour, it was an extremely enlightening experience. It made him feel that he'd been playing down his previous encounters; trying to categorise them as being on the same emotionally insignificant level as any other job of work he'd done. It gave him a sense that there were powerful subconscious elements to what he was doing, the significance of which he preferred not to examine too closely, though he became increasingly aware that the whole area of prostitution was fraught with emotional dangers that might not be apparent at the time, but which could be seen to have been important (and perhaps damaging) only in retrospect.

Interestingly, Ian Gray hired him again the following month, as an interpreter only, and their liaison gradually developed into one of professional respect. It amused Howard that their dealings with each other had an overtone of intimacy that could never have arisen without their previous encounter.

On Howard's second assignment to Ian, at a party conference in Bournemouth, he was introduced to Matthew. Howard's first impression of him was of a supremely confident man. He had a wide smile of orthodontically corrected teeth, and large strong hands with which he gestured expansively. He also had a tendency to dominate any conversation in which he participated. His wife was mentioned at one point, as was his interest in hiring Howard for a Conference Management Services - or CMS as Matthew's company was called - conference in Paris the following month. It didn't occur to Howard, given Matthew's marital status, that there might be a secondary agenda involved.

As it turned out, Matthew was not a pushy man as far as his seductions went. He made a subtle pass at Howard on their first evening in Paris, whereupon Howard carefully explained Matthew's mistake. After a certain amount of awkwardness, an amicable friendship had sprung up between them and Howard enjoyed his five days in the city that had always fascinated him with its contradictory traits of laid-back tolerance and unbearable cultural snobbery. Matthew's interest showed only in charming ways; in his extreme attentiveness to Howard and his desire to socialise with him out of working hours. Matthew was also more cultured than Howard had at first assumed, and they spent a couple of free afternoons going round the Musée D'Orsay and the Centre Pompidou.

By this time, inexperienced though he was at this kind of linguistic work, Howard was beginning to get the hang of interpreting without hesitation, although his need for intense concentration did not diminish. In fact, the attention required for this work, especially when an idiom was being used that had no direct translation, was so tiring that by the end of a two or three hour stint, Howard would feel an overwhelming mental exhaustion that would render him almost completely inarticulate for an hour or so after he'd finished. Matthew was at his best at times like these. On three of the four evenings they were in Paris, Matthew took Howard to a small bar off the Champs-Elysées to buy them both a kir or a kir royale before wandering over the river to a tiny restaurant near the Place des Invalides where they could eat outside in a rear courtyard, beneath a gnarled fig tree.

If Matthew was disappointed that Howard wasn't gay, he didn't show it overtly, and didn't discuss that side of his life. At one point, Howard mentioned the fact that Matthew was married, but he wouldn't be drawn to talk about it (Howard was extremely ignorant of the sliding scale of sexuality and had no idea whether Matthew was gay or bisexual, and, despite a definite curiosity, he found that he didn't have the instinct with which to work it out). They touched on the subject of God, briefly, too, but Howard was still struggling with an ingrained antipathy to religion of all kinds and so was not inclined to discuss the topic because he feared that it would inevitably lead to derision on his part and a kind of infuriating superiority on Matthew's. (Matthew, much later, said to him: "You handle your atheism badly, you know. You're so assiduously anti-religion it's almost a religion in itself.") Instead, they talked of art and travel and culture, and politics, of course, because that was Matthew's world. His job as conference administrator and publicist meant he had a wealth of gossip about many of the top politicians.

He also encouraged Howard to take his career more seriously, pointing out that if he applied himself there was the possibility of earning an excellent executive salary - with Matthew's firm, perhaps, of which he was director. Howard found it impossible to explain that he had no desire to earn twenty-five or thirty-five thousand per annum, or even more. He said that he was already working more than he'd intended to - which is to say, more than fifty per cent of the time. So long as he had enough money to travel, and enough work to keep his languages fully articulate, then what point was there in working harder - and sacrificing exactly those things which he valued and which he earned money *for?*

"But," Matthew told him, "you've got a good degree from Cambridge. If you could get onto the EU circuit, you'd be made. You clearly pick up languages extremely fast; if you could learn Arabic, you'd do wonders in the Middle East..."

Howard had laughed and said something banal about the excessive rigours of the protestant work ethic, and mentioned, briefly, his antipathy to those of his peers at university who had aspired to the kind of life that Matthew was proposing.

"In retrospect," Howard said, "I realise that I spent so much time on the dole after university because I saw it as the only alternative to taking a faceless job in a mighty bureaucracy. In the end I realised that I had no intrinsic obligation to be anything, or do anything, or fulfil any expectation on the part of my parents or *society*. The only person who signified in any way, was myself. It was then that I decided to use my degree for myself alone, if I used it at all, to enable me to live the kind of life that suited me. That may sound incredibly selfish, and it is in a way, but then so is all human behaviour *in a way*, isn't it?"

"As a Christian, I have to disagree with you," Matthew had murmured. "I'm sorry that you're cynical. Cynicism is so negative, I find."

"You say that as though cynicism necessarily renders people unhappy," Howard told him. "In fact, the opposite is often the case. At least I'm not chasing a romantic ideal. And one thing you can't accuse me of is being unhappy."

"No," said Matthew. "I don't know you well enough to know whether it's true or not."

By the time they returned to Leamington, Howard was mystified. He couldn't work out *why* he liked Matthew. They differed in almost every way. They were diametrically opposite when it came to both politics and religion, and yet they found that they could laugh about these differences without animosity. It was clear that, given the coincidence of them both living in Leamington, they were at the start of a solid friendship.

It didn't surprise Howard when Matthew requested him for the Scarborough conference, though he was intrigued to discover that Matthew was also bringing Corinne, his wife. He wondered if she knew that her husband was interested in men, and if so, how she dealt with it.

THREE

1999:

After Howard had paid for his lunch at the Pump Rooms, he left and crossed the road to Jephson Gardens, which was at its spring best. The foliage on the trees was fresh and vibrantly green; the cool arcs of water from the fountains glittered in the sunlight. An exotic tree trailed its branches into the water of the pond suggesting lethargy of the most appealing kind. The place seemed not to have changed in the thirty years since he'd first come here as a child.

He recalled one occasion on which he'd visited the gardens with Matthew, who had been on a high at the time after a successful conference. Remembering Matthew like that, buzzing with adrenalin and bright with smiles, suddenly reminded Howard of the fact that he was, at that moment, ill in hospital. Howard looked down at his own body; so light and healthy, so completely taken for granted, and was prompted to recollect how Matthew had been when they'd first met – physically bursting with energy, sincere, open and cheerful. Cheerful! That was Matthew's hallmark, and it was how he'd been that morning as he lay there in his hospital bed. It was inconceivable that a man could be cheerful when he was so clearly weeks, if not days, from death.

Howard wandered up past where the floral clock used to be and on, under the great, expansive copper beech trees, to the riverside. Here, families played, boats were being rowed, laughter could be heard, and it amazed Howard that he had ever lived in this town - it all seemed so alien to him now, so utterly domestic and provincial. It was strange for him to remember that he'd scaled the fence into this very park one night and lost his virginity here, beside the river, aged sixteen, with a girl from one of the more prim private schools in the town. And now here he was, taller, more assured, more *cynical* as Matthew had often pointed out. And perhaps more uncertain. At least, more aware of the limitations of life. But he was also, he had to remind himself, more relaxed, more centred. As an adolescent he had been a jumble of unsatisfied longings - sexual, material, intellectual. His most vivid memory of that time was of being trapped in a middle-class television-orientated family of conformists. This wasn't particularly true, he realised now, but he'd needed to see his family in that way in order to justify rejecting it.

***

1986:

Howard was in his second year at Cambridge, talking to Jan, his girlfriend of the time. She'd got to that stage in their relationship where she wanted to meet Howard's family, but Howard was desperate to put her off; embarrassed both by how ordinary his family was, and by the unashamedly Thatcherite views of his father. An investment broker by profession, he was a materialist to the core and Howard found that this clashed so deeply with his vision of himself as a free spirit that he had no intention of letting Jan anywhere near him.

"My mother's so cold," he lied defensively. "You'd hate her. She'd freeze you out. My father's the same, too. They argue a lot. In public. It's a nightmare. I wouldn't inflict them on anybody, and especially not you."

She accepted that, but not before she had tried the 'I can be by your side in the face of adversity' tactic, which - for obvious reasons - hadn't worked. Instead, she insisted on taking him home to *her* family for the weekend. Eerily, Jan's family was almost an identikit reproduction of his own, even down to the younger sister who was doing 'A' levels. Jan's father was a solicitor, her mother a social psychologist. Howard felt a weird dissociation on meeting them - they were intelligent, anodyne, affable. As an outsider, he enjoyed their hospitality. Why then, he asked himself, did he feel so prickly, so alienated from his own family, who were, after all, a trio of perfectly pleasant people?

This question wheedled at him for weeks before he realised that he felt distant from them because they didn't fit his own private mythology - the *persona* he liked to present at university: the slightly quirky, unpredictable young man. That persona simply wouldn't ring true if it was known how ordinary his background was. He could have forgiven his family almost anything, but he couldn't forgive them that - the fact that they were ordinary. And so, he began to irrationally despise them, and the more Jan requested to meet them, the more stories he had to make up about how awful they were. No single story, in itself, was particularly extreme - they were mainly of minor neglect and deprivation; of witnessing vicious arguments; of promises made to him and then wilfully broken; of crass behaviour in front of friends and their parents so that he'd been isolated out of school hours; of disloyalty and mistrust. In sum, however, he managed to conjure an extremely unpalatable image.

***

1999:

Howard had long-since come to accept that there was nothing wrong with his family. He had nothing in common with them, that was all. He didn't despise them for that, he just had as little to do with them as possible. He was aware that his life in London was still, in the opinion of his parents, directionless. His father, especially, found Howard's choice of lifestyle infuriating. (How much more so if he knew about the prostitution, Howard thought.) After graduation, he had set Howard up with a number of interviews in The City, several of which had yielded job offers that were both lucrative and full of the possibility of advancement. That Howard turned these offers down baffled his father, as well as making him furious. Howard was intelligent, he was reminded, becoming fluent in five languages, and could, with the right entrepreneurial spirit, do extremely well in the European business arena. With a father's considerable expertise at his son's disposal, Howard ought to do extremely well. Howard's simple answer of, 'But I don't want to, dad,' always elicited a groan of irritation - a groan which somehow underlined the huge ideological gulf between them.

His parents still felt he dissipated himself with travel and lack of full-time work. There was an element of truth in this, Howard acknowledged, but he couldn't explain to them the strangely addictive quality of his restlessness; of his inability to see himself as anything other than a loner. He didn't *want* to be settled. And constantly, restlessly moving on, emotionally if not geographically, could be an extraordinarily creative and sustaining experience. Almost without exception, his most stimulating conversations had been those he participated in when he was idly travelling by the Mediterranean or the Aegean. It was there he'd met people like José, a Spanish poet whose ability to express those things that other people sublimate, was so removed from the usual attitudes of a middle-class resident of Leamington Spa as to be almost within a different dimension of existence. José had become a regular travelling companion over the years and they saw each other several times a year, during which they would conduct the most intense and, for Howard, exhilarating discussions.

Perhaps that was what had attracted him to Corinne. She'd had an other-worldly air about her; a way of seeming to be thinking of remote things, as though her preoccupations were entirely incorporeal. Curiously, considering this, when he met her she'd just bought a florist shop at the bottom of town. It was her first venture into the world of business and, he felt, it was at odds with her volatile and fervent nature. Still, she'd been headily excited about it and, when Howard had first been introduced to her, in the hotel bar in Scarborough, she had talked to him about Athyrium, Acanthus and Lilium Regale.

***

1996:

When he *did* meet Corinne, Howard was surprised by the unruly lurch of desire he felt on seeing her. It was on the evening they'd arrived at the hotel in Scarborough, on the day before the conference for which he'd been hired by Matthew as an interpreter. It was difficult to know whether she reciprocated in any way because everything about her seemed to be full of erotic charge, even the way in which she rummaged in her bag for her business card. Matthew was tired that night and appeared not to notice Howard's slight breathlessness, nor his uncharacteristic hesitancy during conversation.

When Matthew went off to bed, Howard was both pleased and wary that Corinne decided to have a last drink with him before joining her husband. He wondered if he should mention his attraction to her, but quickly realised it wasn't something that needed to be stated. There was no way that he could hide it.

Right up until the moment she went upstairs, he couldn't decide whether Corinne was interested, too, but she kissed him, briefly, as she said goodnight; an intimacy uncalled for under the circumstances. The kiss was both subtle and unmistakeable, and Howard thought to himself, *aha!* It looked as though it was going to be a delicate flirtation and he relished the prospect of it; including the very real chance that it might not come to anything more than flirtation.

When he went up to his room he found it difficult to sleep.

On the following morning, Howard took a walk with Corinne down to the sea. The clouds were high and featureless. Light seemed to be coming from all directions at once and Howard wished he'd brought his sunglasses. He'd shared a table with Corinne for a late breakfast (Matthew having long-since set off for a business breakfast in Leeds), and he'd been trying to work out whether she was interested in him or not.

As they arrived at the seafront, families already staking claim to their area of beach, there came a warbling sound that Howard didn't immediately identify as Corinne's mobile phone. She stopped and, turning slightly away from him, conducted a *sotto voce* conversation as she leaned against the railing. After she'd finished and slipped the phone back into her coat pocket, she said, "That was Matthew," and began to stroll on as though working out something complicated.

Howard looked across at her. She had intense mid-brown eyes, lips slightly parted, and a lock of burnished hair curling across her forehead. She was wearing ankh earrings that day, as though she'd wanted to suggest the mythical. She told him, then, as they walked along past the games arcades to the harbour, that Matthew had had to dash off from Leeds to Manchester for the day to a technical meeting aimed at improving links between CMS and the media. He would not, therefore, be requiring Howard's skills as an interpreter that afternoon as previously arranged.

Howard looked at her as she said this and his gaze must have been particularly eloquent because she laughed and grabbed his elbow as if he'd joked, and she nodded without saying anything, and they began to make their way back to the hotel, walking faster and faster until they were almost running, gasping and laughing by turns.

When they got back to Howard's room they made love for the first time, spending the rest of the morning, and most of the afternoon, in bed, exploring further the promise that had been apparent the night before. After the abandonment of the first orgasm, however, Howard had been almost paralysed by feelings of guilt - Matthew was, after all, employing him as an interpreter for the week, and sleeping with your boss's wife is hardly exemplary professional behaviour.

"But you must know," she murmured to him as they lay together on the static-ridden bedspread, "that he's gay?"

Howard looked at Corinne closely as she said this. Her expression was completely neutral.

"Well," he admitted, "I knew he had *inclinations*, but I kind of assumed he was bisexual or something."

"Oh no," she told him, "there's no grey area as far as Matthew's concerned."

Howard absorbed this remark for a while, trying to figure out in what way this might make a difference.

"The thing is," he said eventually, "I hate doing things behind people's backs. I hate deception. It's so dishonest, and tends, in my experience, to lead to further dishonesty."

"Don't worry about it. I have an unspoken agreement with Matthew. We tacitly understand that seeing as we aren't having sex with each other, that it's okay to have sex elsewhere. It's not dishonest - merely circumspect."

The set up between Corinne and Matthew mystified Howard. She was so unwittingly sensual that he couldn't imagine how or why she might have settled for a sexless relationship. She was electrically sexual from her sparse but beautifully arched eyebrows to her leisurely hips and almost balletically pointed feet (with toes that she rhythmically curled and uncurled during orgasm). Well, if Matthew wasn't going to appreciate her, why shouldn't he...? A part of him was unhappy with this, but he was too wound up in the experience to discuss it further.

They made love until they were sore and Howard's hips and upper thighs ached from having executed a complicated coitus whilst half-sitting in the armchair by the window. Corinne had stubble burn on her inner thighs that looked livid and rash-like but which, along with her extraordinarily unflushed face, managed to heighten her allure as it gave her the appearance of one who has indulged but has not yet been sated.

Howard was surprised at the dangerous quality of their lovemaking; dangerous because it had a recklessness about it that would clearly take a long time to diminish. Their union was one that *demanded* repetition, although they only managed to make love once more during the five days of the conference; a brief, intense moment of rapture before lunch on the second to last day. Howard had whispered something to her, then, about meeting up again in Leamington and she had nodded as though surprised that he had to ask.

Over the next few days, back in Leamington, Howard was haunted by thoughts of Corinne; of her pale hazel eyes, alight with curious flashes of brilliance, like gaudy lights reflected in a nicotine-smoked pub mirror that has started to lose its silvering; of her breasts that dipped gently as she leaned over him; her mouth with its slightly drooping lower lip so that, lips slightly parted, she would show her regular lower teeth when she reached for a kiss. He thought of the attention she had paid to his nipples, circling them with her tongue. She'd licked them with a flicking motion and then pressed the erect tissue gently back and forth using both lips and tongue, and then she'd asked him to do the same to her clitoris - a request that he willingly fulfilled and which caused him to have a sensation of *connection* that he'd never felt before. He thought of how she'd whimpered that day, and how she'd stopped breathing entirely for a few moments when he entered her. It was spectacular, intoxicating and so unexpected that Howard kept experiencing occasional surges of bewilderment as great waves of erotic anticipation would break over him without warning.

It didn't take long before a pattern was established to their relationship. Corinne was working irregular hours; sometimes she would start as early as 3.30 a.m., when certain kinds of fresh stock had to be picked up from the wholesale market, or when complicated wedding or funeral arrangements had been ordered. On days when she started so early, she would knock off shortly after mid-day, so it was easy for them to meet up in the afternoon without Matthew's knowledge (though why Corinne felt the need to be so clandestine, given the circumstances of her marriage, Howard wasn't sure, though he fell in with her secrecy as though it were a game of some kind). But, the down side of her irregular hours was that Corinne was sometimes too busy to see him for several days at a stretch, which he found hard. She also went to stay with her sister in Nuneaton for occasional weekends, which took up further valuable leisure time. Still, a compensation was that Matthew's work often kept him away for periods, too, so there were free evenings and weekends to take advantage of. Even though he wanted to see her more often, he had to acknowledge that she gave him more time than he had any right to expect.

As he came to see how separate Corinne and Matthew were, it intrigued Howard that they were still together. Corinne didn't seem to love her husband all that much; she certainly didn't sleep with him - so what was the point of living with him? Although Corinne never stated it, Howard eventually decided that the capital used to start up the florist shop was either Matthew's money, or a loan secured against Matthew's assets. It was, he supposed, a sad but powerful incentive for the continuation of a somewhat unusual domestic arrangement.

Matthew never mentioned Howard's affair with Corinne, though Howard found it inconceivable that he didn't know. Sometimes, after an afternoon in bed, Howard would find himself dining with Matthew and Corinne in the evening. One thing he'd never been able to do was hide his post-coital glow, and it seemed that Corinne was the same; they would sit at the dining table exuding that smug complacency which accompanies the drenched feeling of absolute appeasement, and Matthew would pour them wine and chat and be his usual charming self, and Howard would experience strange pangs of sadness that it was all working out this way.

He might have felt more guilty, too, but for Corinne.

"He sleeps with his men," she told him one afternoon when she'd come over to his flat. "I sleep with mine. It's not something we talk about - not as such. And anyway, Matthew's too much of a gentleman to begrudge me my occasional pleasure. And it is occasional, too. You mustn't get the idea that I do this kind of thing often. There's plenty of stuff in my life to be getting on with, far too much I sometimes think. I don't have time to look for people to have affairs with. As it happens, you're extremely inconvenient. I'm starting up a new business that requires my undivided attention."

They had laughed at this, and made love again, and Howard had decided to try to stop wondering what might happen to them.

Their intense connection was clearly as much of a surprise to

Corinne as it was to him. If he'd learned one thing from his previous lifestyle, it was to take life moment by moment and not try to mould it. Things would happen. Their affair would progress. Autumn would give way to winter. The linden tree outside his window would lose the last of its leaves. The pond in Jephson Gardens would probably freeze over and he would go down there to feed the ducks, and in the spring he would either still be seeing Corinne or he wouldn't. In the meantime, he decided, he'd better enjoy their relationship.

Over a period of time she let out snippets of information about her past - in fact, she liked to talk about her previous existence, as though for her it was an occasional but necessary catharsis. Although she never gave him a chronological account, Howard gradually built up a picture of what had happened, and it made him yearn to erase some of the great burden of sadness it must have caused in her.

Corinne's closest friend in the family had been her Aunt Gillian, with whom she'd stayed in Wales as a child and adolescent, travelling there by train from Leicester. Gillian sounded like a wonderful lady; cultured, liberated, non-judgemental – someone who provided a haven for Corinne away from her blighted family.

Both of Corinne's parents had become slightly unhinged after the death of Corinne's elder brother, Mark, who had been run over by a lorry whilst on his bike. Corinne had been with him and had narrowly missed being run over herself. She had actually witnessed the sight of her brother going under the wheels of the lorry... He was so completely crushed that, contrary to family tradition, they'd had to have a sealed coffin at the funeral. Corinne had only been eleven at the time, her brother thirteen, her sister, Emma, nine.

She hadn't been ready for the kind of neglect that happens in a family when parents have ceased to be able to function. Unfortunately, Corinne's father was so riddled with preconceptions that he refused to consider therapy for either himself, his wife, or his daughters. Without Aunt Gillian, things might have been utterly disastrous. As it was, Corinne ran the household more or less single handed. She took charge of her father's cashcard and shopped and cooked for the four of them. She would fit in school work when she could - which wasn't often. Corinne's father would return from work looking ashen and empty, her mother would lie on her bed for most of the day staring at the ceiling, or going for gentle walks on her own, or crying quietly for hours at a time.

What amazed Corinne about her parents was that an extraordinary transformation would occur when relatives put in an appearance. Corinne's mother would force herself to smile and go through to the kitchen (cleaned and tidied by Corinne) to make tea and bring cake (bought by Corinne). Her father would laugh at Uncle Chris's jokes and pour everyone a drink - brandy or beer for the men, sherry for the women, and Coke for the girls. And then, when the relatives had gone, murmuring about how well everyone seemed to be taking 'it', the household would implode in on itself and grief would reign once more.

When Corinne could take no more, she would flee to Wales and stay for a few days with Aunt Gillian, who would make a fuss of her and give her love and encouragement.

When Corinne was fourteen, Aunt Gillian died - killed by burglars who broke into her home whilst she was upstairs in bed. She'd come downstairs to see who it was and they had battered her to death with the telephone table in the hall. They'd only managed to get away with a video, two small oil paintings (worth maybe £100 each) and £250 worth of jewellery. Without her aunt, Corinne ceased to have the emotional ability to function as unacknowledged head of the family and had what she later recognised as a nervous breakdown. By this time, her younger sister, Emma, was old enough to lend a hand, and their mother began to take over in small ways around the house. In this way Corinne managed to survive until she was sixteen, when she left school, friendless, and with no qualifications whatsoever.

She began going out with a nineteen-year-old mechanic who had a flat in a seedy area of the city down past the station. After two months she moved in with him, taking a job in a local W H Smith so that she could pay her half of the rent. But she had only used him to get away from home. The relationship itself was a disaster. He was brash, lazy and sexually demanding and, after eighteen months of shit, Corinne walked out on him. The next man she had an affair with was a school teacher - an English teacher, in fact, and although they didn't live together (he was married), he was responsible for encouraging Corinne to go to college to retake her exams, to work hard, to get her 'A' levels and to gradually build up some self-respect. But theirs was another non-connected relationship. In some strange way he didn't regard Corinne as an infidelity. She was a 'project' who also had the added bonus of being sexually available. Apart from being useful to Corinne, however, he was also depressive and would often come round to her bedsit to cry in an eerily disconsolate manner. She had never much enjoyed their intimacy, but she would always try to instigate sex when he was in despair, because it was the only way she knew to stop him from crying. After nearly four years of their on-off affair, he committed suicide by throwing himself in front of a train. In a way it was a relief for Corinne, who had found herself once more in a situation where she was supposed to be in control; to be strong for someone who had become dysfunctional.

And then, when she was twenty-three, she'd met Matthew who was at that time commuting to Leicester twice a week for business. He didn't want her to be strong. He didn't want her to look after him. He wanted to talk to her, and dine with her, and amuse her, and be amused by her. After years of non-communication and demands for either domestic help, or sex, Matthew surprised her with his consideration and restraint. He didn't demand sex, or want someone who would cook him dinner. He wanted conversation, not subservience; discussion not obedience. It thrilled Corinne, who responded immediately by falling in love with him.

"You see," Corinne told Howard, "Matthew saved me. He saved me from the dreadful, bitter person I was on the verge of becoming. I suspected he was gay but I knew that sex wasn't the key to our marriage. And I was happy about that. Relieved, really. And since then, he's done so much for me."

She stopped communicating with her parents, married Matthew, and moved to live with him in Leamington, where they bought their house on York Road. Corinne was content with their platonic relationship and didn't question it. Their marriage continued in its amicable way and it actually rather pleased her that Matthew seemed to be as happy with the set up as she was. Occasionally, she would allow herself a simple sexual liaison, but always on her own terms and always without strings.

"Until you came along to unsettle everything," she said with a touch of irritation.

FOUR

1999:

On the evening of the day he saw Matthew in hospital, Howard took a room in a large impersonal hotel on the south bank of the river Leam. After a generous and over-rich dinner, he went for a walk and stood in the dusk watching the sluggish water of the river as it passed beneath a narrow, heavy-bolted late-Victorian pedestrian bridge. The willow at his side harboured an erratic mist of early season gnats; the area around the bandstand behind him gave the air an acidic tang of freshly mown grass. He wondered, as he leaned back against the cool railing of the bridge, why he had chosen to stay here. He could so easily have driven back to London and returned to the hospital for ten-thirty the following morning without having to get up all that early. Perhaps, he reckoned, it was because there was a certain melancholy edge to places from the past - a pervasive nostalgia that was fitting.

He had crossed this bridge countless times in the year he'd known Corinne. She'd lived with Matthew in an ornate three-storied Victorian house overlooking the tree-shrouded stretch of river in front of him. He could see the top of it from where he was standing, with its second floor bedrooms set into the roof.

It reminded him of the house in which he'd had his flat, on Bindswood Avenue, to the north of the town centre. Unlike Corinne and Matthew's, this place had undergone one of those squeeze-as-many-flats-into-the-building-as-possible conversions in the mid-eighties. In the flat Howard rented, the sitting room had been divided so that it had two thirds of a bay window, whilst the sliver of a kitchen occupied the other, oddly angled, third. The main room was high-ceilinged, with embossed wallpaper, a sturdy picture rail, and an old feel that made Howard think of his grandmother. The bedroom, however, was incongruously modern and box-like and was tucked into a hastily built extension over which the owner was sensibly growing virginia creeper. Here Howard had entertained many women, but none so fulsomely or as attentively as Corinne, who preferred this room to her own more generous boudoir at York Road.

A year.

That's how long he'd known Corinne. How strange that some emotional episodes have a scale that is utterly disproportionate to their duration of physical time. For Howard, his life divided neatly into the period before he met Corinne and the period after she died. Their actual affair somehow didn't have any *space* at all in his sense of chronology. It simply existed as an all-pervasive fact. And Leamington was permeated with memories of her.

***

1999:

Howard remembered snippets: a cool Autumn day after heavy rain when he had gone for a walk with Corinne by the river Leam, up to where it had flooded Welch's Meadow. All along that stretch bright hawthorn berries clustered in the hedgerows. On another occasion he had driven out, on a frosty night, to go stargazing with her on the Burton Dasset hills, where, after they'd wandered off to the edge of the escarpment, cows had gathered round the car, pressing themselves against the bonnet for warmth, licking the gritter's salt from the panels - even from the windscreen, so that Howard had to use his wipers on their return. During the summer he'd rowed Corinne up the river, where, in boisterous mood, she'd wrestled with him and his car keys had fallen into the water. It had taken nearly an hour of diving to find them again in the sludge of the river bed. And, of course, he remembered making love to her. He used to find himself hypnotised into a haze of eroticism simply by her proximity. Perhaps it was something concrete, like pheromones, that caused him to respond to her so inexorably, because even when Howard felt completely unsexual, if he was in the same room with Corinne, she could set him off and engender in him a sense of urgency that he had rarely experienced elsewhere. All Corinne had to do was walk into his flat and drop her keys nonchalantly on the hall table and something in the languorous movement of her arm would make him breathless. But there was something more that was unique to Howard's relationship with Corinne - it was as if there was a suction, somehow, an irrepressible momentum that carried them forward. Howard had always conducted his relationships in the present, and the fact that the future seemed so inextricably wound up in what he was doing with Corinne gave him a sense of having to use each moment to build on the last. This left him with a feeling of brittleness that made him nervous.

Of course, there was more to his relationship with Corinne than sex, though sometimes - especially on those occasions, later, when he felt a melancholy yearning for comfort - Howard could remember virtually nothing else.

No, she also had a brightness to her, and a dry wit.

They'd often conducted long conversations. On one occasion, they discussed Erich Fromm's philosophy and he'd laughed about how completely Matthew was subscribing to irrational workaholism - the 'avoid confronting difficult personal agendas by working all your waking hours' approach to life. Howard also laughed because it was important for Matthew to own a Mercedes (as indeed it was for Howard's father). Corinne, in her turn, laughed at Howard for his impractical attitudes and told him that Matthew would counter his argument by accusing him of having been a parasite for signing on the dole for the best part of four years after his graduation.

One subject that often arose during these discussions was Howard's prostitution. He'd stopped escorting any clients during the period that he was seeing Corinne, and she didn't hide the fact that the subject was fascinating to her.

"But why stop seeing these people?" she asked. "I'm not asking you to stop for my sake."

"Are *you* seeing anyone else?" Howard countered.

"No."

"Why should I, then? Besides, it's not something I've rationally decided for myself. I don't *want* to sleep with anyone else. And I have no inclination to make prostitution my career. I just did it every now and then to make enough money to do what I want. Right now I want to spend time with you. I don't need any more money than I'm getting from my linguistic work to be able to do that."

Perhaps it gave her an erotic frisson to think that she was getting for free what other women had paid so much for. Howard wasn't sure. It sometimes made him uncomfortable to talk about that side of his life - a side he was now beginning to assume he'd given up for good - not because he was defensive about it, or ashamed, but because of the odd timing with which Corinne would raise the subject.

She would wait until she was reclining after sex. A typical posture of hers was to have one of her slim, pale hands behind her head, so that she looked like an artist's model, with one resolute breast raised by her upstretched arm, and the other hand, slightly primly, covering the small triangle of her pubic hair. Then, when she looked timelessly, knowingly exquisite, she'd ask him questions about how it felt for him to make love to someone he did not desire.

"You see, I've done it myself," she told him, "though for much more complicated reasons than money."

But it was something that Howard could never quite capture with words. He couldn't describe why it was okay, profound even, as a prostitute, to make this gift of his body. Perhaps it was narcissism of some kind, or worse, that kept him from wanting to tie the experience down with words, but then again, maybe - and this was a scary prospect for a linguist - maybe words somehow *diminished* this kind of experience. After all, there were no words that he knew to explain why making love with Corinne was different from making love with all those other women that he had sought out over the years; some of whom had been spectacularly beautiful, in many ways, and not just - or even - physically. *Maybe*, he thought, *that is why the word love is one of the least specific words in our language - so that it can encompass so much.* He certainly didn't love the women who paid to sleep with him. But had he loved those with whom he'd spent half the night in profound conversation in cheap hotel rooms beside the Mediterranean before 'making love' with them in the coolness of dawn? Did he love Corinne? Was he wary of answering these questions because he knew that as soon as he defined what he thought an experience was, then he restricted it? One thing; he was wary of jumping to conclusions, being conscious of the fact that a moment of ecstasy could induce a feeling of profundity that might seem absurd with hindsight.

"Do you *enjoy* it," Corinne asked him once, "sleeping with these women?"

"Enjoyment," he replied, "is such an inappropriate word for what I experience."

She laughed at this.

"Do they enjoy you, then?"

"Sometimes they do, as far as I can tell," he said, "and occasionally they don't."

"You mean you've had disasters?"

Howard nodded, shrugging slightly.

"Tell me about one of those occasions, then," she said, half mischievously, half seriously.

***

1995:

Howard, in his first months as an escort, took a commission to spend a week with a woman he'd previously met, socially, in Milan whilst with Ian Gray and his cable tv entourage. Until that moment, all his assignations as a prostitute had been friendly and straightforward.

Unlike Sally, whom he'd also met via Ian, this woman, Marla, was sophisticated and gracious, but also deeply, and rather elegantly mournful - the sort of European aristocrat for whom being unhappy is a vocation. She paid for him to fly down to Florence, to stay with her in the Hotel Grand there. He was suspicious when no one collected him at the airport, and when he arrived at the Grand by taxi (at his own expense) there was a note for him in the renaissance splendour of the reception: *Stuck in Geneva. Florence trip cancelled.*

The following month they'd met at the Grande Bretagne Hotel in Athens. There was no apology or explanation for the Italian bungle. Marla was already three-quarters drunk when he arrived at the hotel, and proceeded to complain about her journey, the hotel service, her servants... Later, she succumbed to a prolonged bout of weeping before, during *and* after they made love. Howard had the impression, during intercourse, that his penis was somehow an instrument of torture, but when he asked if Marla was okay, she'd murmured with desperation, 'Don't stop! Don't stop!' between plaintive whimperings. To say this episode disturbed him was an understatement.

It was clear to Howard, as the week progressed, that Marla was using him in some obscure way to punish herself. She was using him as an audience for her grief - a grief that he tried to get her to explain, but which she refused to share, saying, "I'm paying. You do what I say, and I say shut up."

He spent a number of hours at different times sitting out on the magnificent balcony of their suite in the Syntagma Rooms - much coveted for their views of the Acropolis. But Marla didn't come out onto the balcony that she had paid so much for, except to call to Howard to come in to keep her company, or to make love to her, or to sit and listen to her incessant anguished monologues about how everyone hated her.

She seemed to think that being a prostitute was a vulgar, virtually subhuman profession and she used the word *prostitute* occasionally in a derogatory way to describe people she disliked. It became clear early on that she regarded Howard as no more than a highly paid servant rather than a companion, and that she despised him for what he was doing. It was by no means the first time someone had been openly disgusted by the fact that he was a prostitute, but it *was* the first time he'd been obliged to sleep with a person who regarded him in this way. It both bemused and disturbed him.

Once or twice they went out for walks, up through the old part of the city. Marla wasn't interested in shopping, which was something of a relief to Howard at first, though later on he wished that she could find some activity to occupy herself that would stop him from feeling uncomfortable about their long silences and lack of any kind of mutual conversation. Eventually, Howard began to feel awed at how it was possible for someone to have such an empty existence.

They went out to restaurants in the evenings and sat, mostly in uncomfortable silence, whilst Marla drank herself into a stupor. Any attempt at conversation was futile and Howard would end up nodding mutely whenever Marla embarked on one of her short, bitter complaints. He could see that she had once been beautiful, but he reckoned that it wasn't just the loss of her looks that made her so resentful, it was the way in which she had been used by those whom she trusted. It was easy to see how a person like Marla might end up feeling maltreated by life. She had clearly never grown up - had wanted for nothing, materially, and had therefore become appallingly selfish without ever ascribing that adjective to herself or her behaviour. Never growing up had left her unclear about the difference between love and lust - a lack of distinction that had clearly led to repeated emotional disasters, given her veiled comments about previous lovers. Now, at this stage in her life, he assumed that she had come to the conclusion that love did not exist for her - it worked wonderfully, tantalisingly, for others, but, tragically, not for her. He had an immense sympathy on one level, but in the end, in the face of her dysfunction as a person, and her using him as an outlet for her unhappiness, all he felt was a yearning to be elsewhere.

By the time he returned to England, Howard felt deeply confused about why Marla might have wanted to hire him at all, and it depressed him that she had been so relentlessly impersonal with him. It took a number of weeks, and a couple of successful assignations, before he even began to feel settled within himself. For months afterwards he would have sudden flashes of sadness whenever he thought of her.

***

1999:

Howard was still leaning back against the metal footbridge over the river Leam, lost in thought. He hadn't remembered Marla for a considerable time, and even now the shadow of her sadness made him shiver.

He sighed, and discovered that he'd been standing, unmoving, for long enough to get pins and needles down his right leg. He turned to leave and as he did so, he found that one of the bridge's bolts had dug into his back, a little above his coccyx. He stretched, feeling the beginnings of a bruise there, and, stumbling slightly on his numbed leg, shook his head at the complete absorption that memories can generate.

***

The following morning Howard breakfasted in the main dining room of the hotel - a room of tarnished grandeur, with carpets a little too worn and an atmosphere of stale cigarette smoke and yesterday's cooking. He made do with coffee and toast, then went for a brief walk in Jephson Gardens, the clean morning breeze welcome after the stagnant air of the hotel. There were few people in the park so early on a Sunday, and Howard paused by the mausoleum-like housing for Henry Jephson's statue which stood close to a small ribbed and curved fountain that was burbling in a subdued, comfortable fashion. The water blinked in the morning sun, which was still cool, and Howard had a sudden urge to take off his shoes and dip his feet into the shallow basin in which the fountain stood. Instead, he crouched down and immersed his hands in the clear, cold water and moved his fingers to the rhythm of his thoughts.

Standing once more, he shook the drops from his fingers before rubbing the residue over his bare forearms, enjoying the slightly prickling sensation as the hairs there bristled with the moisture. He looked up at the ornate building in front of him, then climbed the steps to look through the railings and into the interior where the statue of Henry Jephson stood, looking arrogant and private on his pedestal, below a domed roof, a flurry of dust, debris and clots of litter around his base. Holding onto the chill metal of the railings, Howard remembered having stood exactly here, talking with Matthew.

***

1996:

"Pompous old git," Matthew said, looking up at the statue. "I don't know whether to laugh at him or to be grateful to him for what he did for the town."

It was the day after they'd both returned from a CMS conference in Manchester and Matthew was taking one of his rare breaks. He smiled a lot that day and phoned Howard in the evening to suggest a picnic by the sea.

"I've bullied Corinne into taking a day off, too. The weather forecast is fair. Also, it's mid-week, so it shouldn't be too busy."

It was the first time Matthew had suggested that the three of them spend the day together since Howard had begun his affair with Corinne, and he cautiously accepted the invitation.

"I thought we could go to Wales. Fairmouth, on Barcombe Bay," Matthew told him. "It's at the foot of Cader Idris - stunning. Maybe we could stop off at Dolgellau, too, either on the way there or the way back. There's an excellent restaurant out towards Cymmer Abbey. We'll have to start early because the roads are quite slow."

"I'd love to come," Howard told him. "I've never been to Wales before."

"We'll show you around. Bring some good walking shoes."

If he'd wondered at Matthew's motives in making this invitation, he wondered even more in the morning when Matthew turned up at 6.30 a.m. to collect him, alone.

"I'm sorry," he'd said, "Corinne can't make it after all. She said to send her love and to say that she's sure she'll see you soon. So," he added, "it's just the two of us. Do you mind?"

"No, not at all," Howard said, briefly wondering if Matthew was intending to drive him out to some remote location and then murder him for the affair that he was having with Corinne. It was a whimsical thought, and slightly pleasant because it was so absurd.

It was a cool morning, verging on cold, with broken cloud cover. The roads were clear at that time of day and they made good progress in the first hour or so through Kidderminster to Ludlow before traffic began to slow them down. Matthew was quiet and thoughtful as he drove.

"I love this route," he said at one point, "this countryside... Corinne and I came out here for our honeymoon, did you know?"

"No," said Howard.

"As a wedding present an aunt of hers offered us the use of an old cottage on the lowest slopes of Cader Idris, outside Dolgellau. It was a wonderful fortnight. The weather was dreadful, but that only added to the place's charm. I'd always assumed that the best place to go on honeymoon is somewhere exotic, but I don't think anyone could have done better than we did. Really, it was wonderful."

"But I thought Corinne's aunt was dead," said Howard. "Murdered."

"Oh yes, that," said Matthew, giving Howard a wry glance. "It's too complicated for me to explain. Ask Corinne to tell you about it, sometime. Suffice to say, we *did* stay in her aunt's cottage."

Howard wondered if Matthew was raising the subject of his honeymoon in order to tell him something? He wasn't sure. There's no doubt Matthew was a subtle man, but he was also, in Howard's experience, alarmingly straightforward, so Howard tried to put the thought of hidden agendas out of his mind. Matthew again lapsed into silence as he drove, occasionally pointing out the course of a Roman road as they passed it, or naming a favourite hill or village. Howard sat, cocooned in the hushed interior of Matthew's Mercedes, and brooded over his relationship with Corinne.

Okay, she had said that she would never leave Matthew, but then she'd also said that no man had previously drawn her away from her curious, comfortable existence with him - until Howard. Surely now she would begin to see that Matthew had been a useful, even essential, staging post, a point on the journey from her old, injured self, to her new, assured, complete self. Of course, she should be forever and profoundly grateful to him, but, surely, 'completeness' would, by definition, be impossible with a gay man? To Howard it was incomprehensible that anyone could be fully satisfied with a relationship that didn't have a sexual element to it. It was true that Corinne was fulfilling at least some of her sexual needs with Howard whilst still living with Matthew, but there would come a time, and Howard could sense it fast-approaching for him, when this ad hoc arrangement would no longer be enough. It wasn't as if he saw her regularly as it was. One week he might see her every day, and then he might go a fortnight without word, during which he would yearn in the most pathetic fashion. If he contacted her at the florist, or on her mobile, she would be distant and slightly curt with him and say she'd phone him 'soon'.

He smiled as he thought of this. How was it that he'd got into this situation? Only a few months ago the prospect of an intense but simple sexual relationship with an intelligent, entrancing but otherwise engaged woman would have sounded ideal. To have someone who could flit at the periphery of his life without encroaching on his independence or his solitary travelling... it had been a beguiling scenario for his entire adult life. Now that he'd brushed against the reality, however, the fantasy seemed childishly naive.

Howard looked across at Matthew as he drove. His heavy face usually looked serious in repose, but there was something about him that day, a kind of lightness round his mouth, that made Howard feel that he was about to burst into a grin at any moment. Was this journey designed as a piece of mischief? Had Matthew deliberately mentioned his honeymoon and then shut up in order that Howard could brood over it? If that had been his intention, then he had succeeded.

At just after nine o'clock they came into Dolgellau. Matthew pointed to his left.

"There," he said, "that white cottage on its own up there, at the end of the lane. With the hedge on one side and a dry stone wall on the other. That's where we stayed."

Howard looked at it - a roomy house that hardly deserved the epithet 'cottage'. It stood in a formal garden that was splashed with early summer colour - rich reds and blues. The cloud cover was beginning to break up so that the north flank of Cader Idris, rising above the cottage, was mottled with light and looked, somehow, both benign and menacing at the same time. He made a mental note to ask Corinne about the cottage, and her aunt, when he next saw her.

They stopped in Dolgellau in a café that lacked charm, but served a good breakfast, and Matthew chatted a little about work and the next job he would need Howard for. He also talked about the stretch of countryside from Cader Idris up to Snowdon, an area redolent with nostalgic images from childhood holidays. Matthew's enthusiasm was infectious and Howard began to be enveloped by an almost festive feeling of having got away from home. It was his habit to always travel south when he went away, because he naturally wanted to go to places where he could practice his languages, but he did feel, as Matthew eulogised their surroundings, that there was much of the UK that he had missed out on.

There was a fresh breeze that day, so the picnic they ate by the sea at Fairbourne was not as lazy as Matthew had intended, but later, when they walked to the coomb at the back of Cader Idris the temperature was exactly right for rambling up over old rock and moorland.

Howard found the views of peaks, escarpments and the clear glacial lake breathtaking but he thought the dark rocky outcrops and the dirty-looking tussocks of grass somewhat forlorn. He regarded himself as an isolated person and this landscape served to accentuate that aspect of himself. To visit the melancholy beauty of the area for a day was inspiring but he felt that if he lived here he would go slowly mad - though, perhaps, in a rather pleasant way.

In the early evening they dined in the restaurant that Matthew had spoken of. He was right. The food was spectacular. The wind had died down by that time and they ate out on a stone terrace above the river, whose sibilant babble lent privacy to their conversation. Howard had been building up all day to asking the question that had hung, unspoken, from the moment he'd realised that Corinne wasn't going to be coming with them. Eventually, between courses, as he sipped a classic burgundy, he broached the subject.

"Did you plan all this in advance?" he asked Matthew. "Did you always intend to leave Corinne behind?"

"Sorry?" Matthew looked completely uncomprehending. There was no mischief in his expression whatsoever. "Corinne loves it round here. She was heartbroken not to be able to come."

"Yes. Yes, of course," Howard told him quickly, feeling foolish that he'd suspected Matthew's motives at all. It would be against his morality, after all, to be so devious.

The main course arrived and gave Howard the opportunity to busy himself with his food for a time. Whether or not Matthew had engineered that they should be alone together like this, Howard found himself feeling that, regarding his affair with Corinne, what had started as an honest deception (*"I have an unspoken agreement with Matthew"*) was now beginning to feel like an unhealthy breach of some kind of personal trust. Now that he'd mentioned Corinne, he had a certain conversational momentum that allowed him to continue.

"Tell me," he said slowly, after a time, "how much does Corinne know about your... homosexuality?"

"Enough. I never discuss details."

"But, forgive me for being blunt, isn't it a major handicap to your marriage?"

Matthew stopped eating and looked at Howard with his intense, analytical stare.

"No," he said.

"But surely..."

"No," Matthew said definitely. "Corinne and I are fine as we are. Unkind people might accuse me of marrying her under false pretences because I didn't tell her that I was gay at the time of our wedding. But, then, I wasn't absolutely sure of it myself. I thought that sexuality was a malleable thing. As a matter of fact, I've discovered recently that it *is* malleable to a certain extent - but not as far as the basics go.

"I've never been one for deceit, and not just because of my faith. Anyway, I couldn't hide my feelings from Corinne and so, when I became sure that I really was gay, I talked to her about splitting up. But she was adamant that we should stay together. You may not know this, but she's been a little unwell, you know... mentally. She's not a person who could cope well on her own. She had a nervous breakdown at one point."

"Yes," said Howard, "she mentioned it to me."

Matthew paused.

"Good," he said. "Did she also tell you that she's attempted suicide a couple of times?"

"No."

"Hopefully that's behind her. In fact, I'm sure it is. Now that she's got a stable environment with me, and a new business to put her energy into, I don't see why things shouldn't get progressively better for her."

He took a mouthful of mange-tout peas and looked thoughtfully at Howard.

"The situation as it stands is that she is enormously useful to me, *socially*," he said. "You may find that rather sick as a concept, but having a beautiful wife is an incalculable asset, even now. She gives me a certain respectability and I give her a certain stability in return. It works well, and not in a cynical way either. I also care for her a great deal."

"But what if either of you should ever fall in love with someone else?"

"Yes," said Matthew, "I've considered that. You see - and I'm not boasting here - Corinne is very much in love with me. That's why I couldn't leave her. I know its painful for her, in a way, to be with me, but she does need me and she does have depressive tendencies that I understand and can help her with, so I don't feel I have the moral right to push her away. No, I couldn't do that. If *she* left *me*, that would be one thing, but for me to leave her... No. It wouldn't be right. I married her, I have to take responsibility for her well-being. As far as falling in love with someone else goes, I don't think it will happen to Corinne in the near future. Right now I don't think she's *capable* of falling in love with someone else."

"But," said Howard, "I'm..."

Matthew reached out and put his hand over Howard's for an intense moment.

"I know you like her, Howard," he said, "and I don't want to appear spiteful or jealous, but please be careful. Maybe after she's had more therapy and has come off her medication..."

"Therapy?" said Howard. "Medication?"

"Yes. I won't go into it. It would be a little... disloyal."

He removed his hand and took a gulp of wine and gave a long glance that Howard couldn't interpret. Was it pity? Or concern? Or affection?

"So," said Howard after a pause, trying to think of something to say that might disguise the fact that Matthew's mention of therapy and medication had been an emotional body-blow from which he was still reeling, "what about you? What if you fall in love with someone?"

"That's more of a possibility," he admitted. "In fact, I think it might already be happening, though I'm far too cautious to want to be more specific than that."

"What's his name?" Howard asked.

"David," Matthew told him. "He's quiet and gentle, and rather domestic, which, as you probably know, isn't the type I usually go for. But it's one of those odd facts of life that you tend to find things precisely when you're not looking for them."

***

The following day, when he saw Corinne, he asked her about the therapy and the medication. Significantly (and he was aware of this even at the time), he waited until *after* they'd made love before broaching the subject.

Corinne seemed unfazed by the question and smiled slightly at Howard's obvious concern.

"Don't worry about it," she told him. "I try to forget things from my past, but sometimes they come back and overwhelm me for a while. I think I'm relatively well-adjusted now, but you've got to forgive me the occasional slip. It's no big deal, just something I'm gradually - and successfully - working through."

Howard was relieved.

"I'm not surprised you have problems getting to grips with your past," he told her. "I'd never have survived at all if I'd gone through what you have."

"I *am* a survivor," she said, somewhat wistfully, and smiled.

Howard relaxed.

"So," she asked, "you've been discussing my intimate details with Matthew?"

"No, not really. It came up, briefly, but he wouldn't say anything specific."

"Dear Matthew," she said with a curiously hard smile, "I expect he was trying to warn you off me. Poor thing, he's still in love with you himself. It makes him so sad to think that you might be having an affair with me instead."

"Nonsense," Howard objected. "He'd never waste time over someone as unavailable as me."

"If only love could be as rational as that," Corinne murmured.

They sat in silence for a while before Howard spoke.

"And what about this cottage in Wales where you and Matthew spent your honeymoon?" Howard asked. "I thought your aunt was dead."

"Please don't ask me about that," she said. "I don't mean to be mysterious, and the explanation is simple enough, though a little... sensitive. I'll tell you another time, okay?"

Howard felt frustrated by this evasion and wondered whether to pursue the point, but, looking at her vulnerable expression, he decided not to.

"Okay," he agreed, though his curiosity remained undiminished.

FIVE

1999:

As Howard drove to the hospital for his promised visit to Matthew, he shifted in his seat, somewhat hampered by the bruise he'd sustained whilst leaning against the bridge the previous night. He pondered what Matthew had meant when, referring to the accident and Corinne's role as passenger, he'd said *I know what happened* with such certainty. How could he have *known* what happened? Only Howard and Corinne had been in the car. It was a nonsense thing for him to say, though intriguing.

And then there was all this talk of blame and forgiveness. Howard didn't need to talk that one through: he understood and accepted the blame for Corinne's death. He didn't feel that he needed to be forgiven. The idea that he might have to forgive himself? That was an interesting concept, but one which he had yet to find the emotional space to confront. It was so typical of Matthew to talk in this way; to be so ill and to think of *Howard's* welfare - it was so kind and so liberal-Christian in the best sense, despite the fact that he had lost his faith.

Howard had always thought of Matthew as being a kind man - he'd always made an extra effort to make Howard's work as an interpreter as smooth as possible; had given up hours of his time to iron out little hitches. And it wasn't because he'd fancied Howard. He was like that with everyone who worked for him. That was why his complete emotional withdrawal after the accident had been so painful and confusing.

***

1997:

Howard had been invited to dinner by Julia and Ralph, friends of several years standing. Julia was a fellow translator with Sheldon Translation; a specialist in German. Ralph was a GP, with whom Howard and Matthew were registered. Howard nearly didn't bother going - it was still too soon after Corinne's death and he'd only recently begun talking to other people again. He was still feeling raw inside, scoured out, and the thought of chit-chatting at a dinner party was almost unbearable, even to contemplate. But Julia was one of those women who tended to be a balm in difficult times and Howard realised that if he was ever going to keep himself sane it was people like Julia who would help him do it. Her husband, Ralph, was unfailingly sympathetic, so it seemed the perfect opportunity to venture, bruised and vulnerable, into the world. Matthew, it turned out, had also been invited. Julia and Ralph were unaware that he and Howard hadn't spoken to each other since the accident.

Howard was the first guest to arrive and accepted a whisky from Ralph before sitting in one of the formal chairs in the living room. Julia was cheerful and talkative and Howard responded by feeling suddenly cheerful himself, in a frail kind of way. He gave an inward sigh of relief that he had come out into this welcoming atmosphere; felt real again after more than a month of numbness.

He was sipping his drink when Matthew and David arrived. It was the first time he'd seen them out together as a couple and it struck him how appropriate they looked in each other's company; so much more so than Matthew had ever seemed with Corinne. Howard stood quickly and held out his hand, to David first, who took it, giving Howard a look of sympathetic concern. Matthew, standing behind David, looked stricken, somehow, to be so unexpectedly faced with Howard's presence.

Howard tried to summon a smile of greeting, though he could see from Matthew's face that, for both of them, this encounter was causing a welter of painful memory. He felt oddly relieved when the phone began to ring in the hall and Ralph left the room to answer it.

"I must go and turn the oven down," Julia said as a timer sounded from the kitchen. "I'll be back in a moment. Howard, would you see to the drinks?"

After she'd left the room, Howard looked across at Matthew, whose face had turned slightly blotchy.

"What would you like to drink?" Howard asked.

Matthew didn't say anything for a moment and then looked as if he was about to cry.

"I'm sorry, Howard," he said quietly, "it's weird and unforgivable, I know, but I don't think I'm ready to see you again. That must sound terrible of me, but it's just too painful. Did you know I was going to be here?"

"No," Howard told him, "though it's good to see you. I wanted to talk to you, but maybe you're right and it's still too early to talk about... you know, the accident and so on."

"Yes, let's make it some other time," said Matthew. "It's selfish of me, because I'm sure you need to talk it through, but..."

"Matthew, we're friends," Howard said. "We can help each other, but only when you're ready. You mustn't push yourself."

Julia came back into the room, followed by Ralph.

"Ewan and Karen can't make it tonight," he said, "so it's just the five of us."

Matthew didn't move. He was looking bewildered.

Ralph took a breath and stepped forward.

"Matthew, David," he said, "you don't have drinks. What would you like?"

David glanced at Matthew as though waiting for a cue, but Matthew was still looking oddly blank. He turned to David, then Julia and Howard.

"I'm sorry Julia," he said. "This is appalling behaviour, I know, but I can't stay. I'll talk to you, Howard, when I've got myself together a little; when I'm coping better. I find that I've been working too hard recently. As Ralph will confirm, he's diagnosed me as suffering from exhaustion due to overwork, so I reckon I need to take some time off to sort myself out."

There was a brief tableau of embarrassment in which no one could think of anything to say, and no one moved. Then Matthew turned to leave and Ralph, muttering sympathetically, went out with them to get their coats and see them to the door.

"*Well!*" Julia murmured after they'd left. "I'm so sorry, Howard, I had no idea that you and Matthew weren't talking to each other."

Howard shrugged, feeling suddenly washed out.

"I need to speak to him at some point, but clearly he's not ready for it yet," he said.

Ralph and Julia didn't say anything, so Howard took a deep breath and tried to arrange his thoughts.

"He was the only person who could really have shared this with me," he said after a while, "and there are so many details that I don't know, and I was hoping he could fill me in. It wasn't just missing the funeral, either, it was everything about the accident."

He ran his fingers through his hair and found that they were trembling slightly.

"Howard, Howard," Julia said, hugging him, "sit down, please. I'll get you another drink."

Howard's legs seemed to give way and he sank back onto his chair.

"Okay," said Ralph, sitting opposite him, "we're not Matthew, but we *are* friends. Talk to us."

A long shiver traversed Howard's entire body, followed by a sense of release. All these feelings had come to the surface when he'd seen Matthew, and now he needed to let them out.

"I don't remember anything," he said, "or at least not after the car went off the road. I don't remember the impact. When I came round in the hospital it was all given to me as a piece of history; that Corinne was dead; that she'd suffered severe head injuries... but I never saw her. I had to take it on trust, as it were, that she was dead, that she was being buried. And I keep on having these dreams about the accident;

of how Corinne must have looked with her head caved in; I can see it so *graphically* when I dream..."

If it hadn't been for Ralph and Julia that night, Howard might have succumbed to despair. He had managed to express something of what he was feeling, much later, when he said, "I feel doubly bereaved. I woke up to find I'd lost Corinne, and now I feel that I've lost Matthew too."

"For a while," Julia said. "Matthew has plenty of complicated emotions that he has to sort out before he can be rational about Corinne. He'll come round."

***

1999:

The waiting area at the hospital had exactly the same weary atmosphere as it had had the day before. As soon as he walked through the door Howard saw David standing at a vending machine with his back to him, stirring a cup of coffee with a sliver of plastic. He crossed to him and gently tapped his elbow.

"Hi," he said quietly.

David turned. He looked tired, and a little pale, but his eyes had a clarity to them where the day before they had looked completely lifeless.

"Hello, Howard," he said. "I was waiting for you. I'm afraid you've had a pointless journey. Matthew died at five o'clock this morning. I was with him. It was..." He blinked a couple of times and smiled slightly. "It was more or less what you might expect. He wasn't in pain. I've come back to get his belongings now that they've sorted his room out. I tried your London number to let you know, but there was no answer. I knew you were due to come here at ten-thirty, so I thought I'd wait and let you know myself."

"God," said Howard. "He looked ill yesterday, but not that ill. I had no idea..."

"He didn't want you to see how tired he was. But, anyway, I hate this, you know, *telling* people. I'm so bad at it. Matthew would have been much better. He'd have taken you off into a quiet corner and said all the right kind of empathetic things. Well, quite frankly, I feel like shit, Howard, and I can't think of anything else to say."

"That's okay," Howard told him. "Please, don't say anything. Thanks for waiting for me. I'll go now, unless there's anything I can do."

David looked down at the bulging overnight bag at his feet.

"Actually," he said, "there *is* something you can do for me, if you don't mind. My sister brought me over this morning, but she's gone to collect Matthew's parents from the station. I was going to take a taxi back home, but maybe you could give me a lift?"

"Of course," Howard said, pleased to be able to help. "Have you got anything else to collect?"

"No," said David picking up the bag, "this is everything."

He put his undrunk coffee carefully on a table which was stacked with information leaflets, and they left.

Once they were in the car, Howard looked across apologetically.

"I'm sorry to ask," he said, "but could you put your seat belt on?"

David, who was looking out of his window, glanced back at Howard as though he hadn't heard.

"Your seat belt," Howard repeated. "I'm sorry, but it's a bit of a thing with me these days."

"Oh," David murmured, "yes. I suppose it would be."

Howard pulled out and remained silent as they passed St Johns House Museum and along Coten End. As Howard drove, they talked briefly about the traffic congestion and Howard's night in the hotel before David broached a more serious subject.

"How did you feel when Corinne died?" he asked suddenly as they crossed the canal. "Apart from the obvious."

Howard concentrated on his driving whilst he contemplated David's question.

"None of it was at all obvious," he said after a while. "Did Matthew tell you that I suffered from alalia after the accident?"

"Alalia?"

"Loss of the power of speech. It's also sometimes referred to as mutism."

"I've heard of elective mutism," said David.

"There was nothing elective about my experience. I wanted to talk, believe me. I wanted to, but couldn't."

"No," David murmured. "Matthew never told me about that."

"It seems weird now. Well, it was weird then. I didn't actually feel as though I couldn't speak, or even that I didn't want to speak. It was just that if I tried to talk, if I opened my mouth to say something, instead of words, I would cry. And if I started crying, I became sort of hysterical."

"That does sound weird."

"Afterwards it was difficult to explain to people what I had experienced, until I stumbled across a fairly accurate analogy."

Howard stopped at the traffic lights on the Leamington side of the River Avon and glanced across at David, who was watching him intently.

"You know how sometimes, especially during childhood, it's possible to get an uncontrollable fit of laughter? It keeps on bubbling up every time you try to be serious. You go through that phase where you finally feel serious; you feel that you can open your mouth and say something sensible and coherent, but when you do, instead of actually speaking, you burst out laughing again."

"It's odd to think about something like that right now," said David, "but yes."

"It was like that for me, only with grief instead of laughter. I would open my mouth to talk and then, instead of words, out would come this ghastly mewling sound. It was terrifying."

"How long did it last?"

"Nearly a month. I ended up not trying to speak at all after the first few days; and then one day, when I was back at home, I woke up and went out to get a paper. The newsagent said something to me and I spoke back, and that was it - I was okay after that."

"When you say okay..."

"*Relatively* okay. It was nearly a year before I felt centred again. I'm sorry, I'm sure that's not the kind of thing you want to hear."

"What I *don't* want to hear is what everyone has been saying to me," said David. "That I should give it a few weeks and I'll start to feel better. At the moment I can't imagine feeling better, *ever*."

They fell silent again for a time.

"I take it you're still at York Road," Howard asked as he turned into Dale Street.

"Yes, still there." David paused before saying, quietly, "So it took you a year...?"

"I suppose I'd been kidding myself about what the situation was, exactly, with Corinne," Howard said. "She steadfastly refused to leave Matthew, and she was so busy doing her floristry that sometimes it was difficult to see our affair as being much more than just a fling. I sometimes wouldn't see her for a week or more at a time. In fact, looking back on it, we didn't see much of each other at all considering how intense it was for me. It often seemed that if we didn't live together, then we couldn't actually love each other that much. I mean, that's what I thought people did, if they fell in love - live together, get married. Have kids. Naive, huh?"

"Mmm," David agreed. "But I know what you mean. I felt a bit like that when I met Matthew. Marginalised. After we'd fallen in love, his relationship with Corinne stopped us from being able to have a live-in relationship. I went out with him for over six months before Corinne died, so I felt the same as you. There was that whole business of 'are they serious or not? Do they want to live with me or don't they'?"

"Yes," Howard agreed, "that's it exactly."

He pulled in at the kerb.

"Here we are."

"Do you want to come in?" David asked. "For a coffee, or a drink?"

"No, thanks, I'd better get back, and you must have all kinds of things to organise."

"Yes," he said quietly, "I suppose I do. You will come to the funeral?"

"Do you want me to?"

"Yes."

"Then I will."

David didn't move. Howard waited in silence.

"Look," David said eventually, "I'm sorry I didn't get to know you better when Matthew was alive..."

"You didn't have a chance," Howard told him. "By the time you were properly on the scene, I'd moved to London."

"Before that, when Matthew and I first met and whilst Corinne was still alive, Matthew used to encourage me to try and get to know you, but I was too wary."

"Wary?"

"I realise now that I felt threatened by Matthew's feelings for you," David said. "I'm glad that he finally made the effort to contact you again, by the way. He often felt guilty about losing touch. He thought perhaps you moved down to London to get away from the memories of your life with Corinne."

"He was right," said Howard. "But regardless of my reasons for moving, I would have been pleased to talk to him."

"Then why didn't you ever get in touch?"

"You were at that dinner with Julia and Ralph," said Howard. "Matthew said he would get in touch when he was ready, and I took him at his word. I didn't think it was my place to press him."

"How sad," David murmured as he got out of the car, "that something so unnecessary can separate two people who could have helped each other."

He closed the door with a clunk, waved briefly, and turned to walk up the short front path to the house. Howard leaned across the passenger seat to watch David let himself in. He didn't look back.

***

1997:

Alalia.

Howard knew that he could talk. He would lie on his bed in hospital and nod to himself and think, *No problem. I can speak.* And then a doctor or nurse would come along and ask him a question and either his throat would close so that he felt that he was choking, or his whole body would be racked with heavy, juddering sobs.

Sometimes he would wake in the night, crying out, but not with words - with a guttural, brutal anguish. His dreams were punctuated with images of gore. He'd never been interested in horror movies, but somehow that imagery had lodged itself in an endless cycle in his dreams so that he would suddenly, in the midst of an otherwise innocuous dream, find himself zooming in on ripped flesh and washes of blood.

He was post-traumatic. He was told that, in time, the dream images would fade and he would speak again, once the grief and shock had diminished. In the meantime he shouldn't worry about it, or feel that he was intrinsically disordered. Worrying that there was 'something wrong' with him would only make the condition worse. When he was discharged from hospital he should go home and live as normal a life as possible.

Howard, equipped with a pad and felt-tipped pen for the purpose of communication, returned to his flat and discovered that, since starting his relationship with Corinne, he had slipped out of several friendships. No one called, except for Julia and an old school friend that he was in the habit of meeting for a drink every so often. It was crazy, hearing the phone ring and not being able to answer it. He had to let the answerphone take the messages. He dropped a card round to Julia and to Bill explaining that he was convalescent and would get in touch when he was up to it.

Matthew didn't phone.

After several days on his own without seeing anybody, Howard began to forget that he couldn't speak. As long as he didn't see anyone, he didn't *need* to speak. One evening, frustrated by Matthew's silence, he phoned him at home. It was only when Matthew answered that Howard realised that he was unable to say anything. It was extraordinarily therapeutic to hear Matthew's voice, and to sob out some noises that could almost have been words.

"Who is this?" Matthew asked before perfunctorily slamming the phone down.

After he'd replaced the receiver, Howard retired to bed for a night of disturbed, nightmare-ridden sleep. In the morning he took an ankh on a chain out of his bedside drawer and hung it round his neck. It was a memento that Corinne had given him and which he hadn't thought to wear until then. It had the aura of a talisman and he felt that if anything might help him combat the almost supernatural quality of his nightmares, this would. Not because of its religious symbolism, but because it made him feel connected to Corinne in some way.

The strangest thing about suffering from alalia was that, after the first few days, when he was on his own, he spent whole tracts of time without having any words in his head. Occasionally he would have a verbal thought and it's sudden presence in his mind would highlight the fact that for some time previously he'd been existing in a wordless state. For a linguist this was particularly disorientating as he'd always reckoned that most, if not all, his thought processes were verbally based. But now, he spent whole days in a state of weird mental numbness that wasn't uncomfortable or even unwelcome; it was a state in which time effortlessly slipped past.

However, he must have been healing himself in that curious way that minds have, so that one morning he woke up to find that something had settled in the night and that, somehow, he seemed to be functioning normally. When he went out to buy a paper and he said hello to the newsagent, it wasn't until he returned home that he realised what he had done. He had spoken! It was bizarre that something that he'd previously taken so completely for granted - the power of speech - should engender such an extraordinary sense of elation when it returned.

Later in the day he cried properly for the first time since the accident. He didn't count all those episodes of crazy unhinged grief in the hospital. This time he was controlled. He went out and bought himself a bottle of wine and, as he sipped it, he cried for Corinne, and for himself, and for Matthew, and afterwards he'd felt a preliminary sense of healing so that, for the first time since the accident, when he went to bed he slept through the night without dreaming.

**

1999:

By the time Howard reached London he'd decided that he wouldn't go to Matthew's funeral. He'd never met any of Matthew's family and didn't feel that he'd be anything more than an embarrassment to David. There was little point in going for his own sake. Matthew's death, if anything, simply sealed off that section of his life that contained Corinne - had removed it one stage further into the past. To leave it behind now would be fitting.

Nevertheless, he felt a clear frustration that he hadn't had that second, promised conversation with Matthew at the hospital. What was it that he'd been so keen to tell him about Corinne? He would never know. And, probably, that was a good thing.

When he arrived back at the flat, he was surprised to find a message from Dominic Woods, Matthew's solicitor, on his answer machine giving his home number and asking him to phone as soon as possible.

It was only 3.30 p.m. so Howard tried the number.

"Thank you for calling back," Mr Woods said when he answered. "Have you heard the news about Matthew Rickard?"

"Yes," Howard told him. "I was up in Leamington this morning."

"Ah."

There was a short pause.

"Terrible business," he went on. "I'm shocked by how quickly he went downhill. I was a personal friend of his as well as his solicitor, so I am more than professionally sympathetic about your loss."

"I hadn't seen him for over two years," said Howard. "I don't suppose I could really call myself a personal friend of his."

"And yet," said Mr Woods, "he's written you into his Will."

This statement was so unexpected that Howard asked Woods to repeat what he'd said.

"You are one of the beneficiaries of Matthew's Will," he said. "There's David Tanner, yourself, and also someone called Peter Collicos."

Collicos. The name was unfamiliar.

"The reason I wanted to talk to you about it as soon as possible," Woods told him, "is that you are an undeclared beneficiary, which is to say that David Tanner and Peter Collicos will never know *definitively* - unless you tell them - that you are in Matthew's Will."

"Oh," said Howard, "how does that work?"

"Your portion of the estate is left with me, in trust for an undisclosed party. It's quite straightforward."

"Why would he want to do that?" said Howard.

"Matthew wanted to save David the anxiety that might arise from the fact that he chose to leave some money to you. In a way I think it is pointless, because David will, I'm sure, have guessed immediately that the anonymous beneficiary is you. What is perhaps more sensible is the fact that the sum left to you is also undisclosed, so he'll never know *how much* was involved."

"Not all that much, surely?"

"I don't know what criteria you would use to judge quantity," Woods said cautiously, "but in my estimation you would agree that it is a sizeable amount. Matthew had a number of private insurance policies and you were the named beneficiary. I think it will probably amount to several hundred thousand pounds... I don't suppose you'd be able to call in at my office in Leamington, would you, so that we can discuss it further? Perhaps if you come up for the funeral? I talked to David about half an hour ago and he seems to think it'll be either Wednesday or Thursday."

"Fine," said Howard, "fine. I'll come up and see you then."

When Howard went through to the kitchen to get himself a beer, shrugging to himself at the reversal of his decision not to attend the funeral, he realised that he was in a state of mild shock. He opened the door to the refrigerator and winced at the bruise in the small of his back. Without warning, he remembered with the most extraordinary clarity, an occasion when Corinne had had a bruise in the same place...

***

1995:

They'd made love round at Corinne's. Matthew was away in Italy and it was a warm day in late-spring; the first day of the year that had had a high pollen count. Corinne was sniffly, but delighted with the weather and the fact that, as it was Sunday she didn't have to go in to work.

For a reason that Howard never found out, Corinne was always wary of making love in her bedroom. There was clearly something deeply unromantic about it, for her, and she preferred to have sex almost anywhere else in the house. That day, they made love in the darkened dining room amongst the tall, wooden chairs. They'd ended up with Corinne leaning back against the sideboard, steadying herself with one hand against the highly polished dining table. For Howard it had been yet another experience of heightened intensity; it hadn't bothered him where they did it. At his place they always made love in bed, fully naked, without hurry. At Corinne and Matthew's they did it semi-clothed and with a rather whimsical air of naughtiness. It had become a kind of ritual that this was the way things would be.

In the dining room, as he approached orgasm, Corinne cried out, eyes wide and her free arm hugging Howard firmly, her hips pressed forward, her lips parted in her familiar sigh. The timbre of her voice on this occasion, however, had been somehow *harder*, more extreme - a shout, almost - and Howard had lost his rhythm for a moment before he could continue.

Afterwards, he had noticed the sharp edge of the sideboard and was worried that Corinne might have been uncomfortable. She'd laughed at his concern, but the following day he'd gasped at the green/blue bruise on her side, just above her hip, the size of a saucer.

SIX

1996:

Howard was in Cologne. He'd spent a tedious morning interpreting on the subject of railways and rolling stock and, at lunch time, had been intercepted by Matthew.

"Let's skip the official lunch," he'd said. "Cologne has a brilliant collection of modern art. Let's eat in the café at the gallery."

The café was open and airy, and the gallery was excellent, housing an eclectic collection of modern art - from Max Ernst and Picasso to Claes Oldenburg and Andy Warhol. Outside it was possible to saunter down to the river, where crowds of people were sitting in the sun. Matthew suggested that they wander across town to a rambling park that he knew. Howard agreed, and Matthew bought a bottle of champagne on the way. They ensconced themselves in a quiet knoll surrounded by trees and spent an afternoon of unexpected hilarity lounging on the grass. Quite why everything had seemed so funny that day, Howard couldn't remember, but they'd laughed at the intense seriousness of the conference organisers; at the *dullness* of most of what had been discussed; at the formality of international relations, and the patriotism of most of the delegates... The last thing Howard ever felt like on trips of this kind was an ambassador of his culture.

"Unlike the Germans we've met today," he'd said, "I'm not a patriot. I can see the flaws of my culture only too clearly."

"Mmm," murmured Matthew, finishing off the last of the champagne, of which he'd drunk at least two thirds. He leant back to look up at the sky.

"You know," he said after a while. "I wish I could do this more often. I wish I could *relax* more often. I go from beautiful city to beautiful city, but unless I've got someone to share that experience with, it can be a lonely business. I regard it as an immense privilege to be able to share it with you, because you're intelligent and you have the ability to criticise without being judgemental. Sitting in restaurants, or going round galleries on your own can get tedious after a while. I wish you would consider taking a job with us full-time at CMS."

Howard smiled at Matthew's sincerity, but declined the oft-repeated proposal.

"You've got Corinne's company on a lot of your trips," he said. "She's got exactly that kind of cultural mind."

Matthew shook his head.

"That's only an occasional pleasure since she started up in floristry," he said. "And my usual interpreter, Jerry Futerman, is such a self-important fart. He's one of those ardent, slightly evangelical Christians that give the quietly faithful a bad name. Sadly, he's excellent. As indeed are you."

Matthew pulled a strand of grass from beside him and nibbled it.

"Incidentally, did I tell you I met a woman called Catrina Gibson in Milan last month? She says she went to university with you."

"Catrina?" said Howard. "Yes. A gifted linguist."

"She said you were probably the most talented student in the faculty, but that you were also one of the laziest. She said your tutor was furious that you didn't get a First, because you could have strolled away with one if you'd put in any effort at all."

"It's amazing how people mythologise," Howard remarked. "I wasn't nearly as lazy as I made myself out to be. It was an affectation that I'm rather ashamed of now. At the time I had some absurd notions about how important it was to be admired by other people."

"*That's* why I like having you around," Matthew said. "You're never bothered whether you impress people or not. In my profession I'm surrounded by people who are all 'trying to get on'. It's incredibly refreshing to find someone who isn't. Of course, it's frustrating too, because it's precisely your *laisser faire* attitude that prevents you from taking a full time job as my assistant."

Howard sighed.

"How did I ever come to be doing this sort of work at all?" he laughed. "I'm a drifter at heart. It all seems so *contradictory*, spending my days helping people haggle over multi-million pound budgets."

"You do it because you need to use your brain," Matthew told him. "You shouldn't be spending even part of your time dossing around. If you didn't use your intellect, you'd atrophy."

"Misconception number one," Howard murmured. "In my experience, the most intelligent people are stumbled across whilst dossing around. Look at my friend José for a start. He works part time, too, so that he can go out and *experience* life in a way that he needs for his poetry. His kind of intelligence is strangled by too much routine. In fact, the reason a lot of people do drop out is because they're too cerebral to put up with the kind of shit that normal working life throws at them. I've often been intellectually overshadowed to a humiliating degree by the casual wisdom I've found amongst people who would be described by people like you as atrophying."

"You know what I mean, though."

"Not really. And please don't try to label me as 'intellectual'. One of the most dreadful things I've witnessed in people whose minds I admire is this terrible problem that they have of being unable to switch off. You can see it in their eyes - an endless grinding of mental processes. No wonder so many intellectuals burn themselves out. Well, I'm happy to say that I can switch off with incredible ease. I need to do linguistic work to stop my languages seeping from my mind, *not* because of some intellectual imperative. Having several languages is like physical fitness. Stop for too long and you'll find it all starts to slip away."

Howard nodded to himself at how true this was and how tempting to sit back and let it happen.

"The main reason I do this work is for money," he went on. "If I didn't need to, I can assure you I wouldn't. There are plenty of other more pleasant ways of keeping up your languages."

"But you make ten times as much as this doing your *gigolo* work. If it's money you're after, why don't you stick to that?"

"You have a point," Howard admitted, "but there's something about prostitution..." (he could see Matthew wincing at the word.) "There's something about prostitution that is strangely *sapping* after a while. If I give myself freely, it charges me, if I force myself to perform, it drains me. You could examine that endlessly and come up with different analyses every time. All that matters in the end is the fact that I have a certain amount of spare energy, if you like, for prostitution and I am careful not to overextend myself."

"Do you ever get any *pleasure* out of it?" Matthew asked.

"Yes," Howard told him, "and I sometimes find that confusing."

"Perhaps you were unloved as a child," Matthew speculated. "Perhaps you respond to love in any form. It's a pity you don't have God's love."

"Ha ha," Howard said. "Whatever. It doesn't stop that weird profundity with my clients being a real, true emotion, wherever it comes from."

"Maybe you'll end up marrying some sun-wizened millionairess."

"You may laugh," Howard told him, "but I'd rather interact with a desiccated body than a desiccated mind."

Matthew nodded at this as though Howard had scored an important point and rolled over on the grass to prop himself up on his elbows.

"The high life must be quite intoxicating, though," Matthew said. "I'm lucky enough to have stayed in the George Cinq in Paris, but I've only ever had a room, not a suite..."

"Don't be crass," Howard laughed. "As you know, I'd rather have a sandwich with someone interesting like you than caviar with someone tedious. I'd rather go out cycling with a good friend than be tearing along an autobahn at a hundred and fifty miles an hour in a Ferrari. I'd rather sit by myself on a wild stretch of moorland than make love to someone I didn't fancy on a deserted Barbadian beach."

Howard rolled over also, so that he was lying on his back.

"It's taken me a long time," he said, "to realise that the experiences that are the most fulfilling are *not* the most intense highs, the wild extremes of sex, or those blissed-out moments when you're drunk or on drugs, or even the exhilaration of seducing someone new... the truly important moments are those quiet periods of complete calm, of contentment, when you're sitting by the waves, maybe, and the only sound is of the sea and a distant seabird calling across the water - when you're relaxing on the grass and there are no worries pressing in on you. Contentment. I live for those moments."

He nodded to himself and ran his fingers through the grass.

"It's like with sex," he continued. "Men so often imagine that the greatest moment during sex is the orgasm, but actually, for me, the greatest moment is afterwards when you're holding someone and sharing a peaceful hour or two with them. When you're lying still, and content.

"I suspect," he added, "that you can never reach that emotion without having the highs, and especially the lows. But that's the way it is."

"True," murmured Matthew, "but as far as contentment goes, it helps if you have someone whom you *can* hold, and love, and lie beside."

"I get close to it, sometimes, with virtual strangers if I admire their minds - and I guess I've fallen in love, too, in my time."

Howard thought of Corinne and fell silent.

"I don't think I've ever fallen in love," said Matthew. "At least, not with anyone who's reciprocated it. I don't think I've ever experienced that moment of profound peace after love-making."

"I hope that one day you do," Howard told him.

Matthew leaned over to Howard and patted his shoulder, then looked up at the sky and laughed with regret.

"If only you'd slept with me," he said. "That first time I hired you, when I was still under the impression that you were gay..."

***

1996:

Making love with Corinne. Being with her, when they had exhausted themselves and he might have expected to be lying staring in tranquillity at the ceiling, or out of the window, or at her cool, even skin. But sometimes he couldn't do that. He would cling to her and be washed with an almost overwhelming sadness and sense of frailty. Because there was no certainty. He couldn't capture a sense of permanence, because he wasn't sure of anything in their relationship. For the first time, he wanted to be sure, but everything about Corinne suggested caution. If he ever broached the subject of the possibility that they might, one day, live together, she would grow angry and leave. So there was a silence between them where there should have been words. And Howard didn't know what that meant. For him it was equally plausible that Corinne might arrive on his doorstep with a carload of possessions and say 'I've left him' and embrace him and let him help her in with her stuff, or that he'd come home and find a note pinned to his door saying 'It's over'. Whatever else this feeling of uncertainty did for Howard, it prevented him from lying beside her in complete contentment once passion had run its course. He did nothing to try to actively change this situation because he thought that it would resolve itself, that Corinne would make up her mind one way or another and then act on her decision, and that his best course of action was to put no pressure on her. But he felt wistful sometimes, and that mix of emotions that lovers can feel; of sadness and happiness combined.

SEVEN

Howard was sitting in the tacky café in Jephson gardens. He was the only one there to watch the drizzle mottling the surface of the river. There was an hour before he had to go to the crematorium for Matthew's funeral and he was feeling restless and tired after several nights of poor sleep. He was rereading the letter that Dominic Woods had given him earlier in the day when they'd discussed Matthew's Will. It was dated only four weeks before Matthew's death - which meant it had been written when Matthew knew he was ill.

Dear Howard,

How I wish I hadn't let things slip after Corinne died! At first I was too confused to understand my mixture of emotions. I realised, after she died, that I loved you more than I loved her. What a terrible thing to admit! Then I realised that in some ways I was like her - we'd both fallen in love with people we couldn't have. She'd fallen in love with me, and I'd fallen in love with you. It seemed so much easier to let you go to London and not to contact you. So much safer - emotionally. But I had David, by then, whom I love very much. He would have allowed me to be balanced about re-establishing our friendship, but I was a coward and I shied away from it. I cannot tell you how much I wish I had acted otherwise. Please forgive me, Howard, I know I rejected your friendship when you needed it most - when you were in grief and shock. I turned my back on you, despite my faith, which told me to do otherwise.

Now I have lost my faith I cannot make amends in the name of God, but I <u>can</u> do so in the name of humanity. I was inadequate in living up to my faith. Now all I have to do is live up to myself - what a relief!

So Matthew had given Howard all this money in order to 'make amends'. It was absurd. Howard felt a wash of sadness at the two years in which they'd been out of touch. And now... and now it angered him that Matthew might have thought that money would be, in some way, a recompense for that.

Howard was also aware that there was some mischief involved here. Matthew had known of Howard's antipathy to having more money than he needed. And now he was going to be inheriting a 'considerable sum' as Mr Woods had put it, without earning any of it... Part of him felt that he should simply hand it on to David - who had been left the house he shared with Matthew and its contents - and forget about it. Another part of him wondered if Matthew's intention had been that he should experience a materially secure life for a while - and that maybe he should respect that intention. Yet a third part of him felt that he should simply do nothing; that he should put the money to one side, get used to the fact that it was there, and wait for an idea to emerge concerning what he should do with it.

***

The crematorium was a characterless brick building with only the vaguest of ecclesiastical airs about it. From the outside it could as easily have been an electricity sub-station as a crematorium. At least it was in a quiet woodland setting.

It was a grey afternoon. Fortunately the rain that had been falling intermittently all morning had stopped. A squirrel was scampering up a tree trunk as he parked his car and he noticed at once that Ralph and

Julia were making their way into the chapel. Howard felt self-conscious about being present and discreetly followed them inside to slip into the pew at the back, next to Julia, who kissed him, briefly, and squeezed his hand. Some faces he recognised, most he didn't, and he was impressed that a secular service had been arranged. It only lasted twenty minutes, with a brief eulogy from John Deacon, Matthew's second in command at CMS. It ended with a violin solo; Bach's Chaconne in D - both grand and mournful - to finish the service off.

Observing the people present, Howard found himself aware of an unexpected difference in the quality of sadness that they displayed. It took him a minute or two to work out why. It was because Matthew had died so young. Thirty-five! he heard someone whisper in the pew in front of him.

***

Howard remembered the last time he'd seen Matthew before the accident. Matthew had just come back from Lyons and he'd arrived from Heathrow, glowing with pleasure and confidence. He'd taken Howard and Corinne out for a meal and the three of them had laughed and joked together, and, for an evening, Howard had been content with the set up as it was - loving Corinne and being Matthew's special friend.

Then, there was the image from a few days ago, of Matthew lying in bed, apologising and smiling knowingly, perhaps at the thought that he was leaving Howard so much money? What an extraordinary man he had been, and how tragic that Howard's relationship with him had been so complicated...

Howard felt the loss of the time he might have spent with Matthew over the previous two years as an almost palpable presence. It was like a weight pressing down on him and it occurred to him, for the first time, that, although he was only experiencing a light shadow of the full force of it, this was what people meant when they said a person was 'bowed with grief'. Looking around, and judging by the obvious emotion, it moved him that Matthew had made so many friends who might care enough to cry at his funeral.

And then, the remembrance was over and everyone was filing out into the cool, humid air.

David stood shaking hands with everyone as they left, and grasped Howard by the elbow, to show a special emphasis in his greeting. Once outside, Julia smiled.

"I'm so pleased you saw Matthew before the end," she said.

"So am I," he told her. "By the way, I don't suppose you know if Corinne's sister is here?"

"Emma? Yes, I saw her earlier. She's wearing a black velvet jacket with some sort of silver and amethyst brooch on it. Perhaps you remember it - it used to belong to Corinne."

Howard nodded and set off in search of the woman who was wearing it. He found her on the path to the car park, watching the squirrels. She was slightly shorter than Corinne had been, and with a fuller face. She had raven black hair and a stern air about her that was clearly calculated to be intimidating. Howard took a breath and, walking over to her, introduced himself.

"I suppose you're the undeclared beneficiary?" she asked immediately.

Howard was slightly taken aback by her pushy tone.

"I can't say," Howard said carefully.

"That means you are," she said. "Lucky bastard."

He took a breath and ignored what she'd said.

"Matthew told me, just before he died, that I should come and talk to you about Corinne," he said, trying to sound friendly in the face of her unapproachability.

"Because of the accident?" she asked.

"Yes, I suppose so."

"That was over two years ago," she said. "It's not worth talking about. We're all too busy getting on with our lives to spend time worrying about what happened in the past."

"You might be," Howard told her, feeling antagonised by her apparent lack of concern, "but for me, two years is almost nothing."

"That's true in some ways," said Emma, as though stating the obvious. "I just meant that certain *kinds* of worries are pointless. I'm not trying to be indifferent. The pain and the loss will always be there."

"You sound as though you're indifferent," Howard said.

Emma stopped and observed Howard closely.

"Well, I'm not," she said.

Her expression softened as she noticed Howard's anguished expression.

"You really did love her didn't you?" she asked.

Howard merely nodded.

"And you haven't got over it?"

"No," Howard admitted.

Emma gestured, as though exasperated.

"Of course," she said.

Howard didn't know whether to say anything further. After all, he didn't know her. But, he decided, perhaps the fact that she was a stranger to him, and yet had been a confidante of Corinne's, made confession that much easier; that much more appealing. Almost like talking to Corinne herself.

"I haven't been able to *connect* with a woman since Corinne died," he admitted to her.

They were now standing close to each other, Emma suddenly pensive. After a decisive sigh, she spoke.

"I wish Corinne hadn't decided to use you for her vendetta," she said.

"Vendetta?"

Emma turned as the last of the mourners broke away from David and wandered away from the chapel. She touched her brooch briefly.

"Okay," she said, "I'll talk to you for a few minutes, but I must have a word with Matthew's father first. Wait here."

She left and walked up to an elderly man that Howard didn't recognise. As he watched, someone tapped his shoulder from behind.

"You must be Howard?" the voice said with mid-Atlantic precision.

Howard turned. The man was darker-haired than he was, and perhaps six or seven years younger, and an inch or two shorter. His sturdy frame was powerful where Howard's was lean, but there was no mistaking the similarity of their faces. It gave Howard an eerie frisson to catch the gleam from the man's slightly overshadowed eyes and the humorous pucker of his smile.

"Matthew always said we looked alike," he murmured. "I see that he was right. I'm Pete, by the way. Pete Collicos."

They shook hands. Although Howard was the taller of the two, he felt almost diminished standing beside Pete, who was deeply tanned, fuller in the face and brashly self-confident.

Similar yet utterly different, Howard thought.

"You're the Collicos mentioned in Matthew's Will?" Howard asked.

"Aha," Pete said with a delighted smile. "You should be more circumspect, Howard. You've given yourself away as the undeclared beneficiary. How else would you know that I'm mentioned in the Will?"

"There's hardly any point being secretive about it," Howard said, "seeing as everyone seems to know anyway."

"Actually," Pete confided, "Matthew let me into the secret when he was drawing up the Will. The reason he wanted you to be undeclared wasn't because he wanted to be secretive about the fact that he was leaving you something - he wanted to be circumspect about *how much*."

"But David must have some idea how much Matthew was worth?"

"You'd be surprised. Matthew was pretty quiet about his finances."

Howard was about to question this statement, when Emma approached.

"You must be brothers, right?" she asked.

"No," Howard told her.

"Something much more complicated than that," Pete said, taking his wallet out and removing a card to give to Howard.

"I must go, I'm afraid," he said. "Give me a ring soon, I think we should talk."

"Are you sure you're not related?" Emma asked as she watched Pete walking off. "I thought you were twins at first."

"No, really," Howard assured her. "I've never met him before."

Emma turned and began to walk slowly down the gravel path to the car park.

"So," she said, "what did Matthew tell you to ask me?"

"He died before he could say," Howard told her.

She smiled sadly and looked across at the dark foliage of a rhododendron.

"I expect he wanted you to understand about Corinne's state of mind."

"He implied something of the sort, yes."

"I suppose," Emma said quietly, "Corinne told you the story of how our brother died?"

"Yes."

"Crushed by a lorry."

"Yes."

"And she told you about our family falling apart - about how she had to make it all hang together, by herself, when she was only twelve. About how her only ally was her Aunt Gillian, who ended up being murdered by burglars."

"Yes."

"It's all untrue."

Howard was confused.

"How do you mean?"

"We never even had a brother," Emma told him. "There is an Aunt Gillian, but she wasn't murdered. She's still alive and living in Wales."

Howard stopped walking and stared at Emma.

"In a white cottage near Dolgellau?"

"Yes, how did you know?"

Howard felt a horrible exhilaration as he thought about it.

"Matthew pointed it out to me, once," he said. "I knew there was something odd about that story. I asked Corinne but she wouldn't say anything."

"Naturally," Emma said. "She wouldn't have wanted to be found out in her deceit."

"I don't understand," he said slowly.

"It's quite simple," Emma told him. "Corinne created a looking-glass life for herself, but instead of everything being wonderful, it was all dreadful. She suffered from manic depression - you knew that?"

"I knew she had a melancholy streak..."

"It was clinical. She had treatment for it on and off from adolescence onwards. She had a nervous breakdown when she was thirteen-"

"Yes, she told me about that."

Emma closed her eyes briefly, and then looked up into the new foliage above them before continuing.

"It was weird, Corinne having that breakdown, because she'd been so *normal* until then," she told him. "My parents were horrified. I mean, we had such an idyllic middle-class, cosseted childhood. It seemed so wrong that Corinne could be unhappy. None of us could understand it. My parents thought they'd done something wrong, or that Corinne had had some terrible experience at school that she wasn't telling us about. But it was simply this chemical imbalance that happens every now and then in people like her. A lot of the time - most of the time - she was fine, and then she'd start to get *too* happy. Euphoric. Then she'd crash. It was so sad. Especially because we didn't understand what was happening and didn't know how to help her."

"But what has this got to do with her telling lies?"

"She wanted to invent a past for herself," Emma said. "She was intensely self-conscious about being depressive. She thought of herself as being tragically afflicted - which she was, of course. The problem was that she had no reason that she could see for being unhappy. She believed that if she had no external reason for them, then her depressions must somehow be because she was flawed as a person, that there was something wrong with her. *That's* why she started lying. If she could make people believe that she'd been through a series of appalling tragedies, then they wouldn't blame her for being depressive; that, on the contrary, they would praise her for still functioning when other people would have completely cracked up."

"That's certainly how I saw it," Howard said. "I admired her for how well she'd coped with all that trauma."

"There you are," Emma said. "And of course you fell in love with her, which makes a difference."

"Yes," Howard admitted. He was slightly shocked that he had allowed himself to be so open, despite his earlier desire for this to happen. Perhaps it was due to Emma's clinical approach to their conversation.

"Corinne was the only woman I've ever loved in any meaningful way," he said. "Our relationship was certainly the only fully mutual relationship I've ever had. In a way, I feel blighted because, somehow, it seems impossible that I could ever capture that level of mutuality with someone else."

"Because you'll always compare, and the comparison will, inevitably, be unfavourable?"

"Something like that," Howard murmured.

Emma took him by the elbow and steered him along a walkway at a tangent to the car park.

"There is something I think you should know," she said carefully, then stopped speaking as if trying to work out how to express herself.

"Mmm?"

She looked straight into Howard's eyes with extraordinary intensity.

"Corinne never loved you," she told him.

Howard felt as if he'd been physically struck and jerked involuntarily.

"How do you mean?"

"What I say. She used to see me every couple of months for a day or two, and we discussed you often." She paused. "I would never have told you this if your life wasn't clearly blighted by something that was never even true."

"But..."

"She loved Matthew. That's why she married him. It was a deliber-ate act of self-destructive behaviour. It was the perfect way to turn her

– 87 –

lies into reality, the ideal excuse for being relentlessly depressed - loving a gay man. I don't think she did it consciously, but it was obvious to anyone who knew her well that she was looking for someone other than herself to blame her depressions on."

"But she wasn't sure that Matthew was gay when they got married."

"Yes she was. Even better than Matthew, because *he* thought there might be a possibility of change. But the set up suited Corinne very well as it was. Whenever she felt unhappy, she could say to herself 'I'm not *intrinsically* unhappy. I am just in an unhappy situation - it's not my fault'."

"This sounds very implausible," Howard said. "Corinne and I were lovers for over a year. Do you think I wouldn't have known if she didn't love me?"

"I'm afraid *that's* the implausible part - you believing that she was in love with you. Look at it logically. If she was in love with you and not with Matthew, why did she stay with Matthew?"

"Because she felt an obligation towards him."

"Love doesn't work like that. If you're really in love with someone, you want to be with them *all the time*."

"So why did she ever have an affair with me in the first place, then?" Howard asked dismissively.

Emma laughed as if she was surprised he hadn't worked this simple fact out for himself.

"She had an affair with you so that she could hurt Matthew. That's the way unrequited love works - it turns in on itself. It hurt so much that Matthew couldn't love her, physically, that she wanted him to hurt, too. She met you and saw at once that Matthew was in love with you, so it was the perfect set up - she would sleep with *his* object of desire. It was simply too good an opportunity to miss."

"I'm sorry," said Howard, "but this is absurd. I can't believe that Corinne would be so scheming."

"Corinne saw her life as one great tragedy," Emma said. "When you turned up she had the opportunity, through a single moment of instinctive manipulation, to turn her life from a fantasy tragedy into a very real one."

Howard shook his head.

"Go away and think about it," Emma told him. "It's true. I watched it all happening."

"So why didn't you do anything about it?"

"I did. I talked to Matthew, who insisted that Corinne start having therapy again. I think she might have worked her way out of the whole mess if it hadn't been for the accident. In fact, the last time I saw her she had made up her mind to break off with you. She told me so. I told her it was the most positive thing she could do. She'd also decided that her long-term plan was to leave Matthew - which was essential for her emotional recovery. But she had to leave him and live on her own as an individual for a while, and not to rely on the fact that you were in love with her and prepared to offer her a home away from Matthew. If she'd gone off with you it would have been a reverse of the situation that she was in with Matthew - another one-sided love affair. Not a good idea. And, of course, I told her that to get into a full-time relationship with you would have been yet another case of her deliberately choosing an emotional situation that would make her unhappy. She *had* to break that cycle. But her business was on the verge of bankruptcy so she couldn't leave Matthew right then. She needed him to keep her afloat."

"No, that's not true either," Howard said. "Her business was doing fine."

"That's what she liked people to think. But in reality it was on the verge of collapse. Matthew had to sort out the mess of it all. If she hadn't died that weekend, the business would have folded within a month."

As she said this, Emma placed her hand on Howard's shoulder to show that she empathised with how shocking he was finding the conversation.

"She was extremely upset about it," she told him. "Unbalanced, even. If it wasn't for the fact that you were driving when the accident happened, I'd have thought it was suicide."

Howard now vividly remembered Matthew saying that he knew something about Corinne's state of mind at the time of the accident. Was he referring to the fact that Corinne was facing a financial crisis?

"Have you got a contact address or number?" Howard asked. "Maybe I could talk to you again when I've thought this over?"

"I don't think that's a good idea," she said. "Maybe I shouldn't have told you anything. Maybe it would have been easier for you to have gone on thinking that she loved you. But I have this theory that lies are always a bad idea, and that being duped into believing lies leaves us with a kind of subconscious tension - because no one's lies are ever so complete, or so water-tight, that they don't leave disturbing inconsistencies."

Howard stared at her, stricken, for a few moments. She stared back, then looked down.

"Now, really," she told him, as the path they'd taken arrived back at the car park, "I must get going."

She bleeped off her car alarm and got in. As she started the engine, she opened the window.

"I've often wondered if I would ever have this conversation," she said. "I'm so sorry."

Howard gazed after Emma's car, long after it had disappeared. He felt shell-shocked. Overwhelmed. A familiar numbness started creeping over him and he shivered involuntarily. *Deceit.* Had Corinne been deceiving him? He, of all people, understood how deceit could have it's own momentum, how one simple lie could lead to an endless escalation of misinformation...

***

1986:

When Howard was at university he found that he needed to spend time on his own. Although he could participate in, and enjoy, the frenetic socialising that was a part of living in halls, he also found that he had to get out on his own, preferably for a whole day, each week. There was something agitated in him that needed solitude in order to settle. He had a car that he'd bought for himself in his year out before university, and he used it to drive out to take long walks in the countryside. But there was something too formal, too anodyne and comfortable about Cambridgeshire, with its pollarded trees along the river banks and its well-tended flint churches.

When he was at home one weekend during his second year, he found the two-man tent he'd been bought for his sixteenth birthday. Used twice, it had been put at the back of his wardrobe and then forgotten. Now, he pulled it out and felt, in the close weave of the rustling synthetic fabric, a sense of purpose.

The following weekend, the second weekend of March, he drove to the Suffolk coast with his tent, sleeping bag and mat. He went to *Rosemerion*, an isolated holiday cottage that belonged to his uncle. With willows to one side and an uninhabited salt-marsh to the other, he knew that he wouldn't be overlooked or discovered if he surreptitiously pitched his tent on the overgrown back lawn.

He'd been to *Rosemerion* several times before, mostly during his childhood, and hadn't been all that impressed with the place which, to his childish eyes, looked forlorn, exposed and overly isolated. But now, there was something about the place that connected inside him with a profundity that was not to be equalled until, many years later, he fell in love with Corinne.

The cottage itself was built on a rocky outcrop that was slightly raised above a brackish estuary. Now a nature reserve, there were no modern buildings in the area. At the front of the house there was a duckboard veranda, beyond which the reedy bank curved away. Here wading birds wandered, and seagulls raucously dashed. Along from the house there were the still, reedy pools of the salt marsh where more birds roamed, and in the evening he could hear the distant boom of a bittern. Although there were a couple of farmhouses up the track at the back of the house - and some military installations that could be seen from the lower edge of the garden - from the duckboards at the front there were no other buildings in sight, except for the lighthouse two miles away beyond the shingle spit on the far side of the river.

That first night, Howard ate sandwiches and drank a can of Coke and sat on the veranda of the cottage, watching the twin beams from the lighthouse as they raked along the coast. He couldn't remember ever having seen the stars so clearly. He sat out, shivering with cold, looking up at the haze of the milky way and wondering which stars made up which constellation. He lay on the duckboards in front of the cottage, and he felt the sharpness of the dried seaweed that had been strewn there by a storm-tide.

The following morning Howard was up at dawn, as the first light seeped through the orange fabric of his inner tent. He drank some water from the tap at the back of the cottage and ate a few slices of dry bread. He walked through the marsh, calmed by the presence of still water. He went almost as far as the ivy clad ruin of an old farmhouse, sited on the sharp curve of the river where it was still tidal, before turning back and, still cold from the previous evening, packed up his tent carefully before returning to his car.

As he drove back to Cambridge, fighting off sleep in the warmth of the car, he realised that for nearly twenty-four hours he hadn't had a sequential thought process of any kind; rather, he had experienced an intellectual emptiness punctuated by images that were not related to each other: the paleness of the late afternoon sky, the lack of need to hurry anywhere, the murky quality of the brackish water, the peacefulness of the windswept landscape... He knew, with sudden irrefutable conviction, that he would return to this place again and again.

Howard felt extremely wary of telling anyone about his experience. If he'd simply said, 'I went off with my tent', it would sound far too boy scout-ish, too un-Cambridge, too (it was embarrassing to admit this to himself) *unimpressive*. Instead, on his return, when he went for tea with Leon, a fellow linguist, he murmured, "Oh, I went to see someone, that's all."

There must have been something in the way Howard said it that sparked Leon's interest, because he asked for more details. Howard, cornered, refused to give further information and Leon had laughed.

"Who is she?" he laughed. "Anyone can see you've had quite a night of it and you haven't had any sleep. You look positively postcoital. But why be so secretive?"

Howard had shrugged, pleased that Leon was so impressed, and didn't try to contradict him. Instead, he got up and said, "Look, I've got to go back to my room and have a kip. I'm shattered."

Leon had patted him on the back as he'd left and said, "You'd better not tell Jan. She'd do her nut."

At that stage Howard had only recently started going out with Jan. They weren't seeing all that much of each other and he didn't feel he had to explain where he was going and why. The following weekend, when she asked to spend some time with him, he lied and told her he was going home. But he returned to *Rosemerion*. This time he noticed that one of the windows to the extension at the back of the cottage was loose and, using a piece of wire from a rotting fence, he managed to open it and clamber through. Inside there were two small rooms and a lobby area from which it was not possible to gain access to the main body of the house. As he examined the place, Howard realised that this was not an extension at all, but the original dwelling - an old, thick-walled fisherman's cottage. It was the much larger house adjoining it that was the extension.

There was a hand-pump in the back room that poured slightly rust-coloured water into a stone basin from the well beneath the house. He didn't trust it for drinking, but it was fine for washing. It was easy to clear a space for himself amongst the debris of previous summer holidays - a couple of old bikes, a broken canoe, spades, boxes, gardening tools, a lawn mower... He piled everything up in a corner and draped some hessian sacks over it, then swept the old brick-coloured tiles of the floor and put his sleeping mat down.

The following week he brought a small gas-cylinder cooker and a hurricane lamp that he'd bought in Oxfam. He thought of this little room as his 'hideout'. Back at university rumours had flared up amongst his peers about his 'secret life'. He did feel genuinely secretive and possessive about his hideout - his sanctuary - and so it was useful camouflage that Leon had spread rumours which kept that aspect of his life hidden whilst, incidentally, gaining him considerable kudos. There was speculation that the 'woman' he was seeing was in fact the wife of a prominent MP, thus explaining the need to be clandestine. Howard did nothing to scotch these rumours. Rather, he abetted them with a few well placed shrugs and knowing smiles, seduced by the admiration that came his way from the more pushy males in his year.

He still didn't mention anything to Jan, but she caught him out when she phoned his home one weekend when he had, yet again, told her he was going there.

"I was suspicious from the start, anyway." she told him on his return. "You've been telling me all these stories about how dreadful your parents are, so it was unlikely that you'd want to go home all the time. Where *do* you go?"

"I..." said Howard. "I can't say. But I'm not having an affair with another woman, if that's what you think."

"That's what people are saying."

"I know."

"But why the secrecy, Howard? It's crazy."

Instead of answering her, he'd taken her in his arms and kissed her. She had a strong body, not quite thick-set but not far off, that gave her a sense of assurance, almost of severity when taken in conjunction with the dark, bobbed hair that so precisely framed her face. After some resistance, Jan had eventually given in and succumbed to his love-making. Afterwards, and for the next few months, she had carefully avoided asking him about his absences. In the meantime, it became an accepted fact on campus that he was having a secret liaison with an important woman.

EIGHT

1999:

When Howard arrived back in London from Matthew's funeral, he felt that an internal part of himself was floating. It was a feeling he hadn't experienced since he'd spent six months trying out transcendental meditation, more than a decade ago. This time, however, it was as though he was being raised above something that was disintegrating - like being levitated from a floor that was about to collapse.

I'm starting to grieve again, he thought.

But who for? For Matthew? Corinne? Or for the time that he'd spent with her that might have been a sham?

There was a message on his answer machine.

"Howard! It's Sally here. I know I was supposed to be back in the States by now, but Damon's put me off for another week. Are you interested in a long weekend here in Barcelona before I go home? How about the ninth to the twelfth? You can ring me at the Hotel de les Arts and we can have a talk at least. Ciao."

Howard dropped the car keys on the coffee table and went into the kitchen to pour himself a mineral water. He took it out into his diminutive garden and lay spread-eagled on the seven-foot-square expanse of lawn. As he looked at the sky, he became aware of the distinct impression that his world had become inverted. He was no longer looking up at the clouds, but down at them instead. At any moment he would become unstuck and fall forever.

Now that Matthew's left me this money, he thought, *I don't need to go to Barcelona. I don't need to do ANYTHING if I don't want to.*

He stood up abruptly and the world reinstated itself into conventional Above and Below. He was briefly reminded of the Australian Aboriginals who reckoned there were seven points of direction: north, south, east, west, up, down and within.

Within... Howard thought as he finished his water and wandered into the flat.

He phoned his usual travel agent and booked a flight to Barcelona, then phoned the Hotel de les Arts. Sally wasn't there, but he left a message for her with the desk clerk to say he'd be with her at the hotel at around 8.00pm on Friday.

I don't HAVE to, he thought, *but then again, why shouldn't I?*

For some reason this thought brought Corinne to mind. Sally was similar to her in one particular respect - in the way she'd hugged him with such aching tenderness after love-making. In Sally's case this engendered in him a certain kind of empathy. In Corinne it had sparked a terrible sadness. But maybe, for the women, the feeling had been the same?

Didn't Corinne love me, then? the question echoed rhetorically.

Why was he doing this? Why was he flying out as a paid sexual companion to a sixty-three year old woman, when he no longer needed the money? Okay, the accountant had told him that probate might take between six months and a year, but the money would arrive eventually, and in the meantime he had a certain amount of capital of his own. By accepting Sally's invitation he had rendered all his previous explanations and justifications of his prostitution redundant. He sat for a long time, staring out at the bleaching grass of his lawn and the nubs of fruit on the peach tree that he had been training along the south-facing wall. Then a thought came to him; it completely exploded his curious sensation of weightlessness and he grounded with an emotion thump.

I'm lonely, he thought. *I'M the one who's lonely, not Sally!*

He suddenly had a vivid memory of Matthew on one of the occasions when he'd smiled his enigmatic smile and offered Howard a full-time job as an interpreter with his company. Howard had refused yet again, of course. But for what? So that his life could remain empty? At times like this, in the past, he had simply packed a rucksack and headed for the coast, often without thought for where he might end up; on a beach overlooking the Ionian sea perhaps, or in the Carpathian Mountains, or at a street café in Vienna or Zaragoza... wherever. The mere fact of travelling had been an end in itself. It caused an oddly panicky thrill in him to realise that he no longer had a desire to wander anywhere.

His thoughts returned to Matthew's money. *His* money now. How did that feel?

He didn't know.

He went into the bedroom and flicked through his suits, eventually pulling out a dark, classic Filip Andersen that had a hint of red sheen in the silver/charcoal fabric. Who had bought him this one? Not Sally, certainly. Maybe Mrs Molinaro, or that infuriating Countess who'd had the habit of grabbing his crotch so hard it made him wince.

With the suit went a pale cream shirt specially tailored for him in Milan, dark shoes that creaked slightly as he walked, and a hand painted tie from the Burlington Arcade. These were work clothes. They were his lie. They made him look brash and successful and affluent.

But maybe I am ALL these things now, he thought with a frisson partly of exhilaration and partly of disgust.

He ran his fingers through his hair and made a mental note to have it cut - it was too long; too respectable-looking. He could almost wear it in a fringe. He gelled it so that it looked carefully dishevelled. He inserted his heavy gold cuff-links, donned his Oliver People's sunglasses, twisted a gold, onyx and diamond ring onto his little finger, and the transformation was complete. Here, staring from the mirror, was an international playboy. Where this morning he'd chosen to wear smart but inconspicuous trousers and a casual jacket for Matthew's funeral, now he looked as though he'd stepped from a luxury yacht, or an exclusive casino.

Howard laughed at himself. It was so much a case of fancy dress that he nearly changed into jeans and a T-shirt instead. But tonight he was going to be a wealthy man out on the town. He was going to go out and see what it felt like to play the role of a rich person rather than a rich person's companion.

Part of him wanted to phone one of those high-class escort agencies and hire some glamorous female for the evening. He could find out what it felt like to be the one in charge for a change. He'd be intrigued to see if his escort would be able to fake passion as well as he could.

No, the idea appealed on an intellectual level only.

He decided to go out and see what happened.

He started at a bar in the West End where he had a quick gin and tonic before the insistent music, inappropriate lighting and obvious stares from various intimidating women drove him away to another bar near Piccadilly that, although subtle, had more of a reputation as a singles bar. He'd occasionally come to this bar in the past but had previously resented the dress code required to get in. Now, the doorman even bowed to him slightly as he entered, and beckoned a waiter to find him a seat. Howard shook his head, slipped five pounds to both the doorman and the waiter, and went to sit by the bar. A harpist was plucking away on the small stage; a fountain gently played water into a marble-lined pool that appeared to contain real water lilies. The susurration of the water perfectly complemented the lulling sound of the harp.

The place was expensive, tasteful and quite, quite false. Howard resisted a smile and ordered himself a cocktail of Polish vodka, peach nectar and almond essence. He sipped it and looked around at the other people present. There was a foursome of American tourists talking loudly near the harpist; various older, single men; three women who were clearly looking for business. At a table in front of him there sat a woman who was possibly in her sixties, wearing a black dress with a sequined neck band and a gathered waist that showed off her still-trim figure. With her sat a young man who so reminded Howard of himself when he was younger - in predicament rather than looks - that this time he really did smile. The young man looked earnestly absorbed in the woman's conversation - *too* absorbed. It was his hand movements that betrayed him. He kept on stroking his knee with one, and picking at the side of his watch with the other. No, he wasn't absorbed at all, just doing a nearly flawless simulation of it.

At the other end of the bar sat an incongruous woman. She was dressed in what may have been a day-time work suit of carnation red and was not looking round the bar, but into her empty glass instead.

Intrigued, Howard carried his drink over to her, fascinated by the fact that she was clearly feeling alienated.

"Let me guess," he said, "you've been stood up? You don't even want to be here. Your friend told you what a great place it was and arranged to meet you here. And now she hasn't shown up."

The woman smiled and looked at him briefly but said nothing before looking back at her glass.

"I'm right so far, then," he grinned. "Okay. What else? You're going to give it another ten minutes and then you're going to leave. You'll probably want to give your friend a slap in the face when you next see her, but you're too genial to do that. You'll just make a rueful joke about it instead. Meanwhile, you're hating every moment of sitting on your own, waiting."

"Not quite, but close," she said, with a small laugh. "You're wrong about me being all that genial. I enjoy giving people a slap when they deserve it."

She ran her finger through the condensation on the side of her glass.

"Does the rest show that much?" she asked.

"Yes, I'm afraid so. Would you like another drink?"

"No, no thanks," she said. "I really do have to go. I'm here under false pretences, really. I was going to have a drink with a friend, and have a voyeuristic hour or so. I'm not trying to *meet* someone. I'm married. Really, it's all absurd. And I'm *furious* with my friend."

Howard nodded.

"You're okay having a drink with me then," he said. "I'm here under false pretences too."

"Of what kind?"

"I'm pretending to be rich and successful."

"You certainly look it."

"I'm good at pretending."

She looked at his cuff-links and then back at her empty glass.

"So what *are* you if you're not rich and successful?"

"Maybe I'm just rich," he said. "Perhaps I'm pretending about the successful. I'm also not looking to *meet* someone, or at least, not especially. I guess I'm always open to the possibility - but I've almost always regretted picking up people in places like this."

The woman laughed, leaning her head back slightly so that she showed her throat. Howard guessed her to be around thirty.

"Why," she asked, "what's wrong with the people you pick up in places like this?"

"Maybe it's that they're either looking for casual sex, or for some kind of impossibly idealistic relationship. Whereas, with me, I'm looking for neither. Not a relationship... No, definitely not a relationship. But not a shallow, breathless exchange either. At the very least I hope for some intelligent conversation; or a sense of connection of some kind, or even a feeling that I am *real*."

"And you've done this often? Picked up people in places like this?"

"It depends on what you mean by often."

"Once would be often to me."

"Then yes," said Howard, "I've done it often."

"But you sound like you hate it."

"I do really."

"So why come this evening?"

"To confront it, I suppose. To free myself from needing it. Does that make sense?"

She smiled, then stood up and patted his hand.

"Yes," she said, "yes, it does."

She picked up her handbag and held out her hand.

"Thank you," she said. "At least you've given me an anecdote. When I talk to my friend, I can tell her that actually far from sitting on my own all evening, I talked to a strange and attractive man."

She smiled a private smile to herself and looked round the bar as though she wanted to memorise it.

"I'm sure you'll confront what you've come to confront," she told him, "and I'm sure you'll become both rich and successful if you want to be. I'm sure you can find an interesting woman to sleep with, too, if you want to - but given the clientele here tonight, I'd advise you to go elsewhere for that. Under other circumstances I would actually have considered it myself. It's been interesting meeting you, but now I must go. Goodbye."

He watched her leave and smiled a rueful smile. After *that*, he reckoned, he might as well go home. There was no way he'd cap the conversation he'd just had, and so he might as well not try.

He dropped a couple of pound coins onto the bar and left.

As he came out onto the pavement, the woman was standing talking to a taxi driver. There appeared to be some kind of disagreement in progress. Howard crossed to her.

"Is everything okay?" he asked.

"I have no cash," the woman sighed. "I was asking if the driver would take a cheque or credit card."

"I have some money," Howard told her.

"No, no," she said, taking out her mobile phone. "I'll just phone my friend. She was going to drive me back to her flat this evening. I should have been prepared for the possibility that she wouldn't arrive. It's not the first time she's stood me up."

"If she's not free to come and get you, you must accept a taxi ride from me."

Howard stood on the wide pavement, looking across at the trees of Hyde Park that he could see framed at the end of the street.

"She's not there," the woman told him, then murmured with frustration, "And I haven't got a set of her keys."

"Look," said Howard. "Why not come and have dinner with me instead?"

"No, really. Thanks. I'll go and find myself a cash dispenser, then take a taxi."

"Getting a taxi to an empty flat, when you don't have keys... it's a little absurd, isn't it?"

"I can wait."

"On her doorstep? Why not come for dinner? You can phone from the restaurant and get your friend to collect you from there."

"Really, I couldn't..."

"This is a city that can be incredibly depressing to hang about in," Howard said, "especially when you don't live here. I happen to be on my own. You're on your own. You would be doing me a favour if you kept me company right now. That's all. If we go to a restaurant we'll be on neutral ground. We can eat, and talk, and then you can get your friend to come and get you."

The woman looked carefully at Howard.

"Okay," she said slowly, "I'll come, but you must let me pay half."

"Okay," Howard smiled. "If you want to pay half, that's fine."

Howard chose a tiny Polish restaurant in Shepherd's Market, barely a hundred metres from where they were standing. It was small and intimate, and only moderately expensive. He'd intended to eat somewhere extravagant, but if the woman - who's name was Nina - was going to insist on paying her half, then he had to take that into account.

She was not a beautiful woman if judged by the standards of some of the women who hang around roulette tables in Cannes, but she was clearly honest, which was much more attractive. She had the air of not having anything that she wanted to either gain or hide. She was an inch or so shorter than Howard, with straight dark hair cut to shoulder length. Her grey eyes seemed to measure everything, but not in the cynical way that Howard was used to. There were no games of deception to be played here, and Howard breathed an inward sigh of relief that this was the case. It had always irritated him when he was honest with a person, only to have them put up an evasive screen of mystery or falsehood in return (though he had to acknowledge that this was a habit at which he had once excelled).

Curiously, the sincerity that occurred between Howard and Nina was of a kind that he hadn't encountered since he'd given up his travelling. He'd often come across it whilst abroad, or when he'd hitch-hiked as a teenager - that particular honesty that can happen between strangers. The fact that you can talk openly about your fears or insecurities without wondering what that person might think, because you know you will never see them again.

"I lead such a boring life," she said at one point. "My husband, Neil, is just as boring as I am, so we're well suited to each other. He's an accountant. I'm an accountant. We go out a lot - with other accountants and lawyers and mortgage brokers. We eat in expensive restaurants without character, and we fit in."

"You can change that if you want to," Howard told her.

"I know. Maybe I don't want to. Maybe I'm going through that disillusioned phase in my life where I have to face up to the *is that all there is to it?* question about life. Maybe I'm not ready to answer yes. Maybe I'll be a lot happier when I do."

"And what does Neil feel about it, or haven't you talked to him?"

"He wants to have kids. He thinks that's what's missing in our lives."

"And what do you think?"

"I think I want kids too, but I want to know absolutely that I'm having them because I want them and not because I'm bored with my life as it is. I expect there'll come a time in the next year or so when I'll say to myself - *if not now, when?* and give in. And then I'll discover whether it was a good idea or not..."

She laughed briefly. "A bit like Russian roulette in a way. If I wait around thinking, *Shall I? Shall I? Shall I?* long enough, then eventually I'll just do it."

Howard didn't say anything to this and sipped his wine thoughtfully.

"And what about you?" Nina asked. "Do you want kids?"

"There's only one person I've ever met with whom I might have wanted kids," he said. "But she's no longer around."

"Why?"

"I..." He nearly said *I killed her*, but in this context it sounded too dramatic, or self-pitying, or scary.

"She died," he managed, after a pause. "In a car crash. I was driving."

"My God!" Nina put her hand to her mouth. "How awful! I don't know what to say."

"It's okay. Don't say anything."

He took a gulp of wine as the first course arrived - a powerful borscht soup, sweet and vinegary with a feathery strand of dill snaked across the surface.

"I went to her husband's funeral today," he added as he dipped bread into his soup. "It all seems so complicated. He's left me a *lot* of money. That's one of the reason's I've come out this evening. I'm not like this at all, usually."

"But you didn't buy all these clothes today?"

"No, no. These are what I call my work clothes."

He paused to look at her carefully for her reaction.

"Amongst other things," he said, "I work as a paid companion - which is to say a prostitute. I've had a number of designer suits bought for me over the past few years. For going to casinos mostly, and dreary, expensive parties."

Nina didn't say anything. After a while she looked up at him, impressed. Attracted.

"I think you might be the most extraordinary man I've ever met."

He shook his head.

"Please don't think that I lead a glamorous life, or that the tragedy of the car accident has given my life a melancholy beauty. I assure you it hasn't."

She nodded.

"Tell me about this woman," she said.

"Corinne."

"Yes, tell me about Corinne. You sound as if you were very much in love with each other."

Howard remembered his recent conversation with Emma outside the crematorium, and felt a terrible, anguished stabbing of doubt.

"Mmm," was all that he could manage by way of reply. After a pause, and resorting to his professional persona, he tried to change the subject. Nina, however, was not easily side-tracked and, before long, Howard found himself opening up to her in that oddly hyper-personal way that she had done with him earlier.

By the time they'd finished the main course, Howard had been talking about Corinne for some time, thus breaking the great unspoken rule of never talking about other lovers to women that you've just met. When dessert arrived, he also found himself telling her what Emma had said at the funeral - that Corinne had never loved him.

"You can't fake it that successfully," Nina assured him. "If you had an affair with her for over a year, you'd have known whether she loved you or not."

But Howard was unsure. How many times had he convinced the women he'd been paid to sleep with that something profound was happening between them? It was frighteningly easy to fake certain things, and impossible to fake others; but so long as you could fake *enough*...

"I'll never know now," Howard said with a shrug. "Matthew's gone. Corinne's gone. And here I still am. As aimless as ever. I used to be happy about it, but now..."

"You went to a funeral today," Nina told him. "Don't expect to see things as you usually see do. You've had a brush with the past. Of course it's going to unsettle you for a while."

Howard smiled slightly at how odd it was to receive such good advice from a stranger.

"Mmm," he nodded.

"And two years isn't all that long ago, either, as far as a bereavement goes," she added.

He looked at his watch as he took a last sip of his Barsac.

"Shouldn't you call your friend? It's ten-thirty."

"I suppose I should," she said. "But I'm not going to. Is there anywhere round here where we could go on for a drink?"

"My place?" he suggested quietly.

Nina looked at the floor for a moment and then smiled up at him.

"Yes, okay," she murmured. "I think I'd like that."

Howard called for the bill. Nina reached for her bag.

"If you want to pay half, you can," Howard told her, "if you want to use payment as some kind of proof that you don't owe me anything. But money is no problem for me and I'd enjoy making it my treat."

She paused for a moment before nodding and putting her purse back in her bag.

"Okay," she said.

***

When Howard kissed her, in the hallway of his flat, she seemed somehow reticent and forward at the same time. She shook her head when he offered her a coffee and so he steered her straight into the bedroom, and helped her off with her jacket. She had broad shoulders and a flawlessly pale skin. Her breasts were small, almost adolescent-looking, and she laughed when he uncovered them.

"Not much of a handful there, I'm afraid."

He smiled at her and leaned down to take one of her nipples between his lips.

"Don't apologise on my account," he murmured before flicking his tongue over the areola.

She groaned and grasped his head and sank onto the edge of the bed, where Howard proceeded to undress her, slowly, paying attention to each area of flesh as it was revealed: a curiously recessed navel, lightly dimpled knees, feet with sensuously curved arches. When he slipped her panties over her knees he closed his eyes.

You cannot compare, he thought to himself, *you mustn't compare.*

He took a breath, and a fleeting thought seemed to skip across his consciousness - *Did she EVER love me?* - and then it was gone.

He opened his eyes and looked at the moisture-beaded crux, the heart, as-it-were, the focal point, of the physical and emotional tapestry that was this evening. He realised, then, how appropriate it was to him that this opening, this entrance to her body, was a gateway to something within. For himself as a man he was aware that the penis was outside; external. But for a woman it was internal; the act of penetration an accepted invitation to explore within.

Within... he thought and leaned forward to attend to her with his tongue.

He felt overly formal because he was still fully clothed, and when Nina pulled him up, he stood, undressed quickly, and lay beside her - a gap of maybe a foot between them. He traced his finger down her breastbone, stomach, and into her shrouded vagina. She closed her eyes, and he looked closely at her face as she did so, recognising some complicated emotions there. He could see that she was fighting not to participate more fully in the experience - to allow Howard to take control. He'd come across this exact behaviour a number of times before and knew that it resulted from feelings of guilt, as though allowing foreplay to be done to you is somehow intrinsically less of an infidelity than doing it yourself. Well, it was easy for Howard to be in control. It was a role that he understood; in which he was adept - the practice of discovering what made a woman shudder; what made her gradually bloom in her own mysterious, feminine way.

Howard was also practised at donning a condom during foreplay so that it caused the minimum of disruption, and Nina was clearly surprised to see him already sheathed when he broke off from a protracted embrace. Her lips looked almost bruised as he reached forward to kiss her again and he felt the sighing motion of her whole body as he entered her.

For a moment, he was almost overwhelmed by a surging current of melancholy - a common emotion for him, over the last two years, at this point with a woman. Why? Because it was all so ephemeral? So ungraspable? So fleeting? The moment passed, however. The rhythm that was settling between them eclipsed his sadness and, in time, obliterated everything else. Nina grasped his shoulders and hugged him to her with almost vicious strength. Howard read this action and reacted to it by tensing his own body - making it firmer, more uncomfortable, more insistent. He felt himself doing to her what she wanted him to do, rather than what *he* wanted to do, which is to say he thrust harder, pushing her half off the bed so that she felt like flotsam in his arms; almost lifeless. He felt her rippling orgasm and knew that what she was looking for in this sexual encounter was contrast - an escape from what she perceived to be the mundanity of domestic sex with her husband. The pretence, for Howard, of loss of control was a component of building that fantasy. And although Howard was more in the mood for gentleness, a part of him was gratified that he could play his part so well.

He found himself groaning as his climax approached, a habit he had developed, not because he needed to be vocal, but because it was useful to let his partner know what was happening. Tonight, like on so many occasions in the past, the build up to penetration had been the most powerful part of the love-making experience. Now, the approach of his own orgasm was merely inevitable. It was intense in a way, but somewhere in his interaction with Nina's body their connection had been severed.

Howard groaned as he ejaculated and held her tight as he did so, nuzzling her ear and whispering, "Yes!" as if he meant it.

When he rolled onto his back and pulled her gently to lie beside him, she seemed almost to be in a faint. He lay an arm across her and she began to tremble slightly, then to sob quietly. Howard hugged her from behind, caressing her shoulders and murmuring softly for a long time until, eventually, she drifted off to sleep.

Howard wasn't aware of slipping into sleep himself, and awoke with a jump at seven-thirty to find the curtains opened and Nina gone.

He listened and could hear the sound of the shower so he got up, put on his dressing gown, and went through to the kitchen where he made some coffee. He took the jug and two mugs out onto the patio.

It was eight o'clock when Nina came through, dressed in her red suit of the previous evening and, already, carefully made up. She smiled ruefully.

"Alright?" Howard asked.

She gave him a non-committal look, accepted a coffee, then sat opposite him on a wooden garden bench.

"I knew I would regret this," she said.

"Why? Didn't you enjoy it?"

"You can't possibly understand," she said quietly. "I have go to back to Neil. You don't know what that means. I had almost done it. I had almost convinced myself that having babies and being a mother would somehow compensate for the dullness of being with Neil. He's okay, you see. He's not bad. He's not up to much in bed, but I'd convinced myself that it was an absurd fantasy of mine that loving someone else might be more intense. Now I've met you and experienced something so powerful... I've proved myself wrong on so many counts."

Howard began to get up to go over to her.

"No, please, don't hug me. I'll only cry, and I don't want to do that again. Really, I'm grateful. You've shown me that I'd chosen to narrow my horizons down so much that what I've got managed to fill them. But in fact I've got so little, Howard, and I feel almost ashamed to say that I nearly convinced myself that it was enough."

Howard sat down again at the small table.

"The intensity of last night was because you were breaking your taboos," he said. "Don't be tempted to see it as more profound than it was - though I'm not trying to downplay what happened. I'm trying to be realistic. Believe me, I'm not the sort of person who's worthy of inspiring powerful emotion."

Nina shrugged.

"I'd better go," she said.

NINE

1999:

When Howard arrived in Barcelona to meet Sally for the weekend, he found the city too hot. He had never come here at this time of year before and was stunned by the heat as he got off the plane. He took a cab from the airport to the ultra-anaesthetized area of the city that had been developed for the 1992 Olympics, where the architecturally clean, but artistically barren, tower of El Hotel de les Arts stood; one of a pair of skyscrapers that reared up near the edge of the marina. Despite the heat haze, he could make out the twin hills of Montjuic and Tibidabo that were, for him, the romantic hallmark of the city.

The Olympic Village had such characterlessness that Howard found it hard to believe that it could be a part of such a beautiful city. It was a corporate venture in late eighties/early nineties development and made him feel as though he might be anywhere. It was a town-planning version of the shopping mall, which is to say, individual in certain ways, but in sum exactly the same as everywhere else of its kind.

Howard arrived at the hotel twenty minutes early and ordered a cold beer in the bar whilst he waited for Sally. As was her prerogative, she was nearly half an hour late and proceeded, after sending a bellboy off to her room with Howard's case, to give him the most perfunctory of kisses, and to whisk him into a waiting taxi.

"Darling, Howard, am I pleased to see you!" she said. "I've booked a table at the Rio tonight. Have I taken you there before?"

"I've never been with you in Barcelona before," he told her. "Only Madrid."

"Sure, sure, I remember now," she said as the taxi moved off. "*Oh, the heat... New York is bad enough in August, but this!*"

She lay her head gently against his shoulder and sighed. Howard looked down at her dyed blonde hair and felt the comfortable feeling of knowing exactly where he stood with Sally; exactly what was expected of him. He put his arm around her shoulders and hugged her and murmured how good it was to see her again.

Even though the sun had gone, heat still reverberated in the air from the buildings around them and from the tarmac below them. Breeze from the cab's open window served only to stir the warmth in a desultory way without cooling them at all. Fortunately he'd had the presence of mind to wear a baggy white shirt, so that the sweat under his arms wouldn't show as unsightly patches, but trickled down over his ribs to disappear into the damp waistband of his trousers.

"Darling," she sighed, when the taxi stopped after only the most cursory of journeys, "here we are."

Howard immediately paid the taxi driver with cash he'd converted at the airport's bureau de change so that Sally would not be seen to be the one with money. He felt suddenly immersed in his 'other' role; that of slick, sure internationalist. As the taxi drove away, he turned to look at the sea. He was standing on a quayside looking out into the dusk at the flotilla of pleasure-craft in the marina. The murmuring, breezy clinking of wires against masts had a curious sadness to it that made Howard feel briefly mournful. Sally took his elbow.

"Come inside where there's some air conditioning," she said, and set off up the wide marble steps to where large neon letters declared the Restaurante Rio. "I've got us a table by the window, so we can look out at the terrace and the sea in comfort. Apparently the King's daughter, the Infanta Christina, ate here the other day, so you never know who we might bump into."

Howard followed Sally in. She was wearing a white halter-necked top and a silk skirt that was so light it billowed as she walked. Her long gold earrings brushed her freckled shoulders as they swung. She had sunglasses pushed up into her hair, an affectation that wasn't unique to Sally but which obscurely irritated Howard, especially given that the sun had already set.

"Toni," she called to the waiter, embracing him as he indicated their table, "no need for menus, please. I'll have some of your artichoke salad to start, and your special risotto for the main course."

"*Mi tambien, por favor,*" said Howard.

"Hey!" Sally laughed, "in English, please! I don't want to feel left out." Howard smiled.

"I said I would have the same as you," he told her.

"Wine, sir, madam?" the waiter asked.

"I'll stick to beer," Howard said.

"Scotch," Sally told the boy. "Double. Tall glass, a heap of ice, to the brim with soda."

Now that they were in the cool, she put her hand over Howard's. She had deep tan skin that was becoming papery from sun and age. Her fingers were heavy with gold, and her varnished fingernails were the colour of candy floss. Howard took her hand and kissed the knuckles gently.

"*Jesus!*" she said, "I've missed you. Here I am, stuck in Barcelona, waiting for my daughter to get back from Venice. Why she wants to go there in *August* beats me, but it's her first wedding anniversary and she has this idea about what's romantic and what isn't. Frankly, sewer-ridden canals and over ninety degrees of heat doesn't sound romantic to me, gondolas or no gondolas."

She touched her sunglasses, as though to make sure they were still there, then leaned back in her chair.

"I'd have *died* of boredom here if you hadn't shown up. All my friends have gone back to Florida or LA, so I'm all alone. I was even contemplating following Gina down to Venice, which would have been a *big* mistake, even if she *had* invited me."

She glanced around the room, then smiled at Howard.

"As a matter of fact, she did invite me. Of course. But only halfheartedly. I was expected to refuse. Still, at least I've got something that she hasn't."

"What's that?" Howard asked.

"A horny man to look after me. You should see Gina's husband. Well, frankly, he's about as appetizing as a..." she cast her glance around the restaurant once more, looking for inspiration. "About as appetizing as that guy over there, the guy with the paunch."

Howard looked over at the table that Sally was indicating and saw the man she was referring to; a man who was clearly affluent but who nevertheless exuded an aura of failure, and whose gold watch and diamond ring looked as though they had been hired for the evening. His partner gave the impression of being unaware of anything, except perhaps, faintly, that it was necessary to transport food from her plate to her mouth. Just glancing at them for a moment gave Howard an eerie shiver at how people could be both utterly normal and utterly surreal at the same time.

"Gina's husband is called Paul, by the way," Sally continued. "Or *Paulo*, and he's probably oozing sweat all over her at this very moment. Can you *imagine?*"

Howard drained his glass of beer as the waiter brought him another one, and a further whisky for Sally. He smiled, suddenly appalled at himself for electing to come here when he didn't need to. Sally was so much a product of her culture - wealthy, simplistic, demanding, *judgemental*. What could he possibly gain from coming to see her, except for money that he no longer needed?

She appreciates me, he realised. *In whatever crass or superficial way, I am important to her.*

It intrigued him that he had never admitted to himself that this was important to him too - that he should be important to Sally, or to any of the women he'd escorted. He'd always hidden behind the 'I need the money' excuse; had used it to avoid the necessity of further examining motives. But wasn't this another round of that endless cycle that had started with his compulsive travelling in the early eighties, and with his constant search for the ephemeral profundity of casual, mutual lust; something that had gradually become a one-sided business, until it didn't really matter whether he had an orgasm or not, so long as he was perceived to be... to be what? An attentive lover? A successful lover?

And then everything had changed when he met Corinne. Before that, prostitution had been a game, a charade, a titillation: could he do it? Could he be good at it? It had also been something of an ego boost, he admitted; being desired in that way, having money spent on him. After Corinne died, it had become something else, too. Frighteningly, it had become the only stability in his life.

In the first three or four months after Corinne's funeral he hadn't been able to take on translation work, or interpreting. His mind had ceased to function in that way - his concentration had deserted him. But as far as prostitution went, he found that he could lose himself in the pretence of passion, fooling himself almost as well as his partner. He could also lose himself in the small-talk, the whispered endearments, the blatant materialism. Like a foreigner in a strange culture, he participated in this world without being a part of it.

And now, here he was with Sally again, who, despite her raw edge and outward lack of sympathy, was vulnerability itself. He knew that her brash facade covered a well of bitterness and sadness, and three loveless marriages. She had four children, all divorced at least once, who hardly ever saw her; seven grandchildren who relied on her for pocket money and presents. Maybe making love with her was the only truly constructive way he'd ever used his body; as a balm for what Sally perceived as a wasted life. He couldn't mend her life, but he could help her to forget it, for a moment...

Later, when they arrived back at the hotel three quarters drunk and made love, Howard found himself transported, so that he was travelling a weird internal terrain of wordless intensity. He literally shuddered with emotion as he moved within Sally, as his restless energy coiled inside him, as he clenched the muscles of his legs and buttocks so hard that they hurt. She was so soft, so fragile, so receptive. Howard clutched her and hammered his way to an orgasm so powerful and so shockingly intense that he almost passed out.

Afterwards, when his head cleared and Sally, breathless, had pushed him off, she laughed at the ceiling.

"Jeez!" she said, "I'm not as young as I used to be, Howard. You should be more careful."

Howard pressed his face into the pillow so that his panting was stifled. Sally moved over and hugged him.

"I'm not complaining," she whispered to him. "I haven't been fucked like that in years."

She stroked his shoulders gently as she spoke.

"Just as well you're only here for a weekend. Too much of that kind of love would exhaust me far more than the heat ever could."

She kissed the side of his neck and Howard rolled over to gently embrace her.

"How's your car?" she whispered.

Howard focused in on her again and sighed. Then, remembering himself, smiled.

"Great," he told her. "I wish I'd brought it down here. We could have done with some wind in our hair in this heat."

"Mmm."

She was coiled, curled against him, sleepy, content. Howard looked around the room at the impersonal trappings of faceless, conglomerate five-star living.

Once this was enough, he thought. *Once, I'd have lain here marvelling at all this; at the privilege of being in this city, of dining in one of Barcelona's finest restaurants... But back then it was a new experience. The newness of what was happening outweighed the other stuff.*

He suddenly felt overwhelmed by sorrow at the loss of his ability to experience awe.

Corinne, I miss you.

Corinne was the only person with whom everything had fitted; with whom he'd been able to function emotionally, intellectually and sexually; where all these elements were equally important and equally sustaining. That awe-inspiring connectivity had been severed at the same moment that Corinne's neck had snapped; that moment of impact had shattered something in him so completely that the pieces were still unidentified, let alone gathered or reassembled.

Perhaps he would be unable to truly connect with anyone until he had rebuilt himself. But then, even before the accident, he had hardly been the epitome of wholeness. Now, when he thought back, he could see that alienation had been a factor in his life even in his childhood. There was a story that his mother sometimes trotted out at dinner parties, of Howard dressing up as Dick Whittington, aged seven, complete with important personal belongings wrapped up in his mother's headscarf (a pen-knife, Milky Way, apple, plimsolls, pocket atlas of the world and a pair of his father's sunglasses). He'd set off for 'a life on the road' - a life truncated after only an hour, when his father, driving back from work, discovered him walking by the roadside a mile and a half from home. The story, delivered by his mother in a sentimental tone, was always taken as 'sweet', which made Howard shiver because he saw something pitiful in the tale, along with undertones of unhappiness and a need for escape. There were other episodes of this kind, and, of course, the nervous breakdown he'd suffered in his final year at university had been a part of that.

In the air-conditioned hotel room, as he lay beside Sally's sleeping form, Howard felt claustrophobic. He rolled away from her and was overwhelmed by a sudden desire to be utterly and completely alone.

***

1986:

One Saturday in Suffolk, in the second week of June, the weather had been especially warm and Howard, after a quick breakfast of cereal and coffee out on the veranda at *Rosemerion*, had decided to go for a swim. The water was spring-tide-high and, taking his towel, he walked along the narrow path towards the stretch of deeper water further up the estuary where it opened out. The landscape looked quite different when the muddy sand was covered like this and the tide had gently meandered its way into the reed beds. There was a deep, narrow inlet over which he now crossed by way of an old wooden footbridge that had been weathered to a dry silvery grey. From the far bank, Howard could ease himself into the water without having to wade through the weirdly sucking mud.

The water was cool and lapped quietly in the light offshore breeze. It was still only eight-thirty and the sunlight had a quality to it that reminded him of photographs of the arctic, or perhaps midday sun in early October, when the breeze gives a touch of chill to overlay the warmth of the day. As he struck away from the small inlet out towards the middle of the estuary, Howard felt his isolation scouring him clean of the unwanted debris of university life. When he rolled over and, treading water, looked back at the shore, it filled him with a feeling of triumph that he could see no one else; that the only habitation visible on that side of the estuary was the now-distant cottage that he was staying in, and the barn of one of the distant farmhouses. The coolness of the water seemed to be the cleanest sensation he could imagine, and the idle snatches of birdsong above him made him feel suddenly invigorated.

The tide had virtually stopped coming in so there was no current. At times the flow in the channel was so strong that swimming there would have been madness. Now, however, the water was so still that it was difficult to imagine that it was connected to the boisterous churning of the North Sea.

He began to slowly swim back towards the shore, and as he did so, he saw the car. He recognised it immediately as the Peugeot estate that his Uncle Richard drove. It stopped beside the cottage and Howard saw Richard getting out, with Aunt Helen and his cousins, Ruth, Anna and

Alasdair, all looking impossibly small in the distance. His body gave an involuntary shudder as he thought of his bedding mat, sleeping bag and cooking equipment in the hideout.

He swam back to where his clothes were and dressed quickly, without drying himself, behind the footbridge and then skirted his way along the edge of the reed beds to the line of willow trees that bordered the garden. He was glad that he'd parked his own car out of sight some distance away along the lane, behind a disintegrating boat shed, where it wouldn't disturb his sense of timelessness. As he sat out of sight with his back to the trunk of one of the larger willows, he heard Alasdair, his eight year old cousin, cry out, "Daddy, look, the back door's open!" There came the crunch of footsteps on gravel and Ruth's voice: "Yes, look dad, someone's been staying here," and then further voices from inside the hideout.

Howard closed his eyes and wondered what he should do. Maybe it would be best to wander over and admit that it was him, put up with the embarrassment of it, and then, presumably, be invited to spend the rest of the weekend as a guest in the main house. He remembered previous stays, particularly his last one, two years before: leisurely meals, conversations in which he was aware of his inability to fully integrate with the adults, but, just as surely, being aware of his alienation from the childish world of his younger cousins. No, he couldn't give up his precious solitude for that... Instead, he skirted perhaps a hundred metres to where, hidden behind some long grasses, he could see both the front and the back of the house. He lay on his stomach in the warming sunshine and waited, and watched.

Howard mentally rebuked himself for not expecting the arrival of the McLeans at some point. He'd never bothered to wonder if they ever travelled down for the odd weekend from London, assuming that they simply used it for their three week summer holiday. But that was crazy, he now realised, especially given that it was less than ninety minutes drive from their ultra modern home in Thamesmead.

As he watched, Uncle Richard and Ruth - at thirteen, the eldest of his cousins - came out of the front door carrying the kitchen table, which they placed on the veranda. Anna and Alasdair followed, carrying a pine bench and then, later, another one. By the time they'd finished, the table was laid for a late breakfast of coffee, toast and a full fry-up provided by Aunt Helen.

Howard waited until the five of them had made a start on their hot food, then crept back round to the willows and across the rear lawn to the hideout. Looking inside he saw that all his gear had gone. For a moment he closed his eyes in near panic. Should he make a dash for it and leave his stuff behind? It didn't matter about the mat or the food, or even the cooker and hurricane lamp, he thought, but he'd paid a substantial amount for the hi-tech four season sleeping bag and he'd never be able to replace it, especially now that he needed his savings to supplement his grant.

He took a deep breath and crept into the back hallway. He could actually see Uncle Richard's back through the open front door and hear Aunt Helen's deep, endearing laughter (which made him, for a moment, want to laugh, too, and saunter out to join them). At the foot of the stairs there was a large cardboard box containing all his belongings. He crossed to it, picked it up carefully, and then turned towards the back door. As he did so, Ruth walked in through the front door and saw him immediately.

There was a moment of frozen time, when they both went rigid with shock. Howard noticed, in that heightened moment, that Ruth had entered adolescence and he felt a curious sexual tingle along with the adrenalin. She stepped forward and whispered, "Howard!"

"Shh," he said.

"Have you been staying out in the back?"

"Yes," he whispered. "Please, don't tell anyone."

"Why?"

"Please!"

She looked as though she was about to question him further, when Aunt Helen called from outside, "Hurry up, Ruth, the milk's in the cool-bag by the sink!"

Ruth didn't move. She held eye contact with Howard for several seconds and then, crossing to his side so that she could reach him round the edge of the large box that was in his hands, she kissed him gently on the cheek, then stepped back and gave an unreadable smile.

"Coming mum," she shouted and turned to walk into the kitchen.

Howard crept through the back door and out of the garden via the willows and a muddy ditch. He managed to sneak out onto the untarred lane, and then to his car. When he started the engine, the noise seemed deafening even as the engine idled. He put it into gear and crept forward. He could see the Peugeot and the side of the house, but not the breakfasting family beyond. He kept the car to five miles an hour for the couple of hundred metres before the track curved to the left and fully out of sight. Then he put his foot down.

As he drove, he felt an intense mixture of different emotions. Firstly, there was the exhilaration of the narrow escape; then there was curiosity about his weird encounter with Ruth; then - and this was the most powerful emotion - there was an immense feeling of loss and deprivation. He'd been robbed of virtually a whole weekend of solitude in the only place he knew in which he could feel at peace. Following this emotion there came a strange frisson of fear - that perhaps his incognito weekends here were the only thing keeping him sane, and that if he was deprived of them he would go mad. It was the first time he had ever considered the possibility that his obsessive need for solitude might be an indication of instability.

***

1999:

Howard was still lying with Sally in the cool sterile darkness of their hotel room, looking up at the ceiling and thinking back to his days at *Rosemerion*. Maybe his desperate attachment to those solitary weekends *had* been a sign of some kind of dysfunction? Maybe the reason he'd connected so well with Corinne was because she was unstable too, even though their problems had been very different. Howard had never suffered from clinical depression as described to him by Emma. But hadn't he, nevertheless, drawn strength from Corinne because of this unstated similarity? Even a part-time relationship with her had calmed a restlessness in him that had been present since early adolescence. And after Corinne's death, prostitution had provided a semblance of normal sexual functioning that Howard had clung to - was clearly still clinging to.

Sally stirred in the darkness as he slipped out of bed and crossed to the bathroom.

"You alright, hon?" she mumbled.

"Having trouble getting to sleep," he told her.

"I've got some pills in my drawer," she murmured. "I'll give you one."

"No," he said. "No thanks. I'll have a cool shower. It'll be just as effective."

Pills. There was something so seductive about the idea of taking a pill and drifting off, but Howard understood a certain addictive facet to his personality and so steered clear of all intoxicating drugs except alcohol, which he almost always drank in moderation, except, occasionally, when he was keeping up with people like Sally.

Even the cold water of the shower wasn't all that cold, but it was cool enough to be refreshing. Howard didn't dry himself for some time afterwards, but stood naked in the bathroom allowing the water to evaporate from his skin. There was a small vase of flowers by the bath. The delicate blue and yellow blooms were already beginning to wilt after only a day in their vase. They gave off a restful night-time scent that finally seemed to clear Howard's cyclic thoughts so that he could return to bed and slip in beside Sally, who's sleeping form seemed curiously insubstantial in the overlarge bed.

The rest of the weekend with Sally was comfortably predictable. He was calm and solicitous. He pulled chairs out for her at restaurant tables, ordered substantial quantities of beer, wine and whisky, then paid for everything, flashily, by American Express in the knowledge that Sally would pay him handsomely for the privilege of appearing not to be paying. He allowed her to talk about herself and rarely said anything about his own life, except when she pressed him, and even then he didn't mention personal details like Matthew's funeral, but kept to the subject of his linguistic work. Luckily Sally had never asked him about the other women he had escorted in his time (a subject some of his clients were endlessly fascinated by - especially in terms of comparisons). She was either too discreet or too disinterested. Howard reckoned it was the latter and he rather liked her for it. So many people see themselves only in relation to what other people do or think.

By Sunday afternoon he was conscious of the fact that this was the last time he would ever do this. There had been a time-lag between knowing that he would receive Matthew's money and making the conscious decision to stop being a prostitute. Now, he knew, whatever he did with the money, he would never go back to prostitution. He had learned, finally, that, for himself, the profession was nowhere near as simple, emotionally, as he'd thought it was.

When, in those limbo hours between packing and leaving for the airport on Sunday afternoon, he made love with Sally, there was a nostalgic glow to their union that actually brought tears to Howard's eyes. Whatever prostitution may have been, it had certainly been a life-experience. He felt that when he stepped off the plane at Heathrow he would be stateless, somehow, cast adrift, and although that thought was tinged with optimism and hope, it was also tinged with apprehension.

When Sally pulled out her cheque book, Howard suddenly felt that this was all inappropriate, especially given the depth of transition that this trip had caused. He wanted to thank Sally for helping to propel him into a new phase of his life, not take money from her.

"No," he said, "don't give me money. This trip was my pleasure. Please, put your cheque book away."

Sally's face darkened slightly.

"What do you mean?" she asked quietly.

"I don't need the money," he said. "That's not why I came to see you this time."

Sally looked up at Howard, who was smiling slightly at her.

"No," she said, "don't do this to me Howard. I know where I stand when I pay."

"Please, Sally," he said. "The thing is, I don't suppose I'll be doing this again, this kind of... work. It just doesn't seem appropriate for you to pay, that's all."

"Uh-huh," she said, flushing with anger. "Jeez, Howard, I've been through this before with gold-digging young creeps, but I can't believe that *you're* trying it on."

"Sorry?"

"Come on, I know this game. 'Oh, Sally, Sally, I can't do this work any more, please, don't pay me. I feel too close to you for that. Let's be lovers and have done with it'. We all know the sub-text of *that*: 'Sally, Sally, why don't you marry me and then I can have half your cash'."

"No," said Howard, horrified, "really, it's not that."

"Of course," she said, tiredly. "You slept with me because you think I'm beautiful, because you're in love with me, because you can't bear to be without me..."

"No, it's nothing cynical like that."

"Look, Howard, you were good, great even, but no one's *that* exceptional." She quickly wrote a cheque and then sighed. "One thing I get the feeling you were right about, though - I don't suppose we *will* be seeing each other again. Now, I'm going to brush up. When I come back I sincerely hope you will be gone."

She placed the cheque on the bedside table before standing and walking purposefully, and with extraordinary dignity, into the bathroom, closing the door carefully behind her. He crossed the room and looked down at the cheque. It was for US$ 20,000, payable in cash rather than made out to him by name. Even given the fact that, for

Sally, this was a trifling amount, he still felt humiliated. By her sarcasm. By her mistrust. By her generosity in the face of disappointment.

He slipped the cheque into his wallet. Part of him wanted to rip it up and leave it, confetti-like, on the carpet, and part of him thought the gesture would be so pathetic that it would demean him even more. He quickly packed his overnight bag - leaving his toiletries in the bathroom - and let himself out of the suite.

***

"*¡Hola, José, dígame!*" Howard exclaimed, pleased to be speaking Spanish again. "I'm in Barcelona. Are you busy? Can we meet?"

He was in the phone booth in the hotel lobby, talking to his poet friend. He hadn't thought he'd have a chance to meet up and so hadn't told José that he'd be in the city (clients were notoriously sour if he asked for time off to go and see friends).

"Howard!" José's obvious pleasure was reassuring after the recent scene with Sally. "*Where* in Barcelona are you?"

"El Hotel de les Arts."

"I might have guessed. Shall I come and meet you there?"

"No, no. That's *not* a good idea. I'm trying to avoid someone. Maybe I could come to your place?"

"Sure. Come and sweat it out on our balcony if you like. How long are you here?"

"I only have a couple of hours to spare."

"Okay. Come straight over. You know where I am?"

"Of course."

Howard took a taxi to the Barrio Gótico district of the city; the quietly crumbling area, populated by the kind of interesting people that you'd never see at the Restaurante Rio. The streets were quieter than he had expected. Probably because of the heat. José's apartment was in a building that appeared to be more of a jumble of rooms round a court-yard than a building as such. There was a distant sound of classical guitar music as Howard got out of the taxi, and he noticed an inert tramp asleep beneath a tree. Or perhaps he was dead. Everything was so motionless this afternoon that he could believe that someone might pass away like this, so quietly. He paid the taxi driver and then knelt beside the man, taking his dirty wrist gently to check for a pulse. Yes, the man's heartbeat was slow but powerful and Howard carefully let go of his hand, suddenly embarrassed that he'd considered, even for a moment, the fact that he might be dead - his face, now that Howard was so close, was simply the face of a man in the clutch of those empty dreams into which it is a pleasure to sink.

José came to the door and gave him an *abrazo*, a long, tight hug.

"*Howard!*" he cried in his distinctly Catalan-accented Spanish. "*¡Entra, por favor, entra!* I was thinking of England today and how much I would appreciate a little English rain. Come in, come in!"

José was around the same age as Howard, with dark skin and a narrow face that looked both attentive and preoccupied at the same time. It was easy to believe that he might be a man who had visions.

"Lucia!" he called, "Howard is here!"

Lucia appeared at the top of the stairs and embraced him when he reached her.

"*Buenas tardes,*" she said. "*Bienvenido.* Welcome. I have some iced tea, with fresh mint, if you're interested."

Howard nodded and Lucia, taking his hand, led him out onto the shaded balcony. It felt like coming home, slipping so effortlessly into Spanish. It was like waking up to a part of himself that had fallen asleep; like stretching an unused muscle - invigorating.

"Sit," Lucia told him.

There was a small white, wrought iron table with unexpectedly comfortable iron chairs around it. José joined Howard and leaned earnestly towards him, lighting a cigarette.

"I assume you came to Barcelona with a *patroness*?" he said.

"Yes."

"But something went wrong that you have to avoid her?"

"I guess I've come to the conclusion that prostitution is not the career for me."

"So! It's taken you this long to work that out?"

Lucia, coming out onto the balcony with a large tray of iced tea, nodded.

"Howard," she said, "for some people, prostitution is a vocation, a fulfilment, for others it is a burden. You were made for better things than to *pretend* to be in love."

"But so much of life *is* pretence," Howard said.

"Don't!" she laughed. "José has been on and on about pretence in his writing, for months. Illusion. Reality. Even the most real things become false if you look at them hard enough. I'm beginning to think that truth is the first casualty of analytical thought."

"Hey, I like that," José said, "where's my pen?"

"He steals all my ideas and never attributes them to me," Lucia said.

"Not true," José objected, writing in a small note pad, "always, I tell people that you are my inspiration. But, a poet has to take ideas and thoughts from where he finds them. If I had to acknowledge every stranger in every bar or café who has ever said anything profound that I have absorbed and used, then there would be more acknowledgements than poetry. My talent is in drawing life together and re-expressing it."

"Isn't that the job of all artists?" Howard asked.

"Of course. You understand these things. You are an intelligent and educated man. You should try writing poetry yourself."

Howard laughed.

"I've seen how hard it is," he said. "Thank God I have no talent, and no yearning for it. I have no masochistic tendencies. I have no desire to inflict that kind of self-examination on myself."

"It's true," said Lucia. "One has to tear oneself to pieces to see what is inside if you are ever going to be a real poet. Truth lies in the entrails of life, not on its surface, its skin."

"It's clear that you, also, are a poet at heart," Howard told her.

"I don't need to write poetry," she laughed. "I have nothing to prove. There is nothing wrong with having wisdom for oneself. I don't need to share it with anyone except those I love. I think José's need to write and be published comes from insecurity. All art says, 'look at me, look at me!' It doesn't bother me that people don't look at me."

José shook his head.

"Insecurity... No. I am driven, I am *driven* to do what I do."

"But driven by what?" Lucia said earnestly. "And please, don't try to answer that question." She looked across at Howard and smiled. "We must try to preserve at least *some* mystery in life, no?"

Howard sighed his agreement.

"Wait here one moment," José told him, and went into the flat. He came back a few moments later carrying a slim volume.

"I don't know what you would call this. It's not just a book of poems. It's a *distillation*. See what you think of it."

"Thanks," Howard said, pleased. "I'll read it when I get home."

He flicked through the handsomely produced book which was titled, *Vitrinas de la Memorià* - Cabinets of Memory.

"So," Howard asked, "are you still teaching?"

"You think I'm making a living out of my poetry? Of course I'm still teaching. Only twenty hours a week, though, so I can't complain." He smiled at Lucia. "Between us, we manage, don't we?"

She leaned forward and embraced her lover, then smiled at Howard, who sipped his tea and felt a frisson of pleasure at this conversation. What a relief to be talking with people who wanted to express *ideas*. People like Sally, for all her worldliness, dealt with things, and in the end people become things too if you see the world in that way. But the world is full of real people, thinking and having ideas. It's just that you can cut yourself off from it if you're not careful.

"Now," said José, "you must tell me all about the woman that you have been entertaining at El Hotel de les Arts."

Howard smiled and recounted to them something of what had happened, including the embarrassing final moments of accusation in their hotel room. In the retelling, he began to see why Sally might have suspected him of some kind of subterfuge. It was a miserable fact of her life, he thought, that she couldn't bring herself to trust anyone - and rightly so, he supposed, given the amount of opportunists who would claim love, at the very least, to get their hands on her money.

"Howard," Lucia said, "you look sad."

"Sad?" Howard murmured. "Mmm, yes, perhaps I am a little."

"You must let her go," she told him.

"I'm sorry that Sally misunderstood me," he said, "but I can't say she's responsible for making me feel sad."

"No, not Sally. Corinne. I've seen that look in your eyes before. I've seen it in other people's eyes too. It's a yearning that cannot be appeased."

He looked at her, stricken by an almost overwhelming panic. He closed his eyes and took several breaths before he could speak.

"You may be right," he admitted, surprised that Lucia had seen this about him when it had been so far from the surface of his thoughts. She smiled earnestly at him, catching his gaze and holding it for such a long time that José began to fidget.

"And now," José said, getting to his feet, "let's have a proper drink. We still have a couple of bottles of cava from our wedding. Let's open one now, in honour of Howard's visit."

"Wedding?" Howard said. "But you said you would never get married."

"We kept it quiet," Lucia told him as José went off into the kitchen. "To be honest, we needed the presents. It was as cynical an act as that. At heart, we are still living in sin. Although José jokes about us being okay, money has, as you can probably imagine, been getting tighter and tighter over the last couple of years."

Howard nodded, but remained silent. Lucia patted his knee and laughed as José returned and opened the cava, popping the cork so that it flew in a fantastic arc over the rooftops. He poured them a glassful each and they toasted each other, suddenly solemn, before smiling once more. Howard found, as he watched them together, that he couldn't deny a certain envy of their happiness and he consciously tried to steer his thoughts away from self-pity (without complete success) as they chatted about future projects.

When it was time to leave, he went to their toilet and took the cheque for $20,000 dollars from his wallet. As it was made out for cash he was able to leave it for them, on the cistern, with his card; on which he wrote, *Esto NO es un regalo de bode. Creo que a vosotros os servirà mejor que a mí. Con mis respetos, Howard.* (This is *not* a wedding present. I think you'll find better use for it than I could. With love, Howard.)

***

Flying back to Heathrow, Howard felt obscurely liberated. He hadn't felt this way since he'd graduated from university. For the first time in over a decade there seemed to be an uncluttered horizon ahead of him. This wasn't because of Matthew's money, or not directly so, but something in himself, because even before Matthew's bequest, he now admitted to himself, he hadn't *needed* the money from prostitution. And now, of course, he could even pack his translation in, if he felt inclined, and travel round the world for a few years.

He smiled at the thought of this, though somewhere at the back of his mind there was a quiet voice that began to panic at the thought of being cast adrift.

And being adrift is what I thought I always wanted.

He remembered discussing the fear of freedom with Corinne, lying in her arms and feeling that if freedom meant doing what you most wanted to do, then he was as free as it was possible to get. Even at the time, he'd realised that this was a particular interpretation of 'freedom' and that freedom *for a moment* may not be worth it if the journey to that moment is one long compromise. For him, the compromise with which he'd paid for those precious moments with Corinne was in the currency of uncertainty and a yearning for more than she was prepared to give him.

He could remember one day, specifically, when he'd experienced that wordless companionship that is simply itself without the dissatisfaction of reality. Howard had actually said those words to himself that day, 'I'm free'. What he'd really meant was 'in this moment I have no preoccupation, and no desire to be doing anything other than sitting here, sipping cold beer on this roof terrace with my lover'. It seemed so poignant now, that he could have felt this way when so much time since then had been so constricted.

***

1986:

Freedom. Howard had never used that word to himself before, but that was how those weekends in Suffolk had made him feel. Free. Here he was, a budding linguist, and suddenly that word - freedom - seemed the most intangible, indefinable and mystical word he could imagine.

In the week after his escape from discovery at *Rosemerion*, he wondered compulsively if he'd be able to return to the McLeans' cottage. Or perhaps there was some patch of grass further along the estuary where he could pitch his tent undiscovered, even if the McLeans *were* in residence. Or maybe he could go to the official campsite a couple of miles over on the other side of the road, down by the village. (But, no, that would be a nightmare.)

In the end he drove down - with his tent, just in case - to arrive at the cottage mid-morning on Saturday, so that he could see if the McLeans were there. As it turned out, they weren't, but a large padlock had been bolted onto the rear door, and the windows had been made secure with bars and window locks. Howard felt bereft as he stood, looking at his precious sanctuary, now denied him. As he glanced at the lawn, he knew he didn't want to pitch his tent here either. He would feel too vulnerable, somehow, too unwelcome.

As he was about to turn to leave, he noticed the edge of a scrap of paper sticking out from below the bolt. Looking more closely, he noticed that there was something written on it. He carefully took hold of the tiny sliver with his fingernails and pulled the piece of paper out. There were three words printed there. *Under the buoy*. He didn't recognise the handwriting, but assumed it to be Ruth's.

At the front of the house, underneath the nearside of the veranda, there was a large, old rusting buoy that he remembered from his childhood. Now, he went round to where it was lying, as ever, just above the high-tide line. He leaned his weight against the top of it and its large bulk rocked gently forward. Underneath there was a small tin wrapped in a plastic bag. Inside was a key. He took it out and went round to the back, but found that it didn't fit the padlock. It was the wrong kind of key altogether. After a few moments of exasperation, he realised that it must be the spare for the front door.

He let himself into the house and felt like a burglar, or at least an intruder. Still, it didn't take him long to find the key to the hideout - there was a key-rack on the wall behind the kitchen door. He took it round to the back and gained access to those two small rooms that had become so important to him.

He saw the envelope immediately, propped up beneath the water pump. Beside it there were two cans of Heinz Baked Beans and a bottle of Pepsi. He opened the letter and read:

Dear H,

I didn't tell mum or dad about you, but they were pretty upset about the place being broken into. Dad got some men in to put bars on the window straight away. We're not coming down next weekend (21st) or the weekend after that, but we <u>will</u> be coming on the 6th of July, so you can keep away *then. We'll be coming for our three weeks on 27th of July - maybe you could come for my birthday on the 8th of August? I'll make sure dad invites you. I hope you can come.*

R.

Howard stared at the note and felt a thrill of conspiracy, followed by an echo of the haunting moment when Ruth had held his gaze the previous weekend. What were her motives in helping him like this? He looked at the beans and the Pepsi, and smiled at the innocence of the gesture.

It occurred to him that, now he had access to the main house, there was no reason why he had to make do with the concrete floor of the hideout. He could ensconce himself in comfort if he felt like it. But no, he realised, it was precisely the bareness of these two rooms that made him feel so *separate* from his normal life. To move into the house with the comfort of beds and television would be ghastly - and completely pointless.

TEN

1999:

It was extraordinary to think that he'd only been away to Barcelona for three days, because the flat felt oddly unfamiliar when he walked into it, as though he'd forgotten exactly how it was laid out. He poured himself a glass of iced water and wandered out onto the patio. Even though it was after midnight, the air was sultry. He felt as though he'd been constantly *exuding* over the last few days.

When the telephone rang, he jumped. After midnight, phone calls almost always mean disaster of some kind and he warily made his way inside to answer it. The last unexpected call he'd received had been to tell him of Matthew's illness...

It was Lucia.

"Howard," she said, *"Espero que no te hayamos desperado."* I hope we haven't woken you.

"No, acababa de llegar," Howard told her. I've only just got in.

"Good," she said. "Look, we've found the cheque. It is impossible for us to take it from you."

"I tried to refuse it when Sally offered it to me. For me, it's tainted, Lucia. You'd be doing me a favour to take it and use it constructively."

"But Howard! It's such a lot of money."

"Don't tell me you don't need it."

"That's not the point."

"What *is* the point?"

"The point is that people don't give money away like this."

"You need it. I don't. Please, let's not talk about it. You've phoned

– 137 –

up to ask if I really meant it when I left the cheque for you. Well, I did mean it. I want you to have it. If you argue with me I'll get angry and embarrassed and then you'll have spoilt the pleasure that I got from giving it to you."

"Okay, okay, but Howard, it's incredible! I mean, thank you *so* much. José didn't say but he's been on the verge of having to go full time with his teaching, and, fine, we'd have coped, but it would have been bad news for his creative work. Now, we can carry on as we are. I can't begin to tell you what a difference this money will make."

"I could tell you needed it," Howard told her. "I'm so pleased I've been able to help."

"Here's José," Lucia said.

"Howard!" came José's voice. "Howard, what good timing you have. I've opened the other bottle of cava. What more can I say? Thank you. Come and see us soon, properly, for longer - in October, perhaps? We could go to the Sierra Nevada, to my brother's villa. Or maybe we could go later on. Whenever you are free. It is beautiful there all through the autumn and winter."

"I'd love to come," said Howard. "Now go and drink your cava. I'll be in touch soon."

Smiling at how easy it had been to make a difference to José and Lucia, Howard took a cool shower, then lay on his bed, covers thrown back.

***

The following day he felt the need to get started on some work in which he could immerse himself. He had a need to do something to stop a terrible slipping of belief in the integrity of the time he'd spent with Corinne. He needed to do something to stop himself thinking about what Emma had said to him at Matthew's funeral. Perhaps that was what the Barcelona trip had been about - the need to do something, anything, to avoid fully confronting the possibility that Corinne had never loved him.

Her love was the one certainty that he'd clung to over the past two years. Without it, what certainty was there left about anything?

He phoned Colin Farley, his boss at Sheldon Translation, who was relieved to hear from him as three of his staff were either off ill or on holiday. There was an accumulation of basic bread-and-butter leaflets and instruction pamphlets. Howard agreed to take them on and Colin arranged to have them couriered to him that day. Next, Howard phoned John Deacon, Matthew's second in command at CMS, now director. After some formality, commiseration and a brief discussion of how valuable Howard had been as part of their team, Howard broached the subject of work. Yes, John told him, after a brief consultation with his files and his secretary, there was a trip to Berlin, if he wanted it, at the beginning of October. Was he interested in that?

Howard then phoned Pete Collicos and got through to his answerphone.

"Hi," he said to the impersonal device. "Howard Martindale here. We met at Matthew's funeral and you gave me your card. I'd like to take you up on your offer of a talk."

He left his number and replaced the receiver, feeling less than satisfied at the one-sidedness of answerphone conversations, but pleased at the prospect of a forthcoming visit to Berlin.

The Sheldon courier arrived during the afternoon bearing a variety of pamphlets to be translated and Howard lost himself in the technical details of volume control, recording levels, ohms and filters. One thing that work of this kind does, he knew, is to give you a rest from cyclic thoughts, and, in that respect, he couldn't fault the timing of its arrival.

***

For the following three or four days, Howard worked between

twelve and sixteen hours a day, relieving what was clearly something of a backlog of material at Sheldon, and earning himself far more money than he needed, plus a welter of gratitude - something which, as in the case of José and Lucia, he found embarrassing. It was a period of blanding-out, intellectually, and the mindless work was restful in a wonderfully soothing way. The weather was slightly cooler, too, which enabled him to sleep better.

He took two hours off at the beginning of each afternoon, to lie in the sun. It was the same period he'd used to go for a swim, or to the gym, to keep himself fit and presentable. But now that he'd given up on the idea of prostitution, he simply couldn't be bothered to make the effort and the sensation of 'letting himself go' felt extraordinarily indulgent and pleasurable.

On Thursday morning he received a phone call from Pete Collicos.

"I'm coming down to London today," he said. "I've got the evening off. Do you want to meet up for an early drink, or a meal?"

"A drink would be great."

"Do you know Ballans, on Old Compton Street?"

"No, but I can find it."

"Right. Six-thirty?"

Howard had a sudden feeling of ambivalence about this meeting as he put the phone down. Something about the finality of his scene with Sally in Barcelona seemed to have cut off his past. Part of him wanted to simply forget about Sally and the others, to forget about Matthew, too, and let that side of his life slip away. But there was no denying that he was still curious about why Matthew might have felt the need to leave him money, and Pete was likely to know at least something about that. Also, he was interested in anyone who might have known Corinne, however peripherally.

Howard hadn't been to Old Compton Street for a number of years and he was surprised at how gay it was these days. Several of the cafés had tables out on the pavement that were patronised almost exclu-sively by gay men. Ballans, a café-restaurant, was busy and open at the front to let in the warm mid-August air. Pete was already there and came forward to shake his hand.

"Hi," he said. "I hope you don't mind being somewhere gay. I didn't think of that until after I spoke to you."

"It's fine," Howard said as Pete escorted him to a small table by the window and ordered them both a Becks from the waiter.

"It feels weird, meeting like this," Howard said to Pete. "I assume that you knew Matthew well. That much was clear at the funeral. But he never mentioned you to me."

"That, I'm afraid, was deliberate," Pete said with a slight grin.

"Why?"

"I'll tell you, but let's have a drink first."

The beer arrived and Pete raised his bottle, clinking it against Howard's.

"Cheers," he said. "Here's to Matthew."

"Yes, cheers."

"So," Howard asked after a pause, "you knew Corinne?"

"We only met once," he said, "just before she died, but she was wary of me, I think, because I look like you."

Howard nodded slightly and Pete smiled in a conspiratorial way. He leaned forward and touched the small ankh that was dangling on its silver chain over Howard's black polo-necked top.

"Are you religious in some way?" he asked. "I wouldn't have guessed it."

"No," Howard told him. "Corinne gave it to me. It has sentimental value only. I hardly ever wear it."

"Strange that you should choose to do so today."

Howard shrugged.

"I'm not religious myself," Pete told him, "though Matthew was when I met him. Did you hear the story of how he lost his faith?"

"No."

Pete smiled again, but this time without humour.

"It seems he witnessed some sort of apparition when he was at university - I get the feeling it was of the Holy Virgin. Anyway, she told him he should turn to God. He was completely convinced by it. Converted, no less. But last year, at a class reunion, he discovered that the whole business had been a trick carried out using a large sheet of glass and some cleverly concealed lighting. It was an elaborate gag tried on by some of the more theatrical undergraduates. They had a go with several people, but it only worked with Matthew. He was devastated when he found out.

"I felt so sorry for him," he added. "If only he could have kept his faith a little longer, it would have been of some use at the end."

"He seemed extraordinarily positive when I saw him the day before he died," Howard said.

"Yeah," said Pete. "But a man can't be stoical all the time. What about those private moments when the only company you have is your thoughts?"

Howard nodded and sipped his beer, glancing round at the well-groomed clientele. Pete fitted in here perfectly, with his ironed T-shirt and pristine white 501s.

"So," he asked, "what are you doing in London?"

"Seeing a wholesaler," Pete said. "I own a catering business. I owe everything to Matthew on that score. We set up together, with his money. Now I'm the boss. I do all kinds of events, but specialise in conferences - which, as you know, was Matthew's area of expertise. I've done well out of it in the time I've been at it. From zero to an annual turnover of well over a million pounds in less than three years..."

"You look too young to be the boss of a company that size," Howard said, thinking privately that in this light he could pass for twenty-one.

"I'm getting a reputation for delivering the goods," he said. "In business it's results that matter, not how old you are. Matthew and I always delivered the goods. If people are prepared to pay, I've always been able to supply the best. Matthew and I were both perfectionists. It may not seem to make much difference from moment to moment, but in the long run it pays off. I can produce the best dinner for five-hundred in the UK, by a long way. I'm going to be twenty-five next birthday. Barring catastrophe, I'll be a millionaire by the time I'm twenty-seven." He laughed briefly. "It seems so weird, saying it like that, considering how it all began. It sounds like a boast, but it happens to be a simple statement of fact."

"And how *did* it all begin?" Howard asked.

"That," he said, "can wait for now. Let's order something to eat. You might as well eat now you're here. My treat."

Howard picked up the menu and glanced down the list of dishes.

"So?" he asked, "why eat somewhere like this, if you're into catering of that kind? I'd expect you to eat at five star restaurants."

"I do. I'm always checking places out, or looking for new ideas. In fact, there's a place I often go to, round the corner from here - the Tanera Mor. Breathtakingly expensive, but worth it; one of the best restaurants in Europe. But sometimes I like to be informal, too, and go somewhere where I can wear jeans."

He settled for soup and bread, with a salad. Howard ordered crispy potato skins followed by pasta with red, green and yellow peppers.

"Okay," Howard said as they waited for their food. "Tell me a little about yourself. For a start, you're not English, are you? Canadian?"

"I'm from New York State," he said. "American father, English mother. I came over here, to Leamington, when I was sixteen, after my parents divorced, and went to school in Warwick - hence my mid-Atlantic accent. My father lives in New York and I visit him once a year for a fortnight, at the end of which I return to England and people tell me my American accent has come right back. Everyone in England says I sound American. Everyone in America says I sound English."

He gestured in a carefree way.

"My mother lives in a village called Hunningham, outside Leamington, where she keeps cats, tends her garden, and lives off a pittance that my father sends her."

The food arrived and he started on his soup as he continued talking. His eyes had a self-confident glow to them. It was clearly no effort for him to talk about himself.

"I studied catering and management in Stratford-upon-Avon," he continued, "and I spent a lot of time avoiding Shakespeare. My mother eventually persuaded me to come along to a production of *Julius Caesar*. It was okay, but all those death scenes at the end are *so* tedious. She thinks my vocation is too capitalist by far - she always wanted me to be an artist or an actor."

He paused as if wondering for a moment what it might have been like to have taken such a course in life, then shook his head slightly, dismissively, and turned his attention back to Howard.

"Because my mother is English, my fees were paid at the tech, but I had no money to live on. I moved out from home and into a house-share in Stratford because daily commuting from Hunningham was absurd, and I didn't have a car. Also, I wanted to be away from home. Mum managed to scrape together enough to pay the rent on my room. I had to raise money for everything else. That's when I started doing rent."

"Oh..." said Howard.

"Yup, we've got more in common than you'd think," Pete smiled. "I guess prostitution wasn't my first choice, but it was by far the easiest way to make money and still have time for studying. Other people on my course were doing twenty hours a week, or more, of part-time work. I'm not surprised their grades weren't as good as they might have been."

"Is there much business to be had in Stratford?"

"You'd be surprised. There are some big hotels there, and plenty of passing trade. And once I'd bought myself a car I could go to Coventry or Birmingham. That's where I met Matthew."

"You mean he was a *client* of yours?"

"Yup. This is where it all gets slightly complicated. He slept with me because he thought I looked like you."

"Me?"

"Yes. I think it was after some business trip that you'd both taken, to Paris. He'd realised that he was in love with you at more or less the time that he discovered you were straight, and unavailable. You may not have heard of me, but I've *certainly* heard of you! It was pretty weird, I can tell you, being someone else's stand in. I would never have done it if it wasn't for the fact that Matthew was clearly an ordinary guy in an extraordinary situation, rather than a weirdo. Oh, and he paid *extremely* well."

Howard took a breath.

"I find it a bit hard to take in," he said slowly. "I saw a lot of Matthew at that time and I never got even a hint that something like that was going on."

"No, well... when Matthew met you he was in the habit of keeping that side of his life separate. He'd decided that he had no intention of looking for a relationship, and so there was no reason for his sexual life to mix in any way with either his business or his domestic life. He knew that he wasn't going to leave Corinne, because she was so needful of him, so he decided that he would sleep with people when he was away on business, but not when he was at home. Then he met you. And then he met me."

Pete shook his head fondly as he thought back.

"At first it worked extremely well," he said. "Matthew was an intelligent guy. We got on. He approved of what I was studying. The sex was okay. Easy for me, because his needs were so simple. Then it all became more difficult."

"In what way?"

"He fell in love with me."

Howard laughed sadly. "Poor Matthew."

"Yes. I'm afraid I didn't reciprocate. I mean, sure, he was a great guy, I *liked* him, but... I was only twenty-one at the time. I just wasn't interested in having a relationship with someone like him. After a while, I refused to have sex with him because it was screwing him up, and I was getting close to graduation, and I had no intention of continuing with prostitution after that. It wasn't that I hated the profession, or the work, particularly, but I'd had one or two *threatening* experiences, including one that was violent."

"Were you hurt?"

"A little, but I gave a lot worse than I got. I can take care of myself, but that's not the point. The point is that you need to work at something that you enjoy. I could never relax, except with occasional regular clients. And that's no good."

"I've never had to think about safety," Howard said, "given the fact that almost all my clients have been women over fifty."

"There's emotional safety to think of too," Pete said.

Howard nodded his agreement at this.

"So Matthew was one of your regulars, until you refused to sleep with him."

"Yes. It was shortly after that that he came up with his big proposition."

"Oh?"

"That we go into business together. He knew I had a cool business brain, and a real drive to succeed. He suggested that he invest in a catering company that I should run for him. He could supply plenty of contacts in the conference business - all I had to do was supply the goods. It was a brilliant idea, and, as you can see, it worked perfectly. We started making money back on Matthew's investment almost immediately, although in an emotional sense, for Matthew, the timing was terrible."

"Why?"

"Corinne went into business at about the same time as we did. Matthew kept the catering business a secret from Corinne, because of the difficulty he would have had in explaining about me. It caused trouble for both of them because Corinne naturally assumed that Matthew would have money to invest in her if she needed it, when in fact he had overstretched himself setting up RCC."

"RCC?"

"Rickard, Collicos Catering. Not a very imaginative name, but who cares? Anyway, as I say, once he'd set up RCC, he had nothing over to help Corinne. When her florist shop went bust she believed it was because it was undercapitalised and blamed Matthew for its demise. In fact, that wasn't true. But it didn't alter the fact that Matthew had no money to help her out, even if he'd felt inclined to do so. That's how she found out about RCC - when she asked him to raise further money and found he'd already borrowed to the hilt. I think it was a real blow to her, that Matthew had been so deceitful. And when she met me, it was like you could see this dreadful, cold, plummeting look in her eyes. I thought she was going to commit suicide, or something..."

"If she hadn't died anyway."

Pete shrugged at Howard's somewhat bitter tone.

"Yes, well, you can go on, over and over, about what might have happened under different circumstances. Pretty fruitless in the end. Corinne went bust. She died. RCC flourished. Matthew talked of giving up his work in conference organising to go full-time with RCC, but I persuaded him to leave it with me. I managed to raise some capital and bought into a partnership with him... it was all going extremely well. David was on the scene by the time Corinne died, and although I regret that she died, you have to acknowledge that it freed Matthew up to get on with his own life as a gay man. It was fun, and cute, to watch him falling in love with David. They were genuinely happy together. They'd only been together for eighteen months when Matthew got ill."

Howard nodded.

"Poor Matthew," he said.

"Poor David."

"Mmm," Howard agreed.

The waiter arrived with the main course and there was a pause in the conversation. Howard was aware that Pete had been watching him throughout their talk and it made him self-conscious.

"I met Emma, Corinne's sister, at the funeral," he told Pete. "When I last saw him, Matthew seemed quite keen that I should talk to her."

"About what?"

"Probably about the fact that she seems to think that Corinne only slept with me as a way to hurt Matthew."

"That wouldn't surprise me. She sounded as if she was complicated and, I guess, what you would call clinically ill."

"But my experience of her was so different from that. I always found her well-balanced and decidedly sane."

"But how often did you see her? I'm only theorising here, but, given the pathology of her depressive condition, I would guess she'd only have allowed herself to be with you when she was feeling stable - which wouldn't be all the time. I know something of this. My mother has depressive tendencies. Did Corinne have a history of cancelling arrangements to see you?"

"No, but that's because she never made arrangements in the first place. She would phone to say she was coming over, and that was that. It was sometimes difficult for me to adjust to that. Sometimes I didn't see her for more than a week at a time, but I assumed it was because she was fitting around her schedule at the florist, or Matthew's timetable."

"But Matthew was fine about the concept of Corinne having an affair. He had no reason not to be. In fact, if Corinne had genuinely fallen in love with someone to the point where she wanted to live with them, and share with them all her vulnerabilities and difficulties, then he'd have been delighted for her. Of course, it was problematic for Matthew when Corinne chose to have an affair with *you*. For obvious reasons. But he never tried to scupper it."

"I know," Howard murmured. "Matthew was brilliant."

He sipped his beer.

"I feel very confused about all this," he went on. "I find it hard to believe that the Corinne I fell in love with - and I did fall in love with her - wasn't the whole person. The person I saw when she came over to my flat... that wasn't a pretence."

"Howard," Pete said, leaning forward and speaking quietly, though the buzz in the busy restaurant kept their talk anonymous anyway, "does it matter? Corinne was Corinne, you'll never fully understand her, because she's not here to either refute or corroborate what you say.

We all have our opinions of her, but she was a very secretive person and not even Matthew knew everything. Your best bet is to think what suits you most. If you want to believe that she was in love with you, then believe it. Don't forget, Corinne might not have been honest with Emma when she talked to her. She might not even have been honest with herself. As far as my opinion goes, that's irrelevant. I was wrong to express it."

"How simple that sounds, 'believe what suits you most', and how absurd."

"Maybe." He paused for a moment and then spoke with a definite air of changing the subject. "So, what are you going to do with Matthew's money?"

Howard was caught unawares by this question and paused to ponder it.

"I don't know precisely how much it will be," he said after a while. "Quite a bit. But I haven't pressed Mr Woods on that. I'll wait and see. I'm just surprised he didn't leave it to David."

"David's got the house and he owns a place of his own in Warwick that he rents out, so he'll be fine. Matthew knew David very well; much better than he ever knew Corinne. David has very simple tastes. I don't mean this to sound derogatory, but he is a simple man. I admire that, really, that someone as intelligent and sophisticated as David should need so little, materially. If Matthew had left David a large sum of money, he'd be bemused by it, and perhaps a little frightened. He'd probably give it away in some unsuitable manner, or worse, stuff it somewhere and not touch it. Money needs to be *used*."

"But why would Matthew leave it to me, then? I'm even less suitable than David. He knew what I think about money."

"Maybe it was a challenge?"

Howard looked at Pete questioningly.

"I presume you know that Matthew was insured up to the hilt, medically," Pete said. "It was a hobby for him, creating this great web that would catch him if he fell. And he did fall. And it didn't catch him.

And now the money is going to you."

"Don't you resent that? Why didn't he leave it to someone with an astute business brain like yourself? I'm the only one who doesn't deserve a penny."

"Matthew left me his share of RCC, so I'm the lucky one if you ask me," Pete said.

"But I don't want the money," said Howard. "I'm aimless enough as it is."

"Like I said," Pete murmured, "a challenge. Be an optimist. Take it. Use it."

"I really don't know how to do that without wasting it."

"Everything about you tells me that isn't true," said Pete. "You've got this air of yearning loss about you, so I guess you're still hurting a bit? And hurt leaves little room for optimism, I know. But you've done some interesting things in your life, Howard, and you've loved and been loved by some pretty interesting people. Life only stops being interesting when you stop experiencing it afresh. You're too bright and too needful of experience to ever shut it out for good. Close your eyes and jump!"

There was an eerie quality of wisdom in Pete's words. It was almost creepy seeing this immaculate youth being so assured.

"You're right," Howard breathed. "You're right."

Pete smiled smugly.

"I know."

ELEVEN

1986:

Howard accepted the invitation from his Uncle Richard to stay for part of their three week holiday in Suffolk. He arranged to go for four days, over a long weekend - though not for Ruth's birthday - and he wondered what it would be like. At that time he still wasn't sure whether he was in love with Jan or what was happening to their relationship, so they'd agreed not to bother seeing each other over the summer. This was harder for Howard than he'd expected. He spent the second week of his holidays with Leon in Swiss Cottage, which was only a short distance from where Jan lived, in Kentish Town. He found himself, on more than one occasion, suggesting to Leon that they should go for a wander over Primrose Hill - which he knew she visited regularly - on the off chance of bumping into her. He anguished over whether or not to break his promise and go and knock on her door. In the end, he didn't.

Although Richard's invitation to stay at *Rosemerion* had been made to the whole of Howard's family, he drove down to Suffolk on his own. His sister, Elaine, had laughed at him, saying, "You promised you would never go there again after last time. You used to say how bleak it was and how you always got bored."

His mother had tutted at Elaine and said to him, "You'll have a lovely time, darling."

He arrived for lunch on the Friday. Aunt Helen was the only one there when he wandered into the house. She was a short, large woman who had boundless energy so that Howard would often feel energized (or sometimes stressed) by being in her company. She put him in the tiny box room above the porch.

"I'm sorry you can't have the back bedroom as usual, but we've given it to Anna and her friend Karen, who's used to *that* sort of comfort. I hope you don't mind."

"Of course not."

"I've put Ruth in with Alasdair. She's not at all pleased."

There were seven at lunch. The five McLeans, plus himself and Karen, a rather arrogant non-entity, he thought. Uncle Richard had an air of heartiness about him that was completely fake. The ruddiness of his cheeks was caused by his drinking rather than his dedication to country pursuits, but at least he had gusto like his wife and, although Howard felt alienated whenever he talked about his profession (he was a financier), he was at least an affable man and genuinely friendly towards Howard. He was keen that Howard should drive with him into Aldeburgh to hire a sailing boat, or a fishing boat if he'd rather. Although the prospect of a day out on the choppy North Sea depressed him, Howard couldn't bring himself to refuse in the face of his uncle's enthusiasm.

"I'll let him go with you tomorrow, dad," said Ruth, "but he's coming for a walk with me to the old ruins this afternoon. I want to show him something."

As he ate, Howard wished he hadn't come to *Rosemerion*. The place had nothing of the atmosphere that it had when he was here on his own. It was as though the house had been desecrated, somehow, by the presence of other people. The only thing that stopped him from succumbing to misery was curiosity about his forthcoming conversation with Ruth.

They set off after Howard had done the washing up ("You see, a gentleman!" Aunt Helen had cried when he offered).

"Mum thinks you're *marvellous*," Ruth told him as they wandered off. "It's rather sickening."

Howard smiled and looked out across the reeds to their left. A grey heron rose gracefully into the air and flew, with its slow-motion wing beats, off up the river. Ruth watched it, too, pulling her fringe away from her forehead as she looked up. She had a long narrow face, with fine features. Howard felt that if only someone could take the top of her head in one hand, and her chin in the other, and squeeze hard so that her face was somehow compressed, then her proportions would be perfect. As it was she looked rather elongated, like one of those extruded, mythical maidens that seem to float in the air looking wistful and playing pipes in paintings by William Blake.

On second thoughts, he decided, her looks were fine as they were. Another three or four years and she would be stunning. He wondered if she knew.

"Why *do* you come out here on your own?" she asked him.

Howard looked down at the seaweed and straw-like detritus of the high-tide line and stopped to pick up a stick before answering.

"To be alone," he said, swinging the stick loosely.

"But you can do that anywhere. Why did you decide to come and break into *Rosemerion*?"

Howard thought about that for a moment.

"I didn't intend to break in. I came with my tent the first time and pitched it on the back lawn."

"But why here?"

"Maybe because I know the place. Maybe because it's so isolated. It's the only place I know where you can *really* be on your own."

She nodded.

"I only asked because I sometimes feel the same way," she told him. "You're alright, you're twenty and you've got a car. I haven't. I sometimes wish I could come here on my own, but mum and dad would never allow it. I even considered running away for a couple of days last weekend and coming down here to join you. But it's such a long way from the station. And I haven't got any money for the fare anyway."

She looked out towards the horizon, suddenly dreamy.

"I hate being thirteen," she said.

"Nearly fourteen," he reminded her.

"That's no better. Things aren't going to even begin to look up until I'm sixteen."

They arrived at the rickety footbridge over the inlet and Ruth took Howard's hand as she crossed. Once on the other side she kept hold of it, swinging it slightly between them. Howard wondered suddenly if she had started menstruating yet, and felt embarrassed by the thought. He also remembered the kiss that she'd given him when he'd been holding that cardboard box full of his camping gear and wondered if there was some kind of sexual connection between them. He looked at her now as she gazed ahead, the tiniest of smiles playing on her lips. She appeared completely child-like to him at that moment. Virtually asexual.

"I'm glad you found the key to the outhouse," she told him. "I like to think of you staying there. Did you notice that I sweep the floor after you've been?"

"Yes," he said, though he hadn't. "Thanks."

She smiled shyly at him.

"I sort of imagine that it's me staying there - running away and being alone like that. Either alone or with... someone. Someone to share it with. Someone from school maybe, but not like Karen. I don't know why Anna brought her along. She's the wrong type altogether. She keeps wanting to go in to Aldeburgh to go shopping, for God's sake! In fact, there's no one at school that I'd like to be alone with like that. That's why I wanted to run away for the weekend and come down to be with you. At least you like going for walks."

Howard laughed and squeezed her hand with affection, then let it go.

"I can't explain fully why I come here," he told her. "The isolation's an important part of it, but there's something more than that, too."

"I know," she said. "You don't have to explain. I understand."

If it hadn't been for Ruth, that weekend would have been a complete disaster. Going fishing with Richard the following day was a nightmare of back-slapping, beer drinking and sea sickness. The rest of the time Anna, Karen and Alasdair were irritating merely by being present in the house. Aunt Helen was fine, if a little overbearing. Ruth, however, was allowed to stay up drinking cocoa with Howard after her parents went to bed at ten-thirty. He enjoyed her simple view of life, and her desperate envy of all the freedom he had achieved by leaving home for university.

***

Over the rest of the summer Howard only managed a single illicit weekend to *Rosemerion*, but when he returned to Cambridge for the Autumn term, he reintroduced his weekly pilgrimages. It was seventy-four miles to the cottage, which made it reasonably accessible. He'd had a note from Ruth to say that her parents weren't planning to go there before Christmas, but that they were expecting to stay for the entire Christmas/New Year period.

He bought himself a small paraffin heater for his hideout as the evenings drew in and cooled down. He almost preferred the place in driving rain and, later, sleet, because it somehow embodied the internal quality of the experience - he had to huddle into his cagoule when he went for his walks, as though protecting something extremely precious at the core of his being.

He found that he could work well, too, lying in his sleeping bag with the hurricane lamp to one side of him and the paraffin heater to the other. Final year pressures were already building up and it was good to be away from potential distractions, of which Jan was the most pressing. After the summer holidays they had both surprised themselves by being pleased to see each other and they had resumed their relationship. He found her physically mesmerising, although he couldn't work out precisely why. Maybe it was because she had a deeply assured air; a confidence that made him feel confident too, merely by association. Maybe it was because there was an easy momentum between them that seemed to work of its own accord. And sexually, they had always seemed to click without effort. There was still a tension around Howard's secret weekends and the rumours that had arisen as a result of them, but Jan was emancipated and vociferous about the need for independence and so she didn't try to stop him going, although they did have one or two fierce arguments about why he wouldn't tell her *where* he was going; arguments that always ended up with bouts of frenetic love-making and odd conciliatory gestures such as small gifts, or special meals.

In November she managed to corner him regarding meeting his family and he eventually gave in, inviting her to stay with him for Christmas (on the grounds that he could pass off his parents' good behaviour as being festive-season hypocrisy rather than genuine friendliness). She readily accepted the invitation, curious to see for herself these ghastly relatives that he had told her so many nasty stories about. She also accepted an invitation to spend New Year's Eve at *Rosemerion* as part of the Martindale family entourage.

Howard couldn't decide which he dreaded most, Jan meeting the family, or Jan seeing his precious stretch of Suffolk Coast.

At Christmas, Jan instantly got on with Howard's mother, who was a personnel officer and who talked in an intelligent and accessible manner about *people*. She immediately adopted an intimacy with Jan that Howard found rather frightening, especially when Jan started giving him glances of confusion. Where were the arguments? she seemed to be asking. Where was the coldness, the animosity, the subdued violence that Howard had described to her?

She laughed with Howard's father about Howard's 'absurd' notions concerning what constituted equal opportunities, particularly in education; ridiculing Howard, but at the same time, rather cleverly, also ridiculing Mr Martindale for his clearly elitist views and his extraordinary reverence for Mrs Thatcher.

On the first night, when they went to bed, she voiced her confusion.

"You told me all these stories about how awful they were," she said. "But they're not like that at all. They're wonderful. Okay, your father's a bit self-important, but he's okay. I just don't understand why you lied about them."

"Oh, you know," Howard told her, trying to pass it off as insignificant, "I suppose I wanted to impress you or something."

But Jan looked disturbed and turned away when he kissed her, muttering "Crazy!" under her breath.

They settled down with each other after that and nothing further was said but there was, nevertheless, something wistful about Jan during that whole period. She developed an almost passionate friendship with Howard's mother, endlessly discussing feminism with her and sending Howard from the room under the pretext that they were indulging in 'women's talk'. When the five of them made their way to Suffolk in Mr Martindale's Mercedes, she sat in the back and talked to Howard's mother and Elaine whilst Howard sat in silence in the front.

As it happened, Howard's anxiety about sharing *Rosemerion* with Jan was unfounded. It rained for the two days they were there and Jan never left the house, referring to the landscape outside as 'grim' and showing no interest in going outside to have a closer look.

Aunt Helen put Howard and Jan in the little box room above the porch that he'd had on his last visit, and made a suggestive remark about the two fold-out beds that she'd placed side-by-side. In fact, Howard having a girlfriend was joked about to an irritating degree for the duration of their stay and he found himself resenting the fact that he was the oldest of his generation. He didn't see what was so different about Elaine that she should get off without any sexual innuendo at all. She was, after all, seventeen and had had at least two vague, rather virginal relationships.

The revelation at *Rosemerion* was Ruth. She could hardly bring herself to speak to Jan, and ignored Howard completely. She actually burst into tears at the New Year's Day dinner, running from the room and into Howard's hideout to sob loudly, leaning against the wall. Jan seemed to intuitively pick up something that remained unstated and she smiled at Howard as Aunt Helen rushed out to see what was the matter with her. Jan referred to Ruth, later, as 'pathetic', which put Howard into a foul mood that seemed to give Jan smug satisfaction.

TWELVE

1996:

Towards the end of the year that they'd been seeing each other, Corinne came round to see Howard unannounced. He opened the door of his flat and ushered her into the sitting room, pleased to see her. She looked pale, but exhilarated, her brown eyes glinting with a hard light. She kissed him in that strenuous, insistent way that was usually reserved for love-making at York Road, and Howard had the delicious sensation of being caught up in the vortex of her desire. His response was to try to match her desire, to echo it. But, on that occasion, it seemed, he wasn't getting it right. When he thought she would respond to his touch, she seemed oblivious. When he nuzzled her lazy breasts, she didn't look down at him as she usually did. When they made love, their rhythms were so separate that her orgasm, when it arrived, seemed to have come, not from his ministrations, but from some other source. And he thought, *This is how it is, sometimes. Part of loving someone is recognising and respecting their otherness.*

Afterwards, when she admitted to problems at work (though nothing serious, she assured him), she had laughed and said, "It's all going to have to change, isn't it? Really, I've been carrying on as though I could go on like this forever. But I can't. I have to sort myself out and *settle* things."

"What things?" he asked cautiously.

"Oh, things..." she said, and kissed him, and dressed quickly and left.

***

1999:

Howard, thinking back to this occasion with Corinne, was startled by how differently it was possible to interpret the scene with the benefit of both hindsight and information recently received. Previously, when he'd thought that her business was doing well, he'd assumed that if she ever mentioned struggling, it was with the build up to saying yes to making a definite commitment to leaving Matthew, rather than a reference to her job.

Now that he knew she'd been teetering on the verge of bankruptcy; that she'd been on medication (and when he thought back to it, he realised that the curious glint he'd sometimes seen in her eyes had probably been chemically induced), it made him feel that almost anything might have been true about that moment. Why shouldn't Pete and Emma be right about her? Or maybe all three of them were wrong and it was something else again...

The only way out of this conundrum, seeing as answers were unlikely to be forthcoming, was to try and forget it. Howard reacted by heaping more and more work onto himself. He worked even harder than he had before - up to twenty hours a day. This wasn't especially difficult as he'd begun to suffer from insomnia and it was easier to work than to lie listlessly for endless hours on his bed.

He gave up exercising altogether, gave up going out, gave up talking (except out-loud to himself to prove that he wasn't slipping into some kind of extreme psychological state). He gave up shaving and flung towels over the two mirrors in the flat so that he didn't have to see what a mess he was becoming. He gave up sleeping for more than twenty minutes at a time - he even gave up eating on a regular basis. Couriers would arrive with new batches of work almost daily, and the last days of August slipped away in a welter of linguistic concentration. The first fortnight of September continued in the same way. He found himself sipping cold cups of coffee at five in the morning, desultory music filtering from the radio as if through some sort of heavy, deadening material (Howard thought of the black, vaguely bluesy music as 'post-coital' somehow, and restful). It was the most extraordinary release. His waking hours became conveyor-belt-like. It was the first time since the period during which he'd regularly visited *Rosemerion* that he'd managed so completely to push away his preoccupations. It was the first time in over two years that he'd managed to stop consciously missing Corinne. His only acute physical or emotional state was that of exhaustion. He would find himself falling asleep on the job, or phoning out for a free-delivery pizza only to find that it was four in the morning and the pizzeria had been closed for hours. He experienced peculiar bouts of nausea, too, and dizzy spells and a level of weight-loss that would have astonished him if he'd ever stopped to look at himself. Being unwashed was a new experience for him and although he didn't enjoy the itchiness of his scalp, or the way his T-shirt felt greasily cold when he put it on, he *did* feel an almost exhilarating liberation from the need to be presentable.

At the end of the second week of September, Colin Farley called him in to Sheldon Translation's small London office for a talk about some up-coming work. Despite the fact that Howard had showered and put on a suit, he could see that Colin was shocked by his appearance.

"My God!" he said, "you look dreadful! Are you okay?"

"I'm fine," Howard said.

"It's not just the beard," Colin told him, "you've lost such a lot of weight. You're not... ill are you?"

Howard laughed.

"No, nothing like that."

"I knew you were overworking," Colin told him. "You've done the work of half a dozen people by yourself."

"I find I need to work at the moment."

"You look like you need a rest, and you might as well take one, because there isn't any more pressing work in at the moment. I was going to go through a possible project with you, but I can easily give it to one of our in-house staff - there's no hurry. Why don't you take a break? Go away. Eat!"

But Howard couldn't bring himself to go away. He didn't want to take some late summer sun. He didn't want to go down to the Mediterranean, or trek up into the Atlas mountains, or slip out to some dusty oasis in the desert. He felt too listless. All he really wanted was to work and to sleep and to, one day, wake up and find that he understood what he had to do next by some process of subconscious osmosis.

Now that he had no work to do, his insomnia turned, overnight, into its opposite. He couldn't wake up before noon, and then he would drowsily sit at his kitchen table drinking black coffee. The coffee made him edgy, rather than wakeful, and he spent his afternoons in a kind of fugue. The only activity that he indulged in was walking - wandering really - across the Heath, or meandering through the area where he lived, hands in pockets, eyes half-closed, his mind not exactly empty, but numb to anything but the most trivial thoughts, observing people around him in a detached, disinterested way. Sometimes back at the flat he tried to read, but he found he couldn't concentrate. Even José's poetry was beyond him. It was as though all leisure activity became meaningless. Anything that could be described as useful for 'passing the time' or which could, under some circumstances, be seen as displacement activity - reading, watching television, meeting friends, *travelling* - became unnecessary because time passed anyway, effortlessly. He would occasionally think of Matthew's money, but that had somehow become an irrelevance to him, so he found it difficult to keep it in his mind for any length of time.

After about a week, during which he hardly ate anything and washed in only the most cursory manner, he noticed a chill to the air - the first for months. He ran his fingers through his hair and discovered that it was already long enough to have tangles. Leaving it as it was, he put on an old pair of jeans that he usually kept for dirty chores around the flat, plus a checked cotton shirt that had a rip at the elbow. Then, passing the towel-covered mirror in the hall, he retreated into the anonymity of the streets. He wandered down to Primrose Hill. He hadn't been there for a long time and enjoyed the slight formality of the lay-out of the trees in the park, and the incline to the summit. He felt light, almost weightless, as he walked, and had to keep it slow because he became breathless after only a small amount of physical effort these days.

He was comfortable dressed as he was and felt unpressured to *be* anything, and so he quietly hummed a tune to himself as he walked. At the top of the hill, beside a small cobbled circle, there was a solitary woman, looking out at the panorama before her. Howard stood on the uneven stones and did the same. Immediately beyond the park was the odd, tent-like contraption of London Zoo's aviary, and further away endless anonymous tower-blocks, with Telecom Tower standing rather incongruously in the middle. St Paul's Cathedral looked distinctly over-shadowed by the buildings around it, and more distant, only just visible in the haze, the squat regularity of Canary Wharf. There were a couple of planes which, at this distance, seemed silent and motionless when glanced at cursorily, but which were, presumably, approaching Heathrow.

His gaze encompassed the woman at this point and he realised, with a lurch, that he recognised her.

"Jan?" he said quietly.

She turned, clearly not recognising him as he took a couple of steps towards her.

"It's me," he said. "Howard."

There was a moment's pause as he watched Jan searching her mind for a Howard that she might know. Then it clicked.

"God, *Howard!*" she said, smiling with a curious mixture of embarrassment and apprehension. She was clearly shocked.

"I didn't recognise you," she said, hovering for a moment between a handshake and an embrace, then choosing the handshake.

"What are you doing?" Howard asked her.

"I'm on holiday," she said. "I came up here because I have some... memories of this place."

"I know," he said. "You lost your virginity here."

"I told you that?"

"Of course," he said. "We had no secrets from each other. We were lovers for nearly two years, remember."

"Four terms."

"Four and a half, plus the summer holidays."

"I don't think you can count the summer holidays..."

"Whatever."

Howard turned from Jan and looked out across London. He felt suddenly dwarfed by it. There was a dull pall of photochromatic haze in the still, sunny air. Jan was facing away from him when he turned back. He looked down at his paint-splashed jeans and his dirty finger-nails and realised how he must appear to her, which made him feel suddenly embarrassed. Then he caught an emotional echo of the terrible anger he'd felt, all those years ago, when she'd exposed him as a fraud to his peers and he felt a sudden urge to walk away without saying another word. But along with that feeling, now that he had the chance of company, he also felt a desperate need to retain it.

When Jan turned back to him, she seemed to have composed herself She looked slick and professionally disinterested.

"Look," he said her, "do you fancy going somewhere for coffee? Somewhere where we can talk."

She looked at him for some time, clearly vacillating between repulsion and sympathy, and then nodded.

"There's a place on Regent's Park Road," he told her.

They started to walk down the pathway, not speaking. The tarmac was flanked by plane and rowan trees, and there was a slight glistening of late-morning dew on the grass. As Howard glanced across, it amazed him that he'd recognised her at all. Her dark hair was straight and long, where before she'd had it cut in a bob. She was slender, too, now, in a way that made her seem taller than he remembered. Her eyes had a knowing cast, a new cynicism to them that accentuated her intelligence and made her formidable, somehow, where before she'd been open and approachable. When they walked under the chestnut tree that overhung the exit from the park, he spoke.

"You look great," he told her. "I can't believe it's ten years since I last saw you."

"Nearly eleven," she said. "I've been working it out."

He shook his head, then shrugged.

"You look great," he said again.

Jan smiled.

"I'm okay," she told him. "What have you been up to since you graduated, then? Are you working?"

"Yes, of course."

"You look a bit... dishevelled. I thought you might be unemployed."

"I'm not. I do translation work mostly, and interpreting. You?"

"I work for a small media company in Manchester," she said. "I don't really use my Spanish anymore. I'm getting incredibly rusty."

She sighed and looked back at the park, briefly, as they left it. He noticed that she still scuffed her shoes on the ground as she walked.

"I thought Spanish was such a romantic language," she murmured. "I still do. But when I was at college I thought I'd end up living there, being a dark-haired *señora*, you know, in a long, figure hugging frilly red dress and clacking away with my castanets. I was such a child, then, so unformed..."

Howard smiled at the image of this, but found that it collapsed into a gloomy shadow of past emotion.

"I used to think that life would inevitably become what I hoped it would be," he said. "I thought that all you had to do was conceptualise it strongly enough and then it would conform to your expectation."

"Mmm," she smiled. "You always were strange."

They walked on in silence. Howard was surprised by how dark Jan's beauty was, and how angular in an aggressive way. He remembered her as slightly - pleasingly - rounded, with full cheeks that she would press her fists into when she was concentrating. He remembered the dimples in the backs of her knees, and her attempts at dieting. He remembered the energy of their lovemaking - so grown-up to them at the time, but so simple and childish in retrospect.

He looked over at her and realised that she, too, was preoccupied with her memories. She caught his gaze and smiled in a slightly nervous way.

"Howard...?" she began.

"Yes?"

"I can't think of a tactful way of saying this..."

"Say it straight, then," he told her.

She took a breath.

"What's *happened* to you? You look so gaunt and hollow eyed; and that scrappy beard, it's so... my God!"

"What," Howard asked, alarmed by her tone.

"You're not still ill, are you? That breakdown you had in your final year, it hasn't *recurred* has it?"

Howard wanted to laugh at this, but felt tears welling up instead. He looked down at the ground.

"No," he said. "No, at least the possibility of that hasn't even occurred to me until you just said it. I'm going through a complicated moment in my life, that's all. It's not really comparable to what I went through at university."

He thought about this for a moment and then nodded to himself.

"I've had a protracted period of having to be something I'm not," he said. "I've had to be well turned out, fit, immaculately groomed. I chucked that in nearly two months ago and I've been rebelling against it for a while."

"I have to tell you that it doesn't suit you. What form has this rebellion taken - fasting?"

"I've been forgetting to eat," Howard admitted. "I've probably lost a couple of stone over the last six weeks. I've been working pretty hard."

She nodded and murmured, "Crazy."

Howard laughed. "You used to say that all the time, especially when you wanted to change the subject. *Crazy*."

"I still do," she said.

"I must say, I found it incredibly irritating at times."

"That's because I said it to you more than most," she told him. "I knew it irritated you, so I said it when I was angry. Because it was the only way I could get you to be angry too."

Howard absorbed this for a moment, until they arrived at the *Primrose Patisserie*.

"I'll get this," Jan said when they had found themselves a table. "They probably wouldn't serve you. They'd think you were a tramp or something. What do you want?"

"Just coffee," he said.

He sat beside the doorway to the toilets. Here, the wall was panelled with mirrors and Howard caught his reflection for the first time in weeks, which made him wince, visibly. His beard was sparse and dirty-looking - the kind of beard that no one would grow unless they were destitute. There was something haunted, too, about his deeply shadowed eyes, which really looked as though they'd sunk back into his head. With sudden self-consciousness, Howard shifted his chair so that he was facing away from the mirrors and looked instead at the pictures on the walls which depicted either thistles or owls.

Jan arrived at that point with coffee and a large slice of cake each. Howard looked down at his gateau as though even the concept of eating it was an impossibility. Instead, he concentrated on her.

"So," he asked, "have you got a lover? A husband? Children?"

"No on all points," she said. "I did have a husband - technically I still do - but I left him nearly three weeks ago. That's why I'm down here on a nostalgia trip. Actually, it's been a bad idea. Most of my friends have started families, or moved away from London, or drifted off in other ways. I came down to get back into the swing of things, but in fact I've only managed to prove how alone you can be."

"Did it break up badly?" Howard asked.

"If you mean, did we fight, then no, we didn't. Maybe it ended in the worst way possible - it sort of petered out. There was no definite moment when I thought, 'that's it, I've got to get out of this'. I realised one day that it had been over for months, but I just hadn't accepted it up here." She tapped her temple. "I'd been judiciously ignoring the obvious."

"How long were you together?"

"Six years." She took a gulp of coffee after saying this and widened her eyes as if, even to her, this seemed extraordinary.

"And you?" she asked.

"I was in love," he said quietly. "She died in a car accident."

"But that's terrible!" Jan said, and the genuine concern in her voice made Howard wince again, but this time it didn't show. It didn't feel an appropriate moment to talk about Corinne, so he steered the conversation back to Jan.

"So, where are you staying?" he asked.

"In a hotel in Kentish Town. A nasty place. Still, it's only exorbitant rather than impossible. I decided to treat myself to a hotel, but leaving your partner of six years is more expensive than you might imagine and I'm near enough broke. So I chose the cheapest hotel I could find. I'm renting an unfurnished flat up in Manchester in anticipation of buying somewhere when I'm sorted out. I needn't tell you how costly it all is."

Howard looked out at the sky, which was beginning to cloud over. He noticed that people in the tea shop were beginning to look at him in a furtive but obvious way.

"It's funny the way things change," she said.

"Mmm," he said thoughtfully. "You know, I can't remember us ever having been happy together, back then. Isn't that weird? We must have been happy, at least for *some* of the time, surely?"

"Of course we were," she said. "It was wonderful, that first summer term... But I didn't understand your needs. I so badly wanted to be an ordinary, normal person that when I realised you wanted to be anything *but* normal, I was freaked out. That's why I betrayed you to Leon and the others, really, because I wanted to turn you into an ordinary person rather than an extraordinary one. I felt extremely bad about it for a long time afterwards, you know. Partly because I could never bring myself to apologise."

"There was no need. I shouldn't have been so idiotic - fostering all those rumours about me having an affair with some MP's wife."

"You said you didn't make them up."

"No, but I didn't deny them, either, did I? I *allowed* them, which is more or less as bad as making them up. I was flattered by them, which is kind of pathetic when you think of it."

She sipped her coffee and took a forkful of cake before becoming pensive again as she ate.

"You know," she said, "I was terribly jealous of those secretive weekend breaks you used to take. You always looked so *settled* within yourself when you came back. And I knew you weren't having an affair with anyone..."

"That's not what you said at the time."

"I was pretending to be terribly open and liberal, Howard. I thought that if I gave the appearance of allowing you to conduct an affair with someone else, it would reflect rather well on me. It was only the fact that I knew you weren't that allowed me to be so magnanimous."

"How did you know I wasn't?"

"Intuition, I suppose, because I wasn't particularly worldly. And also because there was something so, well... *innocent* about the way you were refreshed and invigorated by your breaks; plus the fact that you used to get work done whilst you were away, which was *completely* inconsistent with having a passionate affair.

"That's what was unforgivable about the way in which I dumped you in the shit, because I knew that what you were doing wasn't smutty or disreputable - I was jealous that you had something I couldn't share, and I was angry to discover that I rather admired you for something that I found so infuriating."

THIRTEEN

1986:

On the Friday of the first week of their final term at Cambridge, Jan seriously challenged Howard.

"Why," she asked, "*why* won't you tell me where you're going this weekend? And don't give me your usual evasive answers because I don't want to hear them. At first I thought it was quite fun, having a lover with a mysterious secret. Now, I'm afraid, it has become exceedingly boring. And after Christmas, when I discovered that all the terrible stories you told about your family were lies, I find that I no longer trust you. If I'm in love with you, and I think I *might* be, then I want the truth from you. I want to begin to be able to trust you again. As it stands this whole situation is crazy. *Crazy!*"

It was incredibly easy for Howard to tell Jan the truth. In fact, he found he'd been waiting for months for her to make this demand.

"I've been going to *Rosemerion*," he told her.

"*Rosemerion?*"

"Yes, where we went for New Year."

He went on to explain how he'd first gone there with his tent, and then, with Ruth's help, had used the hideout without being discovered. He tried to explain about the particular quality of 'aloneness' that he could achieve there; how he could make himself calm inside. But when he described it, it sounded lame.

"So Ruth was your accomplice?" Jan asked.

"In a way," he agreed. "Though since you've appeared on the scene, Ruth has neither spoken to me, nor left me notes to say when the

McLeans will be in residence."

"I knew she had a crush on you," Jan breathed, "I *knew* it."

"That's irrelevant, now, whether it's true or not."

Jan smirked and looked derisive.

"So," she asked, "how do you know that the coast's clear this weekend?"

"I saw Uncle Richard, briefly, at Easter and he told me they weren't going to go down there until June at the earliest."

Jan nodded slowly.

"And you're going over there this afternoon?"

"Yes."

"I want to come with you."

Howard closed his eyes. This was his worst case scenario. How could he explain to her that the intrinsic *point* of what he was doing was that he should be alone? How could he make her understand that there was no way he could feel that sense of profound isolation if there was someone else with him? He realised that this was why he'd kept so quiet - because he feared that she would make precisely this demand.

He looked at her as neutrally as he could manage.

"Well?" she asked.

He sighed, realising that to argue would make everything worse.

"Okay," he murmured, "but you'll need a sleeping bag and mat."

"Lisa's got a sleeping bag," Jan said, "and I can buy a mat. They only cost a few quid, don't they?"

"Mmm," he agreed.

Driving over to Suffolk that day was one of the most depressing experiences that Howard could remember. It was forcibly impressed on him how important these weekends were. To sacrifice one of them, as it were, in order to share it with Jan, was a loss out of all proportion to what he might have expected, given that he was going to go the following weekend, and the one after that. Jan noticed his mood, and so became moody herself.

Things were made worse when, on arrival, it began to drizzle. Had

Howard brought Jan here in the summer, they might have had a chance of constructing a makeshift barbecue and then sitting out, looking at the stars. They could have sunbathed during the day, or gone swimming, or for a leisurely walk to the ivy-clad ruins... Now amidst April showers, their choices were limited. Jan didn't even have a waterproof jacket.

There was an initial sense of conspiracy as they fetched the front door key from under the buoy and then let themselves into the house to find the key to the hideout. But when Jan saw the bare, dusty little room that Howard was proposing that they should use, she rebelled.

"You have the run of the house!" she exclaimed. "Why hole yourself up here when you've got access to all that luxury?"

Howard shook his head miserably.

"That's not the point," he told her. "That's not why I come here. I'd rather go back to using the tent than sleep in a bed."

Jan couldn't see it. Rain was beginning to fall more heavily outside and the noise of it seemed to make her even more angry.

"No," she said. "I'm not staying here. It's cold. It's draughty. The weather's vile. There's a cosy kitchen where we can cook our dinner... come on, let's use it."

The weekend was ruined anyway, Howard thought, so why not?

One thing he insisted on was no electric light.

"I don't know who might be out there to see, but if we stick to lamplight behind closed curtains we should be alright."

Jan agreed to this and seemed to find it romantic to sit and watch Howard cook up beans on toast in the half-light from the hurricane lamp. After they'd eaten she took a torch from the sideboard and went exploring, coming back after a while with a bottle of gin from the drinks cabinet in the sitting room.

"Let's have a gin and tonic," she said. "There's stacks of tonic in the fridge. No one will notice."

Howard felt that his weekend was finally slipping out of control.

"Can't we just leave everything as it is?" he said.

Jan laughed.

"Come on, Howard, where's your sense of adventure?"

Without waiting for a reply she took two glasses out of one of the cupboards and poured them both a stiff measure of gin.

"No ice or lemon," she smiled as she handed him a glass, "so I guess you could say we *are* slumming it."

Howard became even more despondent when Jan opened a bottle of wine from the wine rack under the stairs.

"Relax," she told him. "It's only a basic claret. I haven't touched any of the classy stuff. It won't be missed."

At least getting drunk was something to do, but for Howard, the ultimate desecration was Jan's insistence that they watch the late night film on tv. After that, her suggestion that they sleep in his aunt and uncle's double bed was almost inevitable.

In the morning, as he lay watching the ragged clouds outside, he felt an intense yearning to slip out of bed, put on his cagoule, and go for a wander in the rain. He looked at his watch. It was 7.30. Jan was unlikely to stir before nine, so he decided he might as well go out.

The landscape was absolutely at its best. Moody, windswept, the reeds and grasses still bleached a dry dusty blonde, even though he could see verdant new growth beginning to take hold. The water of the estuary, whipped almost to a frenzy by the wind and the tidal current, was turbulently muddy with flashes of white, and all noises other than that of the sea were subjugated by the rushing of the wind. Howard could feel the bite of rain on his cheeks, and the hard glow that it induced. He felt a wash of calmness starting somewhere in his bowels that crept over his being until he was heedless and serene.

He walked almost as far as the ruins before turning back, and didn't return to the cottage until nearly a quarter to ten. Jan was sitting in the kitchen. Furious.

"Why didn't you ask me if I wanted to come?" she demanded when he explained where he'd been.

"Because you wouldn't have wanted to."

"How do you know?"

"Because of the way you complained about the rain yesterday; the way you hate any kind of discomfort. You don't even like the countryside around here. You called it *grim* at New Year. Of course you wouldn't have wanted to come."

Jan huffed a little at this, but there was no denying that Howard was right, and so she didn't say anything for a while, until eventually she murmured: "You don't want me to be here, do you?"

Howard thought of all the things he'd done over the last twenty-four hours that he hadn't wanted to do: taking up residence in the house, raiding the McLeans alcohol, watching their television, making rather unexciting love in their double bed...

"No," he agreed quietly.

"Right," she said, standing up. "I'd better go, then. You can drive me to the station."

"No," he said. "I'll come with you. I've got far too much work to do to sit around here on my own without any of my books to hand. I'll drive us both back."

He thought of the hours of study he might have done - after Jan's departure and maybe another walk - if only he'd come prepared, and it made him seethe inside that things were turning out this way. Part of him hated feeling like this and wanted to apologise to Jan for the awful time she'd had, and part of him sulked that she hadn't been the one to apologise, for ruining the weekend for him.

As they drove back to Cambridge, Jan was silent for nearly an hour before she spoke.

"I think you're pathetic," she said. "All these spectacular rumours about glamorous secret weekends, and all you've been doing is creeping off to some stupid little *outhouse* in the middle of nowhere. *Christ...*"

She watched the fields for a few moments.

"And you were pathetic about sleeping in your aunt and uncle's bed, too. They'll never know. We put that towel down, so there were no stains. I mean, what did you expect? Your Aunt Helen to come dashing in in the middle of the night to drag us out from under the duvet?"

"I didn't want to sleep *anywhere* in the house," Howard said, "because I wanted to feel that I was in my own environment, not someone else's. I don't expect you to understand that."

"Dead right," she muttered.

There was something so dismal between them that Howard wanted to cry. He had never experienced such a tawdry feeling with someone he'd been sleeping with. His relationships - or *liaisons*, of which he'd had several at university - had never lasted long enough for that. Now he felt curiously humiliated to find himself enclosed in the car with someone so dismissive of him. Presumably she was coming to some kind of deep and negative realisation about him. She kept furtively glancing across at him as though he was a stranger. And he wanted to turn to her and say, "Yes, you never did know me. That was the real me, back there. *That* was the real me. Not this undergraduate *pose!*"

As he pulled up outside Jan's digs, she murmured "Crazy!" to herself and got out without saying anything to him, pulling her overnight bag and sleeping kit from the back and then slamming the door far harder than necessary.

Later, when he was sitting in the refectory with Leon and a couple of other friends, glumly looking down into a cup of luke warm coffee, Jan came in with Lisa. When they reached his table, Jan stopped and smiled at Leon.

"I hope you realise you're associating with a fraud," she told him.

Leon didn't say anything, just raised his eyebrows slightly.

"Having an affair with an MP's wife, my arse," she said. "Actually, he's been going off to the seaside with his tent and playing at boy scouts with a primus stove. Talk about regression! It was like dealing with a five year old."

Then she looked directly at Howard.

"It's not that I hate lying," she told him. "We all do it to an extent.

But that kind of lying - that kind of deceit, I *despise* that, Howard. You've been pretending to be something that you're not and I think that's so pathetic..."

With that she walked off with Lisa, leaning towards her and whispering something. Lisa laughed a braying laugh of derision. Howard gulped the last of his coffee in silence, then stood up to leave.

"Is that true?" Leon asked him.

Howard walked away, and as he did so, he turned slightly to look back.

"Yes," he said. "Yes. It is."

It wasn't so much the embarrassment of facing people like Leon that made Howard cut himself off from them, it was the fact that he smarted so much inside. It was as if he'd discovered that his entire inner being was suppurating in some way, and he wanted to deal with that by himself.

Jan was right. He had been deceitful, in an unforgivably immature way. It made no difference that the MP's wife story wasn't one that he'd invented. He'd colluded over it. It was painful to realise that the reason he'd enjoyed the deceit was because he was insecure, in some deep way, about the validity of what he was really doing - that he feared he *was* being childish in going to *Rosemerion*, and had been covering it up with something that was undeniably adult and sophisticated.

The more he thought about it rationally, the more he began to realise that going away to be on his own didn't need any excuses for it to have validity. There was no reason why he should apologise for it, or hide it. Being himself was hard enough without burdening himself with playing the role of sophisticated Cambridge undergraduate. If he wanted to be alone, then he should be alone. He didn't have to explain that to anyone.

Over the next ten days or so, Howard found that he could hardly bring himself to attend lectures. He didn't want to be with people. He didn't want to be looked at by people - particularly by Jan or Leon. He also found it more and more difficult to talk to his tutors - who were interested in him as an academic being (*And if there's anything I'm NOT*, he told himself, *then it's that*).

One day, he was cornered, literally, beneath a gothic archway, by Leon.

"Look, Howard," he said. "Why are you avoiding me?"

Howard murmured something inarticulate.

"If it's anything to do with this business about what you do, or don't do, with your weekends, then I couldn't give a shit. Personally, I'd much rather take a tent and get away from all this pressure than take on the additional stress of an illicit romance."

Howard hadn't replied to this.

"Listen," Leon told him, "come round to my rooms for coffee sometime."

There was a brief pause as Leon stooped to get eye contact.

"Howard?"

"Mmm?"

"Well?"

"Okay."

Leon prodded him in the ribs.

"Promise."

Howard gave a wan smile.

"Okay."

When Howard set off in his car he didn't articulate to himself how long he was hoping to stay in Suffolk. He took his books with him in case it was going to be longer than a few days. In the end he stayed for a month. But he didn't look at his books. He found himself a relatively dry, flat space out amongst the reeds where he could pitch his tent (*Rosemerion* was pretty well out of bounds because the McLeans might turn up at any time, and besides, the hideout seemed violated, somehow). He bought food and fuel in Aldeburgh and took the precaution of phoning his parents to say that he'd gone off to do some studying, in case anyone worried about him.

In retrospect, Howard could remember very little about that month. He swam as often as the currents would allow, and walked along the estuary without really looking at his surroundings. He would sit for hours at a time and watch the sleepy movement of the tide as it crept in and out of the creek and reed beds near his tent.

The weird thing was that he'd finally managed to define various things about himself that he was not - he was not a gregarious person; he was not naturally deceitful; he was not obsessed by the need to make something of himself. But you cannot define a person by what he is not. He also has to *be* something in his own right. And that was where Howard was stuck.

When, four weeks after he'd driven off from Cambridge, Jan arrived to bring him back, he agreed to come with her without fuss or argument. It was almost as if he'd known that she would collect him when his time was up.

She'd taken the train to Saxmundham, a bus to Tunstall, then walked the six miles from the station to the cottage.

"I knew you'd be here somewhere," she told him. "I found your car straight away, behind the old fishing shed. When I discovered that you weren't in the outhouse, I was at a bit of a loss, but you've made this little path that goes from the footbridge off into the reeds..."

She didn't ask him why he'd left. She didn't ask if he wanted to come back. She didn't mention that he was dirty and unshaved. He packed up, walked with her to the car, and drove them both back to Cambridge.

"I think you ought to know," she said. "I'm going out with someone else now. His name's Jake. He's doing a PhD."

"Fine," Howard told her. "Fine."

After such a low-key rescue, Howard was unready for pyrotechnics with his tutor, who shouted at him, screamed, gesticulated and almost burst into tears.

"You little shit," he yelled, "do you know how valuable a First Class Honours is? Do you *know* what you may have thrown away? I'm sorry, but running off for a month doesn't give you brownie points on the wayward genius front. It just makes people think that you're a stupid prick who doesn't deserve any qualifications at all. How much work did you do whilst you were away?"

"None," Howard admitted.

The tutor nodded.

"None. None! It's hard work and diligence that we like to see rewarded here, not idleness and instability."

Later, before he left for good, Howard realised that getting a First would have reflected well on his tutor and that he'd probably been largely angry on his own account rather than Howard's. But at least he'd had the decency to apologise, after a fashion, when the results were announced.

"A Two-One's fine," he'd said, "especially as you're not gunning for further academic study. And please, don't hesitate to use me as a reference."

Howard didn't know it at the time, but he was never to return to Suffolk, or to *Rosemerion* again. Uncle Richard sold it that summer and the family moved to Winnipeg, in Canada. His parents would occasionally mention how well the McLeans were doing, but he never heard directly from Ruth again.

FOURTEEN

1999:

In the Tea Room on Primrose Hill, Jan sighed.

"When we were first going out together," she said, "I felt so lucky to have you. You were so... I don't know, handsome and three dimensional at the same time. You didn't trade on your looks - seemed almost unaware of them. I loved that about you."

"But?"

"We were kids. Just because we were fucking, we thought we'd grown-up. It was a little bit pitiful, looking back on it, don't you think? Funnily, I was both attracted to and scared by your instability - especially when you ran away like that. That's why I took so long to make up my mind whether to come after you or not. Still, I'm glad I did. I should probably have done it sooner, then you might have got a First. I even contemplated throwing myself into your arms and trying to patch things up. But you looked so wild and unkempt when I found you that I reckoned you were most likely a liability."

"I'm sure you were right."

They talked on for some time, about others on their course, and their tutors. Howard surprised himself by laughing several times. Jan seemed to be relaxing more and more, too.

"You know," Howard said eventually, smiling gratefully, "this has done me so much good. Talking like this."

Jan pursed her lips and looked as though she was about to make some jokey remark, but she stopped herself and looked suddenly so serious that Howard feared she might cry.

"Me too," she said. "I came down here looking for a bit of nostalgia. I didn't expect to meet it face to face."

She looked away briefly, around at the other people there, then back at Howard.

"I've got an idea," he said. "Don't spend money on a third-rate guest house. Come and stay with me for a while..."

Jan glanced at Howard, then noticed his earnest expression. She looked half amused, half embarrassed.

"Are you making a pass at me?" she asked.

"In a way. You're spectacular, Jan. You're beautiful and still as up front and astute as ever..."

She laughed.

"You always did see women as sex objects, Howard."

"No I didn't."

"You hid behind the fact that you wanted to sleep with *intelligent* women. But sleeping with them was the important thing. You obviously haven't changed."

"I was never like that," he objected.

"Of course you were. Why did you have no female friends at university? You either seduced them or ignored them."

Howard took a deep breath, but had been rendered speechless by Jan's remark.

"I mean," she said, "have you *ever* been friends with a woman?"

"You and I were friends."

"Were we?"

"What do you mean?"

"I don't know." She paused for a moment. "Okay, tell me of one *friendship* that you've had with a woman who was single and available."

Howard thought for a while and was suddenly struck by a memory of Ruth, his cousin - of that curious connection that had seemed to exist between them when she'd colluded with him over the hideout; of the walk they had taken out to the old ruins when he'd gone to stay with the McLeans; of how they had held hands and chatted late in the evenings after everyone else had gone to bed.

"Ruth," he murmured. "There was Ruth."

"Ruth?"

"My cousin. Don't you remember, at that New Year when we all went to *Rosemerion*?"

"But, Howard, she was only thirteen."

"Nearly fourteen."

"Well, that's alright, then!"

"I mean, I had a special connection with her, that's all."

Jan laughed.

"If that's all you can come up with," she said, "I think that my point is proven. Aren't you going to eat your cake?"

"I'm not hungry, I'm afraid."

He took a gulp of coffee.

"You should make the effort to eat it," she said. "You look like you're starving. Literally."

He cut off the corner of the cake with his fork, but didn't raise it to his mouth. Instead, he looked up at Jan.

"So?" he asked.

"So what?"

"How about staying at my flat instead of paying for a hotel."

"Really, Howard, don't press the point. Even if I was looking for someone to sleep with, which I'm not, it wouldn't be you. You look like a... like a derelict, or something."

"Oh, that," Howard said. "Well, it's unusual for me to look like this."

"And where do you live?" she asked. "You look as though you've crawled out of one of those ghastly squats we occasionally frequented when we were students."

"Mmm," said Howard. "You once said something to me about how appearances were deceptive - I think you were talking about old Duffy, do you remember? You were surprised that someone so stuffy could be so liberal."

"Okay," she nodded, "point taken. But you do conform to a certain... drop-out image."

"Which is completely erroneous, I'm afraid, though not in a deliberately fraudulent way. I actually own a quiet two bedroomed flat in Hampstead."

"Hampstead?"

"Uh-huh."

"Okay," she conceded, "I guess looks *are* deceptive in this case."

"So you'll come and stay with me?"

"I'm not going to go to bed with you Howard, no. Don't ask me again."

"Forget about that. That's not important," he said. "You've made it quite clear that you don't want to sleep with me and that's fine. The point is, I've got a second bedroom that I use as a study. It's got a comfortable fold-down bed that you could use. How long are you down for?"

"Another six days."

"You've got sod-all to do, I've got sod-all to do. Let's do it together. Let me prove to you that I *can* be a friend."

He gazed at her so hard and so intensely that she looked away. She shrugged and glanced over at the mirrors, then out at the street. It clearly wasn't an easy decision and he could see her weighing up her various impressions of him.

"Okay," she said eventually. "Thanks. I'd appreciate the company right now."

Howard smiled.

"So would I."

She smiled back, and then began to laugh. In a moment they were both laughing so hard that a child at the next table began to cry. Jan simmered down, but Howard laughed himself into a state of hiccups. When he gradually subsided, he sat with tears on his cheeks and an expression of astonishment.

"Hey," he said, amazed, "I'm hungry!"

***

As they walked back to Howard's flat, he told her a little about his life since university. He even mentioned prostitution, but he could see that Jan didn't believe him, or at least he could see that she could only imagine it in the context of seedy fumblings in bushes or back alleys. His talk of jet-set-style pseudo-glamour didn't connect with the person she was looking at and so she seemed to disregard what he said as incomprehensible. He didn't press the point, knowing how absurd it must sound. When he looked down at his clothes he could see why. At one point, as they walked, he gestured in such a way that he held his hands up in front of him and he noticed that even his *fingers* had lost weight.

They stopped off at Jan's decidedly unappealing hotel to collect her bag, and then at a delicatessen on the way to Howard's flat and bought samosas, curried pasties, bhajis, almond biscuits, halvas, oatcakes and marmalade, chocolates, fruit juices and beer. As they set off again, Howard drank a litre of freshly squeezed orange juice with raspberry purée, wolfed down both samosas, a pasty, both bhajis and started on the biscuits. His entire being seemed to be yearning for nourishment - his stomach, obviously, but his muscles too, and even, somehow, his bones which felt as though they were itching slightly at the prospect of calories. Jan laughed at him and accepted a biscuit which she nibbled as she walked.

When they reached his flat, which occupied the ground floor of a building that formed a terrace of rather grand houses, Jan was again visibly surprised both by its location and its decor. The polished wooden floor of the sitting room gleamed slightly in the afternoon sunlight, and the hush made everything, even the air, seem expensive.

"I was seriously dressed down when I met you," Howard told her, pouring them both a glass of lager, "and now I feel embarrassed by it. If you don't mind, I'll go and wash and change, and then we can think of what to do for dinner."

He had a brief, luxurious and energetic shower and then, gently taking the towel down from the mirror, confronted his reflection. His skin had a paleness to it, despite his tan, and there were some incipient spots clustered at his temples. He hadn't lost quite as much weight as he'd thought, though his collarbone was definitely more prominent than usual and he could clearly see his ribs when he breathed in. He held his arms out crucifixion-style and leaned his head to one side, but the Christ-like image didn't quite work. He looked more like a cross between an emaciated Clint Eastwood and Charles Manson at the time of his arrest. He smiled at himself and took out his razor.

It took longer to shave than he'd expected - the razor kept clogging up and had to be endlessly rinsed. Then he dealt with his spots and treated his temples with an astringent antiseptic, and, once his skin had settled somewhat, applied cooling balm to his ravaged face. After this, he went into the bedroom to dress. He chose a simple, slim pair of jeans with a belt studded with ornamental brass oblongs, and a black canvas shirt outside of which he hung the ankh that Corinne had given him. He felt sleek and, when he looked in the bedroom mirror, almost like his old self, though a leaner, more haunted - more *angelic* - version, somehow, with his accentuated eyes. He trimmed his nails, splashed on some aftershave, gelled his hair back, and then went through to Jan.

She had her back to him, and was reading José's book of poetry. She looked round as he came in and double-taked.

"God!" she breathed, putting the book down. "Howard? This is, well, it's incredible, the *transformation...*"

"I *told* you I was dressed down," he said.

"Yes, but, there's dressing down and dressing down. On Primrose Hill it wasn't just the clothes, it was that ghastly beard, your manner - everything."

Howard smiled.

"It's six-thirty. I know it's early, but let's find somewhere special to eat. I'm ravenous."

He flicked through the Yellow Pages for a while and noticed an advertisement for the Tanera Mor - the restaurant that Pete Collicos had recommended. He gave them a ring. Yes, they said, they'd had a cancellation that evening and could fit them in if there were only two of them, but only if they could get there within the next thirty minutes.

Howard called a taxi and they had a breathless ride into town, Howard constantly looking at his watch and sighing, then smiling with incredulity at the sudden change in his life, and laughing out loud about it. Jan found his laughter infectious, and there was something in his sense of importance about this particular restaurant that made her slightly hysterical. The last few blocks of the journey were tinged with an almost frenzied sense of urgency. They arrived at the restaurant five minutes late and were ushered into its plain but sumptuous interior.

"We look so dressed down," Jan murmured as they looked around at the other diners, "all this couture must be worth *thousands*."

The maitre d' handed them their menus and explained that most people had booked up months in advance for a table at the Tanera Mor. He hoped they *appreciated* their meal.

Jan snorted a little at the man's pomposity, then gave a little gasp when she looked more closely at the menu.

"There's a starter here for *thirty pounds!*" she whispered.

"I know. Do you want it?"

"What is this, Howard?" she asked, "are you trying to impress me?"

"No," he said. "I'm doing this for myself, and because of a conversation I had with someone recently. All I ask is for you to try and enjoy yourself, that's all."

"I'll take your word for it, but I'll remind you of it later if you try anything on."

"Fair enough."

The drinks waiter appeared and asked them if they wanted an aperitif.

"I don't suppose a sweet sherry is *de-rigeur* in a place like this?" Jan murmured to Howard.

"Leave it to me," he whispered, then gave some quick *sotto-voce* instructions to the waiter who nodded and slinked off.

"My own individual cocktail," he said. "I think you'll like it. It's flavoured with peach and almond."

"Is it alcoholic?"

"Very."

"Uh-huh," she laughed, "I thought so. You *are* trying something on."

Howard smiled again, but then looked down almost shyly and shook his head. He felt strangely intoxicated to be in Jan's company again and he didn't want to do anything to spoil it.

When the cocktails arrived, Jan sipped hers appreciatively.

"Mmm," she said. "Wonderful."

"Now, choose," Howard told her, indicating the menu, "and disregard the price."

She chose asparagus with a hot balsamic dressing and an exotic salad, followed by Balkan Filo Pie. Howard ordered baked aubergine with raspberries for his starter and a main course of Camargue rice with tarragon, wild mushrooms and spiced truffles. They ordered a crisp 1993 Comtes Lafon mersault and sniggered at the price of it, and, with the dessert of frozen fruit purées in a liqueur syrup, they ordered a chilled 1980 Chateau Climens sauternes that was by far the best Howard had tasted. The meal became a race to find suitable superlatives for their food and the extraordinary presentation that made each dish a work of art. As well as awe, there was also a subdued, though hilarious, undercurrent of mischief.

"I feel as though I've been *transplanted* here," Jan told him. "Look at these people. You can tell that if you told them what your annual income was, you'd instantly become invisible."

"Mmm," Howard agreed.

"Talking of which," she continued, "what *is* your annual income? It must be pretty high if you're eating in places like this."

"I'm just paying to dip my feet into water that I have experienced but never controlled," he told her. "I'm doing it on my own terms for once. As a matter of fact, I've been to much more expensive restaurants than this, but always as an escort. In that world, I'm afraid, the size of the bill is usually much more impressive than the quality of the food."

Jan toyed with her dessert spoon for a moment and watched a drop of syrup linger before dripping into her bowl.

"I'm sorry," she said, "I rather sneered at you earlier when you mentioned that... area of your life. I can see now that all this is second nature to you."

She looked down at a fresh leaf of mint that was decorating a slice of strawberry that had been carved into the shape of a star. She began to laugh again.

"What?" Howard asked, smiling. "What!"

"Oh, I'm sorry," she managed. "It just came into my mind that of all the things I might have imagined you'd end up doing, I'd never have guessed that you would become a gigolo."

"Life is full of surprises," he smiled. "Also, there are plenty of ways of prostituting yourself that have nothing to do with sex."

"I know," she said. "I *know*."

The dinner this evening worked in all the ways that the meal with Nina hadn't. It wasn't serious, for a start. There was the unspoken acknowledgment that they were both amused bystanders in this expensive and rather *precious*, but alien, world.

"You know," Howard said, "the thing that has always interested me about the wealthy is that money should be *liberating*, but the international dinner-party set are the most restricted, etiquette-ridden, self-repressed group you'll find. To fit in, you have to dress a certain way, talk only about certain things, live in the right place... Even the so called 'outrageous' behaviour - the bedhopping, the wife-swapping - has a certain tedious sameness to it."

"And yet," said Jan, "you live in Hampstead yourself. Isn't that bordering on the hypocritical if that's how you feel?"

"Possibly."

"And I disagree with you about the wealthy, too," she went on. "You speak about the international dinner-party set as though everyone who is wealthy belongs to it. You're making a generalisation from very limited experience. The fact is that there are plenty of rich people who choose not to be like that; who really do live how they want to - who would rather give up their money than be a part of the set that you are describing."

"Maybe," said Howard.

He thought of Nina and wondered if the evening they had spent together, when he'd dressed up in his finery, had done her any good. Or had it just been a self-centred act of indulgence on his part; a kind of wallowing in his own indecisiveness? He thought of Jan's accusation that he had never had female friends and recognised the truth in her statement. Of course, there were women like Lucia in Barcelona, or Julia in Leamington, who were true friends. But he had to acknowledge that he had known José before Lucia, and Julia had already been married to Ralph when he'd met her. There were also one or two women who had, briefly, been lovers, who were now settled in new relationships and whom he saw occasionally. He was even a godfather to one of their children. However, he had no female friends whom he had met when they were single and who had simply become friends. It was a realisation that shocked him into stillness. How had he not noticed this before? Did it really mean he viewed women only in terms of sex?

Or perhaps I've spent my life trying to BE something for women, he thought.

Jan, noticing Howard's expression, stopped smiling.

"Are you okay?" she asked.

"It's funny," he said, "in the past I've been so sure of myself, so definite about what I wanted, and yet, I didn't want anything tangible at all. My desires were all entirely negative - I didn't want to be tied down. I didn't want a full-time job. I didn't want to be hampered by commitment."

"But you told me you were in love with someone. That's a commitment, surely?"

"But one I didn't consciously decide to make, though maybe that's the way change comes upon us - it simply happens. Meeting Corinne was like that. I didn't say to myself, 'this is a person to whom I could make a commitment', because I didn't have a rational response to her. I wasn't looking for someone to fall in love with - I was happy with my life as it was. I didn't want it to change. It just did. And then, after she died, I tried to fall back on the life I'd led before. In the last month or two I've been beginning to realise you can't do that. I've stretched that particular point as far as it can go. No wonder I snapped."

"I hate this period," she said. "I hate this limbo that we're both in. It's no help at all when people say it'll pass, because I *know* it will pass. That's not the point, is it? I've just got to wait for my equilibrium to re-establish itself before embarking on anything as dramatic as a new relationship. In the meantime, leaving my husband is like breaking a bone. You know that it's going to take weeks, months, to heal - that the pain will gradually recede, but it will be a considerable time before you're fully functional again. I suppose I didn't really understand that until I left him."

She sipped her sauternes and smiled again.

"Looks like the conversation's getting serious. I hope we're not going to end up being maudlin. I couldn't bear that. I hate self-pity and I've been very close to wallowing in it lately."

"Let me have another dessert," Howard said, "and then maybe we could go dancing?"

"Another dessert? You'll be too bloated to move."

"I guess I've got a lot of catching up to do, food-wise," Howard said. "I really think I could eat a little more..."

He had a slice of summer fruit pie, then paid the bill, which came to just over £350. Jan gasped as he dropped his credit card on the silver platter.

"When have you eaten better food?" Howard asked her.

"Never, but..."

"Then it was worth it."

Jan declined the offer of a dance and they took a taxi back to

Hampstead where Howard brewed some herbal tea. Then they sat for a while, talking about their time at university. At midnight, Howard made up a bed for Jan in his study.

"Have mine if you like," he said. "I'm used to sleeping in here."

"No," she told him firmly. "This is fine."

He lingered in the doorway for a moment, then kissed her gently on the cheek.

"Thanks," he said. "Amongst other things, you seem to have restored my appetite."

"My pleasure," she said. "Goodnight."

Howard took a quick shower before bed. He could actually see in the mirror where his stomach had been distended by his enormous meal, and he suddenly felt a wash of tiredness, despite the fact that he'd been sleeping so much over the previous week. He dragged himself through to the bedroom, idly dropping his towel on the floor and feeling a sudden pulse of nausea. He thought he might be about to throw up for a moment, which wouldn't have surprised him under the circumstances. But after a gurgle or two, his stomach settled slightly and exhaustion overtook him. Even pulling back the duvet seemed an effort. He didn't remember getting into bed.

***

"Let's go shopping," Howard said the following day over breakfast in a local café.

"Shopping?" she said. "You always used to hate that kind of thing."

"I want to see what it feels like from the other side of the fence," he said. "You must let me spend some money on you."

"But Howard, you're not working! You can't afford it."

"I happen to have a bit of capital at the moment that I have no intention of keeping. Let's go and spend it."

Jan clearly thought it was a mistake, but it was equally clear that he was going to spend the money either with or without her, so she went along.

For the first few boutiques and outfitters, Jan shook her head when Howard offered to buy her dresses, skirts, suits or shoes. She helped him choose clothes for himself - baggy white shirts with long collars that made him look like a troubadour, leggy cotton trousers and patterned jeans that were decidedly *un*-jet set; sunglasses that looked more like contraptions than optical devices. After a while, however, Jan succumbed when she saw a dress of palest blue, so light that it reminded Howard of romantic dream sequences from his childhood. She allowed him to buy her a pair of shoes to match, and a scarf with an Escher pattern on it. Howard stopped at an Interflora outlet and ordered £100 of mixed flowers to be sent to his flat, then they went to a delicatessen.

"We could go to a restaurant," said Howard, "but let's go home and enjoy the flowers."

He bought crusty three-seed bread and pale paté and mounds of soft fruit and semi-dried Sweet Bing cherries. He bought bottles of champagne and deep-red wine from an area somewhere near - though, they were assured, superior to - Bordeaux. He bought bottles of cloudy country cider with wired-down corks, and cartons of mango nectar. He bought sweet pickled shallots and raspberries in vinegar. They took it all to Howard's place by taxi and gathered the flowers from the doorstep and festooned the flat with colour and fragrance. Then they lay on the carpet and got drunk and fed each other grapes and strawberries, and laughed a lot and Howard felt light and unrestricted and pleasantly foolish, and time still passed with ease so that he was surprised to find that it was two o'clock in the morning when, having, yet again, eaten as much as he could manage, he went to make them some chamomile tea.

When he returned, he lay back on the settee with Jan's head against his shoulder and looked up at the ceiling.

"You're so weird," she kept murmuring. "You're *so* weird."

They fell asleep like that, with the window open, to the sound of an insistent, distant car alarm.

In the morning, Howard took her out to breakfast again, then down to Chelsea to see what they could find. He saw a pair of conspicuous jeans that suited him well, but he couldn't decide whether to buy them in red, blue or yellow - so he bought all three pairs and Jan laughed at him, and he laughed back and bought her a pair of lush culottes with brocade panels.

They lunched that day in a restaurant overlooking the river, and they laughed together because the waiters clearly thought they were in love, surrounded as they were by bags and packages that attested to Howard's reckless extravagance. In the afternoon Howard bought matching jackets for them, and hats that shaded their eyes and more sunglasses so that they could pretend that they were famous. Later, they went to a nightclub where they drank champagne cocktails and danced together in an expansive style. Afterwards, walking through the cool air, Howard leaned over the embankment and threw his remaining coins into the river.

He felt as though he was participating in a fantasy landscape, a jewelled replica of the world he knew, that did not seem to have the same rules as his 'normal' life, which had, for this period of time, been completely suspended. Jan acted as though she was part of some strange psychological test and went along with everything with good cheer, but with an obvious underlying wariness.

On the third day Howard ordered a hamper from Fortnum & Mason and they blustered down to Brighton with the hood of the car down. They sat on the beach in late-summer sunshine where the ice cream vendors were still open to catch the last of the season's trade. The next day they went to the New Forest where they picnicked by a pine wood, a small herd of deer not far away, grazing and watching them mistrustfully. When it was time to return home, Howard put the hood of the car up and Jan laughed.

"For someone who supposedly isn't into materialism, this car is rather blatant, isn't it?"

Howard ran his hand over the sleek maroon bonnet and grinned.

"It's one of those things," he said. "I would never have bought it for myself, but now I own it I *am* attached to it."

"You look like the kind of man who would drive a car like this," she said.

"*Don't!*" he grimaced.

They dined at the Tanera Mor, where Howard bribed the Maitre d' each evening with breathtaking tips to make a table available for the following day.

On Friday, four days after Howard met Jan, he woke up with a hangover and a sour taste in his mouth from too much wine, and an unspoken yearning. He sat for perhaps an hour on a chair in his sitting room, watching Jan through the open door of her makeshift bedroom. She lay, spread-eagled on his fold-out bed, surrounded by boxes, bags and packages of *stuff* that Howard had bought for her. She looked dishevelled but content, and extraordinarily beautiful. Howard sipped a glass of mineral water and enjoyed the scent of the flowers he'd bought on the first day, that had yet to wilt.

That morning, after he'd showered and shaved, he woke Jan and they went out for breakfast, as usual, before travelling on to an arty shop in Battersea. They wandered around and every time Jan 'oohed' over an item, he bought it. He bought a set of mirrors with *papier maché* surrounds, curious silvered tea cups, a set of saucepans that looked more like spaceships than kitchen utensils, a rug with a design of a gaping mouth on it, a coffee table made of bullet-proof glass, a solid gold 'salt saucer' with spoon that was clearly intended for cocaine. When the shop assistant asked for his address, he turned to Jan.

"Where do you live?" he asked.

"Why?"

"Because these are for you."

"I couldn't accept all this," she said.

"A flat-warming present from me," he said.

After some more persuasion, she gave her address and Howard arranged delivery for the following week.

"Howard," she said as they left the shop, "this has been the most surreal five days of my life. No-one has ever spent thousands of pounds on me, just like that. It's incredible. It's definitely made me forget my problems. But we have to talk."

"No," said Howard. "I know what you'll say, and I don't want to hear it. Later. We'll talk about it later."

"But I'm going home tomorrow."

"Then we'll talk about it at the Tanera Mor tonight."

Howard had discovered a company that did chartered helicopter flights over the city, and they dropped by the company's office to book a flight. The clerk was clearly impressed by Howard's brash insistence on a flight that afternoon, and managed to sort out a slot for them. They spent a couple of hours in the Tate as they waited, then a whirlwind hour flying over Tower Bridge, and Big Ben, and on up to Hampstead where Howard's flat seemed distant and insignificant as they swooped past it. They flew out to Hampton Court, following the Thames, then back over Syon House and landed, deafened and exhilarated, in time for tea.

Later, when they arrived at the Tanera Mor, the Maitre d' shook Howard's hand warmly and took them through to a table by the window, where their usual cocktails were brought to them by a smiling waiter. The food, yet again, was without comparison and the wine excellent.

"So," Jan said as they were served their dessert, "tell me, how much have you spent over the last five days?"

"Ten thousand?" Howard said. "Perhaps more."

"Have you got that much money?"

"I'm being left some money that I don't deserve," Howard told her, "so it's all meaningless in a way."

"But why spend it so recklessly?"

"Fun?"

"Come on, Howard..."

"I wanted to prove," he said quietly, "I wanted to prove that this whole business of throwing money about doesn't mean anything. I've witnessed it often enough, and it seemed to bring a certain brittle pleasure to those who slung the stuff around. But it's like confectionery isn't it? A few squares of fine chocolate can be exquisite, but force yourself to eat a pound of it every day and you'd soon puke at the sight of it."

"But where do I fit in?" she asked.

"You were playing the part of the person I used to be. You were completely indispensable. That's the whole point about chucking money about. You chuck it at yourself, of course, but there's got to be someone else there, especially an outsider, someone who doesn't belong in that world, who's role is to be impressed."

"I *am* impressed, though I've found it kind of scary too."

"I didn't mean to unsettle you," he said. "I meant to unsettle myself."

"And did you?"

"Yes."

The waiter arrived with two flaming Sambuccas and they sat in silence for a while watching the small blue flames.

"Tell me about this woman," Jan said. "The woman who died. This is your last chance. Whatever it is that you've been doing these last few days, you've been doing it because of her."

Howard sighed and blew the flame out and said, "Okay."

He found it surprising how long it took to tell Jan the story of Corinne. He hadn't finished when the restaurant closed, nor did he stop in the taxi home. He was still talking at 2.00 a.m., lying full stretch on the settee with Jan on the floor leaning against the sofa, head back, eyes closed. And she was still listening. The only time she asked for further explanation was when Howard talked about suffering from alalia after the accident. She asked him for further details about what alalia was, and nodded when he gave them.

"I can understand why Corinne might have wanted to invent a past," she said eventually, in the silence that followed Howard's protracted and cathartic outpouring. "Just think how much easier it would be, for example, if I could invent some ghastly story about Paul. Of deceit and betrayal and violence. It would be so much easier than saying that we petered out with each other. I would get so much more sympathy, for a start."

"We're always lying to ourselves, if not to others, about our relationships," Howard said. "Most people do it most of the time. Not blatantly, perhaps, but they still do it."

"I'm not sure what you mean?"

"I'll give you an example," Howard said. "Something happens in your life, and you know you were in the wrong. I don't know, maybe you're in a bad mood and you shout at your lover when you know they haven't done anything to warrant your anger, and then you reinvent the situation so that you can forgive yourself. You tell yourself that actually your lover's been moody lately, or that you're stressed out at work, or your biorhythms are low. And then you can forget it, and you can get out of apologising, or at least you can apologise in one of those general ways, saying 'I'm sorry but it's been a bad day today', and you can let it go without ever facing the fact that you've acted badly. And you never learn not to act like that again because it's so easy to explain to yourself that it's perfectly understandable, perfectly *normal* to act badly every now and then in our high-pressure culture; that that's what we do, how we are. Sometimes the whole business makes me sick."

"You've obviously thought about this a lot," Jan said. "What makes you so cynical?"

"As a prostitute I've spent a lot of time watching wealthy people deceive themselves in the most appalling manner, justifying what they do by saying, 'I deserve it', when they don't, and by saying 'It's my money, I can do what I like' which really amounts to saying 'I'm only going to think of myself'."

"I hardly think that's an area reserved only for the wealthy," Jan said with a smile.

"No, no I know. But it's that much more blatant, that much more *obvious*. I suppose I'm sensitive about it because I recognise that trait in myself and I despise it. I thought, I really thought, that Corinne had none of that. There seemed to be something so beguilingly open and honest about her, and it's been disheartening to find out that it wasn't true."

"No," Jan said, "that's the wrong way of looking at it. The reason you found her so beguiling was because she probably *was* being honest with you about those areas of her life that she allowed you to share."

"But hiding relevant facts *is* a kind of dishonesty."

"I can't agree with you there," she said and closed her eyes for a moment to think.

"Okay," she said after a pause. "You've obviously got a big thing about honesty. Why?"

"Because all the relationships in my life that might have worked, failed, because either I or my partner was dishonest."

"And do you include our relationship in that statement?"

"Yes," he said. "If I'd told you about my trips to *Rosemerion* right from the start, then it would never have become a point of conflict between us."

"I don't see why. You still wouldn't have invited me to join you, and I would still have felt left out."

"Maybe," Howard said. "But honesty *would* have made a difference."

Jan drew her fingertips along her eyebrows, as if smoothing away a memory, and then smiled at Howard.

"How many people have you told that you are a prostitute?"

Howard looked slightly nonplussed at this.

"I don't hide it," he said, "but it's not the first thing I tell people when I meet them. Of course, sometimes the subject doesn't arise, in the same way that I might not mention to a person that I'm a linguist, or that I went to Cambridge."

"But prostitution isn't an idle fact, like the colour of your eyes, or which university you went to, Howard. Have you told your parents about it, for example?"

"No."

"So, in what way is keeping your prostitution a secret from them different from Corinne keeping her manic depression secret from you?"

"There are differences," he murmured.

"No. In some way, you're ashamed - or at least embarrassed - about your prostitution, like Corinne was ashamed of her depression."

"I'm not ashamed of it," Howard said. "I told you about it, didn't I? I'm neither ashamed nor embarrassed."

"So why haven't you told your parents?"

"Why should I? They'd be unnecessarily upset."

"Precisely," Jan said. "And isn't that *exactly* the reason why Corinne didn't tell you about her depressions? You could argue that some things should always be left unstated. It's not a matter of deception, but of sensitivity."

"I take your point," he said, "and in a way you're absolutely right."

He got up and went into the kitchen to put the kettle on again. When he came back with the drinks, Jan had wandered over to the window and was stooping to smell some orange roses that were finally beginning to shed petals on to the wooden floor.

"So," she said, accepting a mug and returning to sit on the settee. "Let's go back to the Corinne story for a moment. This aunt? Aunt Gillian. Corinne said she'd died, but in fact she's still alive?"

"Yes."

"And were they confidants, or was that a story too?"

"I don't know."

"Have you spoken to her?"

"No."

"If Emma saying that Corinne never loved you has troubled you so much, you should talk to someone else who's likely to have a valid opinion."

Howard thought about this for a moment.

"Perhaps I should leave it be."

Jan sipped her tea in pensive silence. Howard picked up José's book and flicked through it, telling himself that he really ought to get around to reading it properly.

"Of course," he said, "I know where Aunt Gillian lives."

"What?" Jan asked.

"Matthew once took me on a day trip to Wales. We stopped off at a town, Dolgellau. He pointed out the house where he and Corinne had spent their honeymoon... Matthew said something in passing about an aunt of Corinne's vacating it for a fortnight whilst they stayed there. He didn't mention the aunt's name but..."

"Could you find it again?"

"Yes, it was out on its own, on the slopes of Cader Idris. Very distinctive."

"You should go and see if she's still there."

FIFTEEN

1999:

"Howard, it's Dominic Woods here, I'm sorry to phone so early, but can you come and see me in Leamington as soon as possible?"

"I'm off to Berlin tomorrow."

"How about today, then? I'd like to clear this up with you as soon as possible. I'm afraid it's rather urgent."

Howard agreed to see him in the late afternoon and replaced the receiver. He felt a buzz of anticipation. How awkward! He'd hoped to drive up to Wales to see if he could find Corinne's Aunt Gillian. Still... that could wait until he returned from Berlin if necessary.

He drove Jan to Euston and saw her onto the train. Considering their platonic relationship over the previous six days there was something melancholy - he hesitated to use the word romantic - about their parting and their promises to see each other again.

After dropping her off, Howard headed out of London towards the M25 and M40. His parents had retired to a small house in the countryside between Oxford and Bicester and he'd phoned to ask if he could drop in on them for a couple of hours on his way up to see Mr Woods. Howard's mother had sounded genuinely pleased to hear from him.

On his arrival, Mrs Martindale had lunch ready and fussed over Howard in a way that he hated. She was tall and slightly stooped but with a haughty grace to her that made Howard think of finishing schools and 'the season'. His father poured him a gin and tonic ("I'm driving, so just a splash of gin," Howard told him). He mentioned as he sat down that he'd bumped in to Jan again.

"Now there's a girl that I liked," his mother told him.

"Astute mind," his father said. "I expect she's done well for herself."

"Is she married?" his mother asked.

"Was. They split up last month."

Mrs Martindale shook her head sadly and went off to the kitchen to get food. Howard sipped his gin and tonic and found it to be full strength. He left it behind a few minutes later, undrunk, when they went through to the dining room.

There was something over-formal about family meals and it occurred to Howard that moments such as these are when estrangement - so easy to hide at other times - becomes glaringly obvious. There were no newspapers or books to read, no television to pretend to be interested in; no chore to use as a distraction. The only choices were conversation or silence and on this occasion there was a halting mixture of the two. Talk was largely inconsequential. Mr Martindale continued with his hobby of restoring antiques, which might have been diverting if it had been described in general rather than specific terms - none of which Howard was interested in. He would have been intrigued, for example, to know why a certain kind of porcelain might have become popular in the eighteenth century, but he was less interested in the chemical composition of the various glazes used to decorate it. It was typical, he thought, that his father should choose for himself a hobby that substantially increased the value of his capital investment.

"Your father's become quite addicted to auctions these days," his mother told him. "He'll go all the way to Norfolk just to look at a piece that he may not even bid for."

"I got a set of six rather ropy Victorian dinner chairs there last year," his father told him. "With exquisite heart-shaped backs. Paid seven hundred pounds for them. Should be worth four or five times that when I get round to doing something with them. They're in the garage at the moment. I don't suppose I'll sell them on, though. I expect we'll keep them and use them to replace the ones were sitting on now, which you could have, if you wanted."

"No thanks, dad," Howard said.

"You've promised them to Elaine, anyway," his mother pointed out.

"I know," he said, "but Howard could have had them if he'd wanted." He looked down at the plain Edwardian chair that he was sitting on. "But I knew he wouldn't," he muttered.

Howard took a mouthful of potato and looked out of the window.

"And what about you?" his mother asked him. "What are you up to?"

"The usual," he said. "You know."

"Have you been off travelling anywhere lately?"

"Not really. I did go to Barcelona for the weekend in August. And I'm off to Berlin tomorrow, but that's for linguistic work so it doesn't really count. I'll have almost no time for sightseeing."

"Barcelona is a long way to go for a weekend," said his mother. "What were you doing there?"

Howard suddenly remembered his conversation with Jan about honesty and, involuntarily, it made him smile.

"Did I say something funny?" his mother asked, noticing Howard's expression.

"No," Howard told her. "I just remembered something someone said."

"Oh?" She leaned forward slightly, inquiringly.

"We were discussing the fact that you would probably disapprove of what I get up to."

"Surely our disapproval is a prerequisite before you do *anything*," his father said.

Howard shrugged.

"You never give us the chance to disapprove," his mother said. "You don't tell us what you do. How do you know we'd disapprove?"

"Promiscuity isn't something I want to hear about from my son," said his father. "It's a sordid subject."

"What do *you* know about promiscuity, dad?" Howard asked. "Or is there something you've never told me?"

His father glowered, furious.

"And anyway," Howard continued. "I haven't been what most people would describe as promiscuous for a number of years. Not since I met Corinne."

"Who's Corinne?" his mother asked.

"A woman I fell in love with; a married woman."

"Alright, alright!" his father exclaimed. "Married women... really, *I don't want to know.*"

"You mean separated?" his mother asked.

"No," Howard said. "She was still with her husband. But he was gay, so it wasn't how you might expect."

"That's enough," said his father.

Howard stared across at his father's frowning, disapproving face and turned to his mother.

"Now you know why I don't tell you anything," Howard said to her. "Dad makes everything I do sound dirty. As a matter of fact, I loved Corinne. I thought she would leave Matthew and that we would live together. Perhaps get married... have children."

"But, of course, it didn't work out, did it?" said his father.

Howard surprised himself by finding tears of anger welling up in his eyes.

"No, it didn't work out," he murmured. "She died. She died in a car accident. And I was driving. I killed her. Typical, isn't it? Typical Howard, always getting into messy scrapes. I fall in love for the first time in my life and then I go and kill her. That was a bit negligent of me, wasn't it, dad? Why can't I be a little more *careful*?"

There was a silence for a moment.

"And I didn't even get in touch with you, did I, when I was suffering from shock and grief? How much does that say about the support I felt would be on offer?"

He took a gulp of water, and, feeling years of momentum behind him, he continued.

"And whilst we're on the subject of things I've never told you," he said, "I might as well add - so that there are no secrets - that I've been working as a prostitute for the last four and a half years. You asked why I went all the way to Barcelona for a weekend? The reason is because I was seeing a client. A client who paid me a *lot* of money. At least you can't accuse me of not knowing how much I'm worth on *that* score, dad."

***

In the kitchen, as he was collecting his coat, Howard's mother came in. She had clearly been crying.

"Why did you say that, Howard?" she asked. "Even if it's true, why did you have to say it?"

"I hate having secrets," he said. "Dad thinks the worst of me anyway, so why not confirm his fears. As a matter of fact, I've given up being a prostitute, but it's still true to say that I used to be one."

"If you're not doing it any more then there's even less reason to have mentioned it."

"*I'*m not ashamed of what I've been doing. *I* don't think I live a sordid life. Precisely the opposite, in fact. I don't expect you to understand that, and I think dad's incapable of understanding that. But, as far as past work goes, my conscience is clear."

***

As Howard drove to Leamington he felt deflated. Had he caused unnecessary pain for the sake of some minor intellectual point-scoring with Jan? It seemed so unnecessary. Truth, he reminded himself, does not become truth simply because you broadcast it... The only important person, as far as honesty went, was himself. Outside that, what did it matter what other people knew or didn't know - what they believed or didn't believe? Would his parents' ignorance of his prostitution have been so bad?

Suddenly, and with extraordinary clarity, he understood the reason for Corinne's silence about her depressions - understood it in a way that he hadn't when he'd talked to Jan about it the previous night.

***

Leamington looked decidedly autumnal when he parked along the edge of Jephson Gardens, the sycamore tree on the corner of Euston Place was already more than half bare and the air was still, but cold. Woods greeted Howard in his office with a firm handshake.

"Please, sit down."

Howard did so and looked expectantly at the solicitor.

"I might as well tell you straight away, it's bad news," Mr Woods told him. "I'm afraid Matthew's insurance company have scuppered the payment of money that we thought was due on his insurance policies."

"But why?" he exclaimed, "and how?"

"There's an HIV exclusion clause..."

Howard was startled.

"But Matthew didn't die of Aids?"

"No, of course not," Mr Woods said quickly. "But he *was* HIV positive. That, it seems, is enough to disqualify him from cover, even though he was asymptomatic and the illness that killed him had nothing to do with his HIV status, *as far as we know*."

He stood and turned from Howard to look out of the window.

"That is the main problem," he said as he looked out over The Parade. "We can't prove that there is no link between Matthew's HIV status and the cancer that killed him. The circumstantial evidence that we have would only give us grounds for a rather tenuous appeal, given the wording of his policy."

Howard looked down at the floor for a moment whilst he absorbed Mr Woods' words.

"Does that mean I don't get any money?" he asked.

"Not a penny, I'm afraid. We'll be appealing anyway, but there's a negligible chance of success. I have to tell you that I am personally *furious* about this and won't leave it without a fight. It's of vital importance that people understand what they're signing away when they take out insurance policies for themselves."

Howard nodded, but was thinking of Matthew.

"Did Matthew know he was HIV positive?" he asked.

"I don't think so. I talked to David about it. Matthew's HIV status was only discovered when he was in hospital. It was as much of a shock to David as it was to you, or me. When it all came to light, the consultant talked to David about it straight away and they decided that there was no point in telling Matthew, seeing as he was so ill anyway. But, of course, it went in his records."

Howard stood and walked over to stand by Mr Woods at the window. He looked out at the ragged clouds that were beginning to gather to the south.

"God," he said. "I spent over £10,000 last week in anticipation of this money."

Mr Woods turned and gave a half grimace of sympathy.

"I'm sorry," he said, "It didn't occur to me that there was going to be a problem. I didn't personally know about Matthew's HIV status until the insurance company contacted me."

"And is David okay?"

"He's had a test and he's negative."

Howard shook his head in disbelief for a moment and then, gradually, from somewhere deep inside him, he felt a strange welling of mirth. It took a while to arrive, but when it did, it surprised and shocked Mr Woods. Howard let out a second short, loud belch of laughter and shook his head again.

"That's that one sorted," he said. "At least I don't have to worry about what I'm going to do with the money."

The more he thought about it, the more it was inconceivable that Matthew hadn't known about the exclusion clauses in his policies. He was such a fastidious man.

"I wonder if Matthew did this deliberately," he murmured.

"Pardon?"

"Maybe Matthew *did* know his HIV status. Maybe he left me the money in the knowledge that, after a period of *thinking* I was going to get it, in the end I would get nothing."

Mr Woods shook his head emphatically.

"Matthew would *never* do that," he said.

"No," Howard nodded, "I suppose not."

SIXTEEN

1999:

Driving up to Wales, Howard felt close to Matthew. Not Corinne. He vividly remembered the day Matthew had taken him to Barmouth Bay, more than three years earlier. Then, it had been a blustery mixture of sunshine and cloud, but now it was a bright, cloudless day in mid October. He'd finished his five day stint in Berlin, feeling adrift and irritated with himself for not having made the trip to Dolgellau before he left, in spite of how little time there had been in which to do it. Berlin had been marred by an insistent regret, and a feeling of urgency about the need to try and find Aunt Gillian, to see what she could tell him. Even Berlin's Tiergarten, where Howard liked to stroll when he was in the city, had made him feel anxious to return to England; and the interpreting that he'd been doing whilst he was there had been dull, dull, dull...

Still, there had been an intriguing 'prodigal son' quality to his return to work for CMS. Despite the fact that he hadn't been with them for some considerable time, it felt like he was slipping back into a familiar set-up. Jerry Futerman was over-friendly with him, which highlighted Matthew's absence more than anything. John Deacon was formidably efficient, though not as welcoming as Matthew had always been. He'd shaken Howard's hand at the hotel and said, "Glad to see you again, Howard. I hope we'll be seeing more of you in future, now that there's no, um... problem... with you working for us."

Howard's only real pleasure during his stay in Berlin was reading José's book, *Vitrinas de la Memorià*. Howard, never a poetry lover, was struck by the simplicity of José's language and the freshness that he'd managed to bring to the basics of life - food, work, leisure, love and sadness. There was an openness to his work that was new and didn't fall into the trap of sentimentality or self-indulgence, though some of it did reflect a certain anguish that Howard had seen in José, and which was, perhaps, a common denominator in all poets whose work was so intense. It occurred to him to wonder why José had never had his work translated into English before, although he understood that the rendering of poetry was the ultimate challenge for a translator. How to find the corresponding images and subtleties? How to match the rhythms and yet keep the nuances of meaning?

Now, as Howard drove up the M40 with the roof down, wearing a cap and scarf, he felt the fresh air stilling his cyclic thoughts about the possibility of meeting Aunt Gillian. There was no reason why she should be there, he told himself, given that it was more than three years since he'd seen the place, and that he hadn't been able to contact her first. She might not be living there any more, and if even she was, she might not be at home. If so, he'd have to leave her a note, with his phone number, to say who he was and why he'd called. And if she *was* there, he didn't know what he could ask, apart from, 'Tell me what you know about Corinne'.

A line from one of José's poems about regret ran through his mind:

Todos nos vendamos las heridas como hacen las chinas con sus pies.
We bandage hurts like Chinese feet.

How apposite for me, he thought. He was beginning to realise that by having a loose structure to his life - especially over the last two and a half years - far from freeing himself, somewhere along the line he'd reined himself in too much and had stunted some part of himself that he couldn't identify. He knew that this journey to see Corinne's aunt was one last attempt to free himself from the stricture that was Corinne's legacy. She had caused him to grow out of his old life of wandering, but he had failed to find the balance within himself to settle for any other kind of life.

And however much I denied it at the time, he thought, *prostitution DID make me feel differently about the way I use my body to interact with women.*

Even contemplating the possibility of forcing himself to have sex with someone solely for money now made him feel almost physically sick. How strange that this should be the case, only a few weeks after being with Sally in Barcelona. He remembered being overwhelmed by sex with her and he thought, *What WAS that? I couldn't do it now.*

He was grateful to Jan, who, simply by listening to him talk, had helped him to leave that phase of his life behind. And what a *relief* it had been to be freed of the prospect of trying to seduce her. She was right on that score, though it was something of a humiliation to admit it: that he *had* been limited in his view of women.

Of course, that was why he'd made such a good prostitute.

He remembered that last morning with Jan, in his flat, before taking her to the station.

"You've helped me so much this week," she'd said. "You're very attractive still, and I'm glad nothing sexual has happened between us. Anything I do now will be on the rebound and I still don't trust myself to make a sensible decision. Thank you for being so un-pushy."

She had invited him to come and stay with her in Manchester, saying with a laugh, "Don't expect to get the same lavish hospitality. But we're both vulnerable, emotionally, and we can offer each other more support than those who wish us well but aren't going through what we're going through. And you *must* tell me if you manage to meet up with Aunt Gillian..."

***

Howard could see Gillian's cottage even before he arrived in

Dolgellau. The bulk of Cader Idris loomed pale in the slightly misty air - the blue of the sky had a washed-out winter quality to it as he stopped at the foot of her lane to close the hood of his car. The hedgerow that had concealed the track to the cottage when he'd last come past here had been heavily pruned this year, and now the approach looked less wild and other-worldly. The garden of the cottage was a dour, autumnal monochrome green/brown, where before, when he'd been with Matthew, it had been awash with spring colour. Still, it had the same quality of juxtaposition; of ordered garden next to wilderness; of whitewashed walls standing out from the heather and grasses behind and higher up.

There was a battered Renault 5 parked on the turning circle beside the well-tended but moss-ridden lawn. Howard pulled up in the shade of a dark holly bush whose unripe berries were pale orange. He got out and patted the bonnet of his sleek car; the car that he was now going to have to sell in order to pay for his extravagance with Jan. He shrugged at the thought of it - at how genuinely unconcerned he was that he was going to have to part with it - and smiled to himself. He crossed to the sturdy wooden front door and rapped the brass door-knocker against its weathered plate. There was no answer and so he tried again. He had no idea how long he should wait here to see if someone might turn up. Should he go away and come back later? It was mid-day, so maybe Gillian had gone somewhere for lunch. Or to work, perhaps? He had no idea if she had retired, or moved away from the area, or even if she was still alive.

As he was pondering this, a woman appeared round the edge of the house wearing an anorak, an old tweed skirt, gardening gloves and carrying a trugg over her arm. Her grey hair was piled up untidily and was held by a tortoishell comb from which wisps strayed down onto her shoulders. She had a small nose and a narrow but not unfriendly mouth. He recognised her as having been present at Matthew's funeral.

"I thought I heard the door," she said. "Can I help you?"

"Maybe," said Howard. "Look, I'm not sure if this is an appropriate time to have called, but my name is Howard Martindale. I'm sorry I didn't have the opportunity to tell you in advance that I was coming..."

"Ah," she said, "Howard. Corinne's young man. Hold on."

She put her basket down and pulled off her gloves, then extended her hand.

"I'm Gillian. I'm so pleased to meet you. I'm sorry I'm not more presentable, but I've been in the vegetable garden sorting out the winter spinach. Would you like to stay for lunch? I'm cooking up some soup."

"I don't want to intrude," Howard said, "I just wanted to ask you a few questions."

"You're not intruding," she said. "I'm afraid I do have to go out in a while, though not for another hour or so. Until then, please, come in."

Howard smiled.

"Okay, thanks," he said.

She had a slight roll to her gait, possibly from arthritic hips, and Howard guessed her to be around seventy, though she had an air of youthful energy about her.

"I've heard quite a lot about you," she said as she opened the front door, "so there's a fair amount that I wouldn't mind asking *you*, if it isn't too intrusive."

He followed her through into the expansive open-plan kitchen where she began to wash the greens that she'd picked. She engaged Howard in superficial conversation about his journey whilst he sat at the sturdy wooden kitchen table. She exuded vigour and vitality and a kind of no-nonsense approach to life. Her eyes were an enigmatic brown/green that reminded Howard of the colour of army jackets. She had a disarming tendency to look down at her hands for a moment and then suddenly look round to stare intently into Howard's eyes. The slope of Cader Idris could be seen behind her, through the kitchen window, and the word 'idyllic' fleeted through his mind.

"I used to look forward to Corinne's visits," she said, leaving the pan to simmer and coming over, with a pile of spinach and a chopping board, to sit opposite Howard at the table. "They weren't easy," she told him, "but they were always rewarding. This cottage was a bolt-hole for her, as I'm sure she told you."

"Actually, she told me you were dead."

"Hmm, yes, that's right. Emma told me about that. Well, that's something else altogether."

She seemed to ruminate over that for a moment as she chopped the greens.

"Anyway," she continued, "as I said, I was always pleased to see Corinne because, usually, I could genuinely help her to overcome her depressions, or at least look after her until they passed. The down side of her visits was that she only came to see me when she was in crisis, which meant that I had the function of doctor, counsellor, healer - whatever you want to call it - instead of friend. Still, no one else seemed to be able to offer her that service, except perhaps Matthew, later on, after she married him. But, latterly, he was *part* of the problem and she couldn't allow herself to accept help from him."

"I suppose she was hard work at times?"

"She made me feel useful. What you have to understand is that, although Corinne was competent and sure of herself in many ways, in one part of her being she was still a little girl, hurting. This thing - this depressive tendency - happened to her in her earliest adolescence. It was so frightening for her, it was as if some terrible force would drag her away from her normal way of functioning and into a fugue state of unhappiness and depression. It was beyond her control, almost as if it was something external... no wonder in the middle ages people believed in the powers of possession and bewitchment, because that's how it seemed to her; that some force that was other than her took her over, and made her feel and behave in a way that was against her real personality. She never got over the feeling that she was compelled to succumb to depression against her will. She also thought that giving in to depression was a weakness - that if only she could be strong, she'd be able to fight it off. You see, she'd always been taught that good people are happy; that happiness is the natural by-product of being an intelligent, functional *good* person. If she wasn't happy, then she must be bad. When she became an adult, she didn't verbalise it in this way, but essentially, that's how she saw it."

Gillian nodded sadly to herself and sighed, then carefully stood up to go and put the spinach into the soup.

"Do you think she harboured suicidal tendencies?" Howard asked.

"Yes. Well, it's not a matter of opinion. I talked her out of suicide several times. And these weren't cries for help. They were serious 'I don't think I can cope any more' situations. I don't blame her, either. She went through deep, deep sadness, sometimes. I can see why she might have often felt suicidal."

Gillian opened the bread bin and took out a crusty loaf which she began to slice and lay out on an earthenware dish.

***

1996:

Corinne. Being with her in Chamonix, in the French Alps, after a CMS conference in Geneva. It was only eighty kilometres from Geneva to Chamonix and Matthew had booked an off season suite for himself and Corinne for the weekend after the conference finished, and rooms for Howard and Jerry Futerman in the same hotel as a reward for services rendered over a hectic month.

Matthew was toying with the idea of taking up rock-climbing and had been persuaded, by Jerry Futerman, to try a beginner's face on Mont Buet .

On the Saturday, Matthew and Jerry went off to a morning service at one of the small churches there, before meeting up with their climbing instructor. Corinne and Howard spent the day in bed. For Howard it was another of those drenching experiences, where afterwards every muscle seemed lush with satiety and torpor.

They went out onto the balcony, Howard wrapped only in a towel, Corinne in her dressing gown, and looked out over the snow-capped mountains. It was surprisingly warm. Howard had expected icy winds and ski slopes, but it was nearly summer and the air was rich with sunlight and the smell of grasses.

They were standing on a first floor balcony which had a little gate in it.

"For when you're snowed in," Corinne said. "If the snow is too deep to get out downstairs, you step out onto it from here."

She unlatched the gate and pushed it open, then turned to him for an embrace. Holding his elbows, she leaned back, laughing, from the gap in the balcony's railings.

"Careful!" Howard said, laughing with her.

And then she let go of his arms.

There was a moment that lasted only a fraction of a second when Howard didn't understand what was happening. Then, in the space of time it took his heart to beat one nightmarish thump, he managed to grab her before she could fall backwards from the balcony.

"Corinne!" he gasped, stunned, his knees buckling slightly as a hot flush of shock flooded through him. "Jesus! You might have fallen."

She was still smiling and absolutely calm, looking at him almost clinically, as if she'd just set him a test and was working out whether he'd passed it or not.

"You might have been killed!" Howard choked, suddenly angry.

"But I wasn't," she said. "You caught me."

"I might not have."

"But you did."

***

1999:

Howard, took a slice of bread and pondered what Gillian had said about Corinne's suicidal tendencies.

"Did you encourage Corinne to have therapy?" he asked.

"Matthew convinced her, with my help, to try it. As far as I could see, what she needed was not to try to overcome her depressions - because they would recur whether she wanted them to or not - but to regard them instead as inconvenient periods to be got through. Rather like going down with a nasty cold. You get the symptoms and you think, 'here we go again, I'll just have to sit tight, go to bed with a hot drink, and keep my head down until I feel better.' If only Corinne had learned to do that, to dig in in the knowledge that the misery would pass, then she would never have killed herself."

"Killed herself?"

"Well, whatever."

"Please," said Howard, "what do you mean by that?"

Gillian gave Howard a compassionate glance before replying, and then carefully chose her words.

"In my opinion, Corinne was suicidal at the time of her death. Don't you think it extraordinary that she should be feeling suicidal, and then die by 'accident'? A little too convenient for me to accept it as a coincidence, I'm afraid."

"But I was driving the car," said Howard, "*I* crashed. It was *my* responsibility."

"Like I said. Whatever."

Howard took a long breath.

"Okay," he said. "Let's talk about another aspect of this. I know this sounds like a weird question, but... do you think she was in love with me?"

Gillian shrugged.

"I don't think we'll ever know the answer to that."

She brought the soup over and placed a bowl in front of him. Then, taking his hand in hers, she held it fast for a moment. Something in the sincerity of her voice made Howard breathless.

"Emma told me," he said, "that Corinne never loved me."

Gillian smiled sadly.

"Depression can cause a sort of mild paranoia," she told him, "and because of this Corinne was often confused about what she did and didn't feel. Whenever a person is depressed they see the world in negative terms. It wouldn't surprise me to find that, at her most despondent, Corinne could question practically everything - especially her relationships - in a way that would seem ridiculous to her when she was feeling well. So in many respects what she may have said to Emma doesn't prove anything one way or another. Now," she added, "less talk. Eat."

The soup was thick with tomatoes and onion, as well as the spinach, and had a piquancy that might have been chilli, or perhaps Worcestershire Sauce. Gillian dipped her bread into it, and Howard followed suit.

"What makes you think that Corinne was suicidal at the time of her death?" he said after a while.

Gillian nodded as if to some internal dialogue, before looking at Howard.

"She had been so careful to just *have an affair* with you," she said. "She put a lot of effort into hiding the fact of her depressions from you..."

"She succeeded," Howard murmured.

"Think what would have been involved if she'd left Matthew and set up home with you? She would have to come clean about being clinically diagnosed as a manic depressive, she would have to let you see her when she was unwell, paranoid, demanding... she was scared that you wouldn't be able to cope with it. That you'd leave her."

She took a mouthful of soup.

"And maybe she was right," she said.

"But I loved her," Howard objected, "I would have helped her, if only she'd allowed herself to share these things with me."

"You say that in ignorance of what it is like to look after a person with severe depression. I know you mean it, so we'll leave it at that. But there are other considerations too. Matthew was dedicated to Corinne. He was one of the most kind and charitable people I have ever met."

"I know. But I would have been prepared to put in at least as much effort as he did."

"And Corinne," Gillian said. "Imagine what a prospect it must have been for her to contemplate leaving Matthew, to contemplate leaving the security that he offered her? I can see why it scared her. And then there was her business. It was the first time she'd ever set out to prove herself in the world, and it failed. How do you think that made her feel, when she was so frail in other ways?"

"I can't imagine," Howard said truthfully.

"No. Whether she loved you or not, deep down she thought she wasn't 'good' enough for you, that you would reject her when you saw how 'bad' she was."

"But that's absurd..."

"That was her reality."

Gillian finished her soup, dabbed her mouth with a paper napkin, and stood.

"Now," she said. "I'm sorry to stop things just there, but I must go out. I have to run an errand for an elderly person in town. I'll only be gone a couple of hours. I wish I could put it off, but I can't. Please, stay here if you like, or go for a walk. I hope we can continue the conversation when I come back?"

"I'd like that," said Howard, trying to overcome a feeling of impatience that the discussion was being truncated.

He watched as she went into the hall to pick up her coat and her car keys.

"If you go out, pull the door to. Don't bother to lock it."

"Is it alright if I make a phone call?"

"Of course."

After she'd gone, Howard stood in the hallway, reeling inside from their conversation. He went out to his car to get his address book, then came back and phoned Jan's work number. It rang several times.

"Hello," she said, "Jan Cowan."

"Jan, it's Howard."

"Did you meet Aunt Gillian?" she asked, anxiously.

"Yes."

"And?"

"She thinks that Corinne was suicidal at the time of the accident."

"What?"

"When it was explained to me it seemed to make sense. I can't go into it in detail now, but..."

He paused, looking down the hall and into the well-ordered sitting room.

"I feel so confused," he said.

"Have you finished with Gillian?"

"No. She's had to go out. We're going to talk some more in a couple of hours."

"Give me a ring as soon as you've finished. I'm going to be at work until six. After that you can get me at home. Come straight here after you've finished talking to her. Manchester is much closer than London, anyway. Don't go home, Howard. Come to my place and we'll talk it through, okay?"

"I don't want to impose."

"Come over, Howard. Please, let me help you."

He was surprised by the urgency and sincerity in her voice.

"Okay," he said.

He went for a wander round the garden but found himself too distracted to do anything but glance cursorily at plants that he recognised but didn't know the names for. In the end he took José's book from the car and went to sit and read it in the sitting room - a low, beamed room with leaded windows that looked down into the valley to the edge of Dolgellau.

At first José's words seemed meaningless, but as he concentrated -

especially on *Vitrinas de la Memorià*, the prose poem about regret, he gradually became absorbed.

No es estallar,
sino el ahogo del estallido,
lo que provoca un duradero dolor.
Entonces nos vendamos las heridas,
como hacen las chinas con sus pies,
y, a pesar de andar a tropiezos,
aún ocultamos en público
los lazos de nuestro obstáculo.

The words echoed with the most extraordinary personal significance and Howard took out his pen and an unwanted invoice from his wallet on the back of which he jotted down a rough English translation. It was extraordinarily difficult to reflect the nuances in José's use of language and the poem's informal structure. Nevertheless, after an hour or so, he felt he had grasped the first part of the poem and rendered a pleasing translation:

CABINETS OF MEMORY

It is not the blow
but the suppression of the scream
that causes lasting pain.
So we bandage hurts
like Chinese feet,
and though we falter,
the roots of our impediment
are hidden from public eyes.

This was only the first quarter of the poem, describing a messy split-up of José's from seven or eight years previously: Howard could remember the event well. It was just before José met Lucia, and the woman in question - was it Teresa? - had dumped him in the most public manner at someone else's wedding. Taken out of context, the words were particularly apposite to himself and Howard kept reading and re-reading the poem. It ended:

Durante un tiempo me preguntaba
cómo fuiste capaz;
ahora sólo puedo asombrarme
de cómo te atreviste
a dejarme en las ascuas
de aquella mañana,
cuando con sólo unas horas más
habrías ahorrado
a mi alma abiertamente sangriar.

Where once I used to question
how you could,
I now can only wonder
that you dared
leave me in the ashes
of a morning
when a few hours more
would have spared
my soul such open pain.

Howard sat and looked at the English text and felt that he had achieved something meaningful by reflecting José's words. It occurred to him as he sat there in that cool, pale room, that this should be his next project. To translate José's book. He had often complained that there was no challenge involved in every day translation and interpreting. He could take *Vitrinas de la Memorià* and spend a month or two of the winter translating it. He had enough money to cover himself for that time - the sale of his car would more than pay for his extravagance with Jan, and he also had what he'd earned during his manic six weeks work in August and September - half of which had yet to come through.

The thought of taking on a new challenge with language was attractive. So what if he couldn't sell it? Maybe it would lead to other projects, maybe it wouldn't, but at least it would be *something*...

This prospect came as a completely formed idea. He knew absolutely that he would do it. There was no need to wonder further whether it was a good idea.

As he stood to go and see if he could make himself a coffee, he heard the tyres of Gillian's car crunching on the gravel. He went to the window and she waved to him as she got out. Howard tucked his translation into the cover of *Vitrinas*... and went through to put it on the hall table. Gillian came in at that moment and smiled at him.

"Hello my dear," she said. "I'm glad you're still here. I kept on imagining that you might have run away. Look, I've been given a cake. Let's have some now."

Howard looked down at her slightly gnarled knuckles as she held the cake for him to see.

"It looks delicious," he said, and followed her into the kitchen once more.

She prepared a tray for afternoon tea - pale china plates and cups with slightly fluted edges, a pot of tea and slices of fruit cake. Howard hadn't experienced afternoon tea for years and felt strangely childlike as he carried the tray through to the sitting room. His parents had insisted on afternoon tea at weekends until he was ten, whereupon his mother had declared that both she and Howard's father needed to lose weight and that, until further notice, cakes were out of the question.

"Right," Gillian said, as she poured him some tea. "I've been thinking about this and I've realised that I can't form a real picture in my mind about what happened on the day that Corinne died. Until I know that, I can't really claim any meaningful opinion on the subject, can I? I know I said that I always assumed it was suicide, but that was presumptuous of me, wasn't it? Perhaps you can tell me what actually happened?"

"We were in a smash up, that's all," Howard told her. "I was driving. I lost concentration momentarily."

Howard felt suddenly reticent to talk any further about what had happened. He hadn't actually spoken of the accident in detail to anyone. Not even the police. They'd questioned him whilst he was still suffering from alalia and, from notes he had written to them on a small memo pad that one of the nurses had supplied him with, they'd accepted that he had almost no memory of the crash. They'd reached a verdict of accidental death regarding Corinne, and that was that. He never had to admit to his lapse of concentration, and had never subsequently discussed it.

"Were there any other cars involved?" Gillian asked him.

Howard paused for some moments before he spoke.

"No... I went off the road. The car struck a tree on the passenger side."

He closed his eyes.

"How did Corinne come to be in the car?" Gillian asked.

"I can't remember."

"Try."

"Look, I don't feel comfortable about this at all. Corinne died because, for a moment, I looked away from the road. Can't you see why I don't want to talk about it?"

"Why did you look away?"

He opened his eyes and stared at her with irritation.

"I just looked away, that's all. There was something wrong with the seat belt. It wasn't anything sordid. She wasn't giving me a blow job or anything."

Gillian didn't react to this. She looked sympathetically at Howard and took a small bite of her cake.

"I wasn't trying to suggest anything of that sort," she said after a pause. "Am I right that you haven't talked this through with anyone?"

"Yes."

"Then it's time you did."

Howard shook his head.

"I can't," he whispered.

"You must," she said firmly.

A line from José's poem ran through Howard's mind, then, *we bandage hurts like Chinese feet*, and he felt a tear trickling on his cheek. It came so suddenly that for a moment he thought the moisture had fallen from the ceiling and he involuntarily looked up.

"I never saw her body," he said quietly. "I'm told she was in a bad state when they cut her free from the car. I was unconscious, but only suffered a couple of cracked ribs, bruising to the face and concussion. I thought it was a blessing that I didn't see what I'd done to her, but now I regret it because of all those terrible dreams..."

He tried to pick up his cup to take a sip of tea but found his hand was shaking too much and so he left the cup where it was.

Gillian nodded.

"Right," she said, "let's get outside. Sitting here having tea is far too formal. I'll take you to out to Pennant's Meadow. It's not far, and it's sheltered, and the view is particularly fine. Then, we'll be able to talk."

They went out to the hallway where she pulled on a coat, and lent Howard a pair of gloves to go with his hat and scarf. They set off from the back door, in silence, and walked a short way up the hillside before turning east and making their way along a ridge that led towards a wood. Gillian kept up a good pace and Howard admired her for her sureness, and for giving him the chance to calm his thoughts.

The grass was tussocky, with patches of heather and bilberry. The trees, when they reached them, were mostly birches that cast long shadows down the hillside in the late-afternoon sun. Gillian chose a flat rock to sit on, from which they could see down into the valley and across to peak after peak that disappeared to the north.

Although Howard could hear a susurration of wind above him, it was almost completely still on the rock, and consequently he wasn't cold.

"Well," Gillian asked, "do you feel up to continuing?"

Howard nodded.

"Right," she said. "Tell me, how did the day of the crash begin? What were you doing?"

Howard closed his eyes again. He couldn't bear the sympathy and concern in her gaze.

"I was driving Corinne to the National Exhibition Centre near Birmingham..."

"Why? She had a car. Why were you driving her?"

"Her car was being serviced. Matthew was away, and so we went in his Mercedes. Corinne never drove the Mercedes. She always said it was too tank-like and that she never felt in control when she was driving it. So she asked me if I would take her. Of course, I was delighted because it meant spending some time with her. There was some floristry and gardening trade thing on at the NEC and she wanted to have a look round."

"Her car *wasn't* being serviced that day, you know," Gillian told him.

"How do you know?"

"Matthew told me. It was one of the things that mystified him about the whole incident. Corinne's car was fine. There was nothing wrong with it. There was no reason to have gone in the Mercedes at all."

Howard felt a confusion descend on him and he sat, paralysed almost, unable to work out what this information meant. Why would Corinne have lied about whether her car was working or not?

Gillian gestured as though putting that information to one side for the moment.

"What was Corinne's mood that day?" she asked.

Howard gathered his thoughts before replying.

"The same as usual," he told her.

"Are you *sure?*"

Howard looked out at the expanse around him and tried to focus his memory.

"Well, she was quiet, I suppose. Yes. Almost silent, and seemed excited, somehow."

"Exhilarated?"

"I wouldn't go so far as to say exhilarated, no, but sometimes she had a sort of *sparkle* about her. It wasn't unusual for her to be like that."

"And she was *sparkly* that day?"

"Yes."

Gillian nodded thoughtfully before she spoke again.

"So, you were driving along..."

"I hadn't put my seat belt on because it was stuck. It wouldn't pull out from the inertia reel at the side, so I didn't bother with it. It was one of those things I'd never been good at, anyway, wearing my seat belt. Corinne was more fastidious about it. She always made me put it on as soon as I got into her car, but I was very lazy about it myself. That day she didn't mention it until we were out by Balsall Common. Then she noticed I wasn't wearing it and asked me to put it on."

"She didn't mention it when you first started off?"

"No. There's a fast section of road at Balsall Common, when the dual carriageway starts. It's a notorious accident blackspot, so it was logical that she should think to check that I was wearing my belt as I speeded up."

"How fast were you going?"

"Matthew's car was such a pleasure to drive I always drove faster than I should. I suppose when we got onto the dual carriageway we must have been doing eighty-five or ninety."

"So, when you were driving at nearly ninety miles an hour, you put your seat belt on?"

"No. I gave it a good pull, and then told Corinne that it was stuck. She said she would steer whilst I quickly looked to see if it had snagged on anything."

"You let go of the steering wheel?"

Howard felt Gillian's surprise as a criticism and instantly became defensive.

"It may sound ludicrous now," he told her, "but it seemed logical at the time. When I was a kid and my father used to drive me to school, I would steer the car for him sometimes, in the winter, whilst he took his coat off. It was a kind of game. It was no big deal. In fact, I steered once for Corinne when a buckle snapped from her shoe and she wanted to slip it off. It's not that unusual, and besides, Corinne had an incredibly intense way of asking you to do something when it was important to her."

"I know," Gillian assured him.

"It seemed so reasonable at the time. Of course, since the accident, *I've* had a neurosis about seat belts, so I can understand why she might have been so adamant."

Howard grimaced slightly to himself at the memory.

"So, you were doing eighty-five miles an hour..." Gillian prompted.

"No, I'd taken my foot off the accelerator. We were slowing down. We were probably doing sixty or so when the car left the road."

"So, how *did* it leave the road?"

"I don't know. I only looked down for a moment, whilst I traced the seat belt with my fingers to see if anything was the matter, and then the car suddenly slewed to the left, over the grass verge, and smashed into an ash tree, which came down onto the car, crushing the passenger side. The car didn't go over, so the fact that I wasn't wearing a belt wasn't crucial for me. I was buffered by the driver's air bag."

"And Corinne was wearing her belt?"

"No. The police said she wasn't. I couldn't understand that at first, but now I reckon she must have released it for the few seconds in which she leaned over to take the wheel."

"And you were knocked unconscious?"

"Yes. I woke up in hospital."

"So the last thing you remember, you were looking down, to your right, whilst you were feeling to see why the seat belt was stuck?"

"Yes."

"And you didn't see what Corinne was doing with the wheel?"

"No."

Gillian looked at Howard and opened her arms in an expansive gesture.

"I was right, Howard, don't you see? It *was* suicide."

"No," Howard said, shaking his head. "No."

"You say that Corinne always used to wear her seat belt?"

"Yes."

"But she wasn't wearing it at the time of the crash."

"No."

Gillian leaned forward so that she could look into Howard's eyes.

"You don't have to take your seat belt off to be able to reach the steering wheel of a car from the passenger side," she told him. "Just visualise the inside of the car for a moment and you'll realise that I'm right. Corinne took her seat belt off deliberately. She took the wheel from you, then, when you were sufficiently distracted, she deliberately steered the car off the road in order to make it crash."

"No."

"*Yes.* Listen. She'd worked the whole thing out. She wanted you to be driving, but it couldn't be in your car because she needed time before you arrived that morning so that she could do something to make the seat belt mechanism stick. So, she pretended that her car was being serviced and asked you to drive Matthew's instead, knowing that you wouldn't be able to resist the offer of driving such an exciting car. It was all premeditated. That's why she was so *sparkly*. She was pumped full of adrenalin because she knew what she was about to do."

"But why?"

"Because it fitted, don't you see? It was completely in line with her highly developed sense of tragedy. She thought of herself as a failure as a person, a failure as a businesswoman and, except in the most superficial way, a failure as a lover. I knew she was in a bad way. I'd talked to

Matthew about her only a few days earlier and we were both worried. So was her therapist."

She took Howard's elbow gently and squeezed it. Howard, leaning forward slightly, put his head in his hands, still shaking his head slightly.

"No," he said. "I killed her. *I* killed her."

"She killed *herself*, Howard, and she tried to kill you too. We'll never know exactly what she was thinking that day. Perhaps she thought that if you were in the driving seat it would absolve her of the stigma of committing suicide - it was a way of killing herself and making it look like a terrible accident. Covering it up, in fact, just like she covered up her depressions. Perhaps she didn't want to leave you behind, especially given that Matthew was in love with you. Who knows for sure?"

Howard stood up abruptly and took a couple of paces forward. The afternoon was fading and the sky was pale on the horizon, but aquamarine above. He pressed his forehead against the trunk of a birch tree that was beside him.

Of course, he kept saying to himself, *of course*.

That was why he'd never gone through it in his mind before, not in detail. Because it didn't make sense properly. Only by not examining what had happened could he fully take the blame. That must be what Matthew had meant at the hospital when he'd said *I know what happened*. He'd figured it out logically, if not in precise detail. Just like Gillian.

Howard turned to her and leant back against the tree.

"You talked to Matthew!" he said. "That's why he wanted to see me."

"Mmm," she nodded. "I was the one who convinced him that Corinne had deliberately caused the accident. It was the only way I could explain what happened. Once he'd accepted that I was probably right, he realised how terrible the whole experience must have been for you. He wanted to talk you through it, but he never got the chance."

Howard turned away again.

She killed HERSELF, he thought.

He was suddenly struck afresh by the line from José's poem: *We bandage hurts like Chinese feet.* It was true. As he sat, he felt an unfurling within himself. An appalling restriction was beginning to ease, and although in one sense it was a relief, the pain of it was overwhelming.

"Howard?" said Gillian.

He pressed his forehead hard against the bark of the tree so that he could feel it prickling his skin.

"Howard?" she asked again.

He could hear her coming over to him and involuntarily shrank as she put her hand on his shoulder, afraid of the reaction that her sympathy might cause in him.

"I..." he said, but it came out as a strangled, almost guttural noise. He tried to speak again, but there was nothing there, just a great yawning gap where once he had been so sure. For as long as he had believed that he'd killed Corinne, the details of their relationship had been so simple, the blame so easy to apportion. But now...

He tried to say something again, but this time no noise came out at all, just a blurring of tears.

Gillian put her arm round him and hugged him silently for a long time.

"Don't try to speak," she said eventually. "Matthew told me that this happened to you after the accident. Then, it was part of the process of blaming yourself. Now, it's part of the process of releasing yourself from blame."

Howard turned back to the tree and pressed his forehead against it once more, but harder, so that a knot pressed into the bridge of his nose causing a sharp pain that emptied his head of other thoughts. Gillian took his hand and held it without pressure, to assure him that she was there.

"When you're ready to speak," she said gently, "you'll speak."